# Worqenesh

## A Story of Renewal

Wega Miller George

Black Rose Writing
www.blackrosewriting.com

© 2012 by Wega Miller George

All rights reserved. No part of this book may be reproduced, stored in a retrieval system or transmitted in any form or by any means without the prior written permission of the publishers, except by a reviewer who may quote brief passages in a review to be printed in a newspaper, magazine or journal.

The final approval for this literary material is granted by the author.

First printing

ISBN: 978-1-61296-136-1

PUBLISHED BY BLACK ROSE WRITING

www.blackrosewriting.com

Printed in the United States of America

*Worqenesh* is printed in Times New Roman

For my grandchildren,
Will, Carly, Evan, Emily and Ian

# LISTING OF CHIEF CHARACTERS

Asfaw Yilma - Dejazmach (Governor) of Begemder
Wishan Kinfu - his wife
Worqenesh - their eldest child, marries John Bell
*Giyorgis* - their eldest son
*Haylu* – their son
*Welde* – their son
*Ribca* – their daughter
*Haile* – their son
Welette Tekle – Wishan's grandmother
Welde Tekle – Welette's brother

Kassa Haylu - Wishan's Uncle, future King Tewodros

Menen Liban - Galla Queen
Ras (equivalent of a Duke) Ali Alula - her son, chief of all the tribal rulers in Abyssinia
Tewabach - his daughter, marries Kassa Haylu

Goshu Zewde - Dejazmach in northwestern part of Abyssinia
Birru Goshu - his son

John Bell - an English explorer and adventurer, marries Worqenesh
Susan Jewubdar Bell - their daughter
John Aligaz Bell - their son
Mary Belletech Bell - their daughter

Walter Plowden - an English adventurer
*Fenta Tadesse* - Asfaw Yilma's friend
Ayto Cassai - a merchant, Bell's friend
Abune Salama - Coptic Metropolitan
*Abba Guebra Barhe* – an Orthodox priest
*Issete* - a slave, Worqenesh's companion
Gabriote – John Bell's servant

Theophilus Waldmeier - a Swiss missionary
Karl Saalmuller - a German missionary

(*italics denote a fictitious character*)

# Worqenesh

## A Story of Renewal

# Mid 19th Century Abyssinia

# Chapter 1

The tinny shaking of the *sistra* caught the beat of the priest's drum, and both seemed to match the rhythm of her own heart. It was Meskel, her favorite time of the year. The long rains were over and the sun blazed on the bright yellow flowers in the fields. Worqenesh felt she would burst with joy, but knew she must contain her happiness and behave with the decorum that was expected of a member of a noble family. Wishan looked down at her young daughter and smiled. This child had special attributes, both of enchantment and fortitude. She would need great quantities of the latter growing up in Abyssinia in the 1830's.

The priests, dressed in their white robes and turbans, began to climb the hill to the Church of Iyasus just above the town of Debra Tabor. Suddenly they broke out into the traditional song for Meskel, the feast day of the Holy Cross. It was the first chapter of the book of Habbukuk. Antiphonally, they tossed the words between the prophet and God back and forth in the crisp highland air. "Oh Lord, how long shall I cry, and thou wilt not hear! even cry out unto thee of violence, and thou wilt not save!" The answer came, "Behold ye among the heathen, and regard, and wonder marvelously; for I will work a work in your days, which ye will not believe, though it be told you."

Indeed, this was a time of violence. Just two years before, the town had been sacked by an army of the neighboring province, Lasta, and it would continue to reel from the forces that ebbed and flowed across this ancient land. The times were known as the *Zemina Mesafint*, or "the age of the judges", because the power of the hereditary kings had collapsed and, as in the days of the judges of ancient Israel when there was no king, "...every man did that which was right in his own eyes."

The ties of Abyssinia to ancient Israel were well known. The royal family was touted to have descended from the union of King Solomon and the Queen of Sheba. Unique on the continent of Africa, Abyssinia had enjoyed the unifying force of a single dynasty, a long history of Christianity and geographically unassailable highlands. But for nearly the last one hundred years the fabled royal family had been in the control of the country's various provincial powers.

Today, the people of Debra Tabor followed the procession of priests in holy disarray. Worqenesh skipped along beside her mother, waving to her friends and looking for a chance to kiss the cross carried by Abba Guebra Barhe. As she and her mother approached the colorful circular church at the top of the hill she could see her father, Asfaw Yilma, standing with other important men in the community. She waved to him, hoping that he would notice her. Asfaw Yilma was the Dejazmach, or Governor, of all of Begemder, the province where Debra Tabor was located. He was a man who could command thousands of horsemen within hours of beating the local military drums. He did notice the gangling youngster with her mother. There were other children in the family, but this was their golden child. Even her name began with the native word for gold. Both he and Wishan believed that she was special and that her life would take an unusual course.

As the people approached their church, the priest carrying the Tabot and leading the procession moved on into the circular quiet of Iyasus to place this most sacred object into the innermost sanctuary. The square Tabot, decked in silks, represented the Hebraic Arc of the Covenant that Solomon's son had brought to their country when he had taken up the reigns of government as its first king. That real Arc was reputed to be sequestered in Axum in the Church of St. Mary of Zion, but each Christian center throughout the land maintained its proxy in deepest reverence. Only on the most holy days were the local Tabots brought before the people. The priests bearing crosses followed the Tabot as far as the outer circle of the sanctuary and, when the music ceased, the festive excitement dropped. The people of Abyssinia seldom entered their churches, but rather gathered in groups around the structure. Even less often were they troubled by a sermon. The music had finished, and the faithful began to drift away.

Worqenesh reached behind her back where she knew she would find the hand of her little slave, Issete. Asfaw Yilma had brought the Galla child home with him as a spoil of battle, and the children had grown up together. More like a sister than a servant, Issete shared every hour of the day with Worqenesh, and most of her thoughts. Issete knew her own fortune in attending a noble family's daughter. There was always sufficient to eat. They shared lessons with Abba Guebra Barhe whenever he was able to travel to Diddim, so that both knew numerous of the psalms of David and parts of the gospel as written by St. Luke, and both could write the thirty-nine letters of the Amharic alphabet. Most of their contemporaries could do neither, but with the other local children they roamed the hills surrounding their village, Diddim, always mindful of the need for caution against wild animals and of the danger of losing their way; and together, after their evening meal, they pulled their shared leopard skin over their shoulders and snuggled together for the night like the little creatures of their forest. Worqenesh loved all of her family, but Issete was the counter beat of her heart.

"Let's pick Meskel flowers on the way home," Worqenesh offered. "We can fill our arms with gold," and she laughed at the play on her own name.

"Let's take the upper path," cried Issete. "Maybe we shall see the baby dikdik."

The path from Debra Tabor to Diddam was well traveled over the hilly countryside of Begemder, and yet the village was remote, and far enough away from the provincial capital that marauding soldiers, or even armies, seemed to pass it by in ignorance. Asfaw Yilma and Wishan followed the girls at a distance, and there were occasional neighbors along the path as well. It was never safe for children to venture far into the countryside by themselves. Recent years had seen a constant struggle in Abyssinia's political arena, which meant war between the Rases (Dukes) vying for guardianship of the King. For now, Sahle Dengel was on the throne in Gondar, but only at the pleasure of Ras Ali who controlled the country along with his ambitious mother, Menen. She had acted as regent during his minority, and had never relinquished her reins of power and influence. Both she and Ali had residences in Debra Tabor, but were absent on this glorious day.

Worqenesh had heard her own family history many times. Children of Abyssinia were taught the importance of family, and to trace their ancestry back for at least seven generations. When her father was at home, she and her little brothers would sit in the evenings and practice the recitation of names that held significance. She knew about her great grandfather, Haylu Wolde Giyorgis, who had been the Governor of Quarra, the western province of Abyssinia that bordered on Egypt. Haylu's first wife, Welette Tekle, had been described by a visiting European as a great lady of Gondar, and her son had been given land in the provinces of Quarra and Dembea on the northern shore of Lake Tsana. This was grandfather Kinfu. Dejazmach Kinfu, under the tutelage of his mother, Welette, had governed the two provinces with a firm hand, and continued to do so to the present time. Welette had a brother, Welde Tekle, who shared in his sister's ambitions and who had guided the military development of her son. The family was also acutely aware that a much younger son of Dejazmach Haylu, by a second wife, was now gaining attention in the western province of Quarra. This new presence was Kassa Haylu, and while he was the same age as Wishan, he was actually a sort of half uncle. His was a name that they would have to watch.

It was because of grandfather Kinfu's position that by 1837, his daughter's husband, Asfaw Yilma, came to hold the province of Begemder. By now, Dejazmach Kinfu was known as a great warlord who defended the western boundaries of Abyssinia against the Egyptians. Only this past season he had repulsed their incursion at the battle of Rashid, but defense of the country was a continuing challenge. There was a rumor that Kinfu's half brother, Kassa Haylu, had helped in the fight and that he had proved to be an impressive strategist. Now the combination of Kinfu and Kassa would catch the attention of Ras Ali, and he would begin to fear the possibility of a coalition between them and the Dejazmaches Goshu, south of Lake Tsana, and Ras Wube in the Simien mountains to the north.

This Meskel evening, however, none of this mattered as Worqenesh and Issete scampered along the pathway home and hummed the Meskel tunes of earlier in the day.

"Shh," whispered Issete. "There she is!" A dikdik fawn was standing by a field of *teff* (an indigenous grain) in the strong afternoon sunlight. With a slight turn of its head the little animal disappeared into the edge of the woods. Coming up from behind, Asfaw Yilma and Wishan guided the two little girls away from the trees and upward along the path.

"But she is so perfect," cried Worqenesh.

"*Isshi, isshi* - of course, of course," responded her father, "but we must not go into the forest without a weapon."

Just before evening they approached the circular huts of Diddim, nestled together on the side of a hill that was part of a lower mountain range. The air was turning chilly as the little group moved past a stand of fir trees and entered the beckoning warmth of their village. Worqenesh and Issete hurried toward the aroma of the evening meal that had been prepared by Asfaw Yilma's mother. There was a wonderful stew simmering over the fire that they would scoop up with pieces of *injera* (a flat bread made from the grain, *teff*). Later, they might hear the distant roar of a lion in the valley below, and they would fall onto the animal skins in their corner in the warm security of the home guarded by Asfaw Yilma – a luxury not shared by many in these unsettled times. There would be a light mist brushing against the fir trees in the morning. The year was 1837 and Worqenesh was eight years old. Before long, as a child of Abyssinia, she would be considered an adult.

# Chapter 2

---

The women of the household were the first to emerge the next morning. It was they who were responsible for almost all of the home and farm chores. from cooking and baking and carrying water from the nearest stream for both domestic animals and people, to most of the farming and even mucking out the stables. Men did plow, but unless they were one of the few great agricultural lords or of the mercantile class, their chief occupation was hunting and warfare. This morning there was already freshly baked bread and *tej* (mead) to fortify the family against the morning cold. The sun was barely beaming its light through gaps in the mountains when the family turned out to begin the day.

Wishan was fortunate to be part of a family that was singularly well known and powerful, so that she supervised, rather than bore, the heavy daily labor of grinding grain or weeding the family's fields. Her more usual occupation was to spin the yarn that a weaver would turn into the cotton cloth for her family's clothes, but today was to be different. Asfaw Yilma was going back to Debra Tabor to purchase a replacement horse for himself, and he had promised to include Wishan and Worqenesh in the day's outing. In Abyssinia, mules were used to carry one for any distance, and were the only animals ridden by women, but when there was the least threat of conflict, a man immediately exchanged his mule for a horse. A man's horse could be as well known as he himself, and was carefully named to project a desired image.

The family set out early. Asfaw Yilma swung Worqenesh up in front of him on his sturdy mule, and little Issete in front of her.

Wishan, dressed in her long, embroidered shirt with trousers to match, looked elegant on a cream colored animal to his side. Then there were the inevitable well-mounted guards – four in number – to discourage any sort of adversity along the way. An Abyssinia that could no longer boast the strong, central government that it had enjoyed some eighty years ago made brigandage attractive to the poor and the destitute. Worqenesh's younger brothers, to their dismay, were left at home with their grandmother and a large contingent of servants and warrior guards.

"Father, could not the boys ride with the guards," pleaded their sympathetic sister, watching her youngest brother, Haylu, jumping up and down in anticipation, but Asfaw Yilma had serious matters to address this day, and would not brook their distracting company. Along with choosing a horse he was concerned to check on the readiness of both his militia and his *negarete*, a group of drummers who announced all important communications to his people. His sons would have to wait for another day.

The little party began to descend from Diddim's mountainous perch. Two of his guards led while Asfaw Yilma followed with Wishan close to his side. The other two guards came behind. Asfaw Yilma had nothing to prove this day by going ahead, so the little family group had a seldom enjoyed opportunity for intimate conversation as they rode toward the market at Debra Tabor.

"Yilma, have you heard anything of my Uncle, Kassa, in Quarra," queried Wishan.

"Yes, Father, is he not very clever and brave," echoed Worqenesh.

Asfaw Yilma's answer came in grudging mumbles. "He has helped to keep the Egyptians near Matemma away from the border, but he is an upstart. I hear he sometimes acts as a bandit and steals from travelers to feed his soldiers. There is no bravery in that." Worqenesh wiggled more snugly into her father's comfortable chest. She was vaguely aware that for many in her country life was precarious, but she was young enough to feel amply protected in her father's arms.

"Father, what do you suppose he is fighting for?"

"Some say he wants to be *Nigus* (King), and not only Nigus, but

*Niguse Negest* (King of Kings, or Emperor). He may be your mother's Uncle, but that does not mean that he is descended from King David," and he laughed at any pretensions that his wife might have to the royal Solomonic line. She smiled in return. Wishan did not require a royal lineage to assure herself of her own worth.

The undulating countryside gave way to a plain covered with a generous crop of *teff* and highlighted with occasional clumps of the bright Meskel flowers. A slow incline showed the way to the busy town of Debra Tabor. They passed the Church of Iyasus where they had celebrated the holy holiday yesterday, and jogged on past the two large, wattle structures that sometimes housed Ras Ali and his artful mother, Menen. Debra Tabor was the seat of Ali's government and sheltered most of his officials and followers in a scattering of houses and huts. Asfaw Yilma reflected on the benefit of his own dwelling and campsite in Diddim, comfortably removed from this corridor of influence. Riding across the top of the town of Debra Tabor, he could look out over a series of hills with a haze of blue mountains in the distance. Named for the biblical Mount Tabor, the location of the town was said to have been selected with supernatural help.

The market was on the northwest side of the town, with the collection of saleable horses and mules at its farthest end. Asfaw Yilma left two of the guards with Wishan so that she could enjoy friends in the crowd and examine market wares – chiefly, materials of different sorts such as silks, calicoes and velvet, as well as red and blue bunting. There were silver beads for adornment, tobacco for the men and even frankincense from Arabia, which the people liked to burn to scent their homes.

With the two other guards and the two little girls, Asfaw Yilma moved on to the area where horses were for sale. Everyone knew that the best horses were bred by the Wello Gallas east of the big bend in the Blue Nile. These animals could gallop across a field pockmarked by clumps of grass and little holes dug by burrowing animals, turn in an instant and slide down steep hills leaning back on their haunches. But everyone also knew that the Wello Gallas would only sell an animal that was damaged, or not of the first quality. Most of the horses here at the market came from Were Himano at the edge of Amhara, and were the closest second to the Wello Galla horses available. Certainly, they far out performed any animal raised to the north in the Simien Mountains or in Tigre.

Asfaw Yilma needed a fleet horse and one that could be easily maneuvered in battle. In his mind it should be not too tall and it should be able to turn in its own length. He hoped to find a bay with a white forehead and white legs, and he pictured an animal that would pick up its knees as it ran so that it would seem to float across the ground. A typical Abyssinian, he valued speed and agility over stamina.

It was Worqenesh who spied the gelding first. He was not what Asfaw Yilma had imagined, but a soft gray with a white streak on his forehead, black hoofs and a black tail. Beautifully proportioned, the creature had glanced up with the intelligence of recognition at the youngster's voice, and her father immediately saw a cohort in battle and a companion. "Look, Father, he is beautiful, and he seems to know us!" cried Worqenesh.

The horses of Abyssinia were generally docile, good natured and even notably social creatures. A little on the small side, they were never shod and extremely hard of hoof. Occasionally, one might feel the need to shape the hoof, but because of their constant use, both in battle and in mock engagements, paring was seldom required. The gray began to follow the little group with his eyes, and when Asfaw Yilma approached he nickered, and then let out his breath with a gentle snort. The man ran his hand across the animal's cheek and then, with a seemingly effortless vault, he was on the gelding's back. There was a feeling of inevitability about it all. "I shall call him Selpha," declared Asfaw Yilma, "for he will fight with me like a sharply pointed lance."

By the time that Wishan caught up with her husband and daughter, Yilma was leading his new acquisition with the little girls astride Selpha's back. Already, the horse was adorned with a headpiece for the halter which would from then on seldom be removed, as immediate use might be required at any time; and Yilma had purchased a bright *benaicka* consisting of a series of highly polished brass rings descending to the tip of the horse's nose. When Selpha tossed his head the rings flashed in the sunlight.

"You are pleased, I can see," smiled Wishan.

"He is a fine animal," replied Yilma. "I have a feeling about him. Worqenesh discovered him. Selpha will bring me luck. Come, I must see to the *negarete* before we return to Diddim."

In olden times, under Abyssinia's unbroken line of kings descended from Israel's Solomon, the country had been partitioned into areas of authority under hereditary tribal chiefs who enjoyed a myriad of privileges and responded with feudal armies to support their liege lord. With the disintegration of the royal line, few of the old traditions remained, but as compelling an ensign as any flag were the *negarete*. For Ras Ali, the current ascendant Duke, this amounted to eighty-eight drums that were carried in pairs on mules, with the drummer seated behind. The Ras, at his pleasure, bestowed a set number of *negaretes* to his loyal dejazmaches. The number of these delegations ranged from forty-eight down to twelve, and Asfaw Yilma, as Dejazmach of Begemder, was responsible for twenty-four drums carried by twelve mules ridden by twelve drummers. The *negarete* precede a great warrior on the march and into battle. If they are taken by the enemy the battle is lost.

Asfaw Yilma took enormous pride in his contingent of drummers – in their mounts, their instruments and their uniforms. Their skills, both as riders and as musicians, were never left to chance. Today, they were to briefly pass before Yilma so that he might review them, and then they would return with him to Diddim. The drums would not beat. Their rhythmic pulse would always collect a crowd and there were no proclamations or calls to battle today, but Yilma would carefully examine men, mules and equipment. It was his responsibility to supply both mules and accoutrements, and he wanted to be sure that these privileged drummers amply reflected his position.

Against all precedence Worqenesh, with little Issete seated behind her, continued to bestride Selpha while Asfaw Yilma stood beside them to review his *negarete*. "Father," whispered Worqenesh, "the third man lacks a cape," and Asfaw Yilma made a mental note of the need for another leopard skin to cloak the drummer's shoulders.

For the most part all was well, although one of the latter drums was woefully in need of repair. The saddle cloths for all twelve animals were identical as were their leather girths. There was the omni present headpiece for each halter. Each bit had a single iron ring that passed below the mules' under lips, and the bridles were made of hippopotamus hide, as were the straps to balance each set of drums. The stirrups, as for all Abyssinian equestrians, were small and light and designed to accommodate not a boot, but the big toe of the rider, and the toe next to it, for this race of warriors and mountaineers had long ago learned that both fleetness and balance on their rough terrain were best managed in their bare feet.

As the *negarete* completed their review, a large contingent of Begemder's militia began to filter onto the field. Frequently, such groups became boisterous, with shouts of recognition and bravado, and brief flurries of competitive horsemanship. Today, the atmosphere was one of muted gaiety and deference. Woisero (the lady) Wishan and her daughter were with the Dejazmach, and any sign of ribaldry was sharply muted in respect. There was a brief moment of hesitation as Asfaw Yilma reorganized his little family group and then, newly mounted on Selpha, he wheeled about and trotted back toward the center of Debra Tabor with Wishan slightly behind and to his right and the little girls, now seated on his supplanted mule, led by a guard behind. Next streamed the *negarete*, and then followed an informal grouping of the militia. As this small reminder of authority passed through the center of the town, people turned to bow, and any who were mounted touched their heads to their animal's mane. Asfaw Yilma was known as a brave warrior and a fair arbitrator, and people were happy to acknowledge his leadership.

## Chapter 3

The calendar of the Christian Church in Abyssinia was replete with holy days, Saints' days and days of prayer. Some claimed that at the very least, a third of the year was spent in fasting. In any case, it was shortly after Timket, or the feast of Saint John the Baptist, that toward the end of January Asfaw Yilma announced to Wishan they would visit her grandmother, Welette Tekle, in Gondar. As the mother of Dejazmach Kinfu of Quarra, the older woman still exerted influence in the realm of politics, and could be incorrigible in her exercise of power. The family was quite aware that ten years earlier she had declared her ambitious younger brother insane and locked him in chains. Welde Tekle had fortuitously appealed to Samuel Gobat, a visiting European missionary, who claimed to cure the gentleman of his madness by copiously bleeding him, and the siblings were reconciled. In any case Asfaw Yilma felt a need to escape the political confines of Ras Ali's capital and enjoy a wider look at the country's state of affairs. He was interested in accessing both Welette's and Welde's opinions of the direction the country was taking, and felt that this was an auspicious time for the family to convene and consult with one another. This time, Worqenesh's little brothers would be allowed to join the party. The trip would be relaxed and would allow the children to see another part of their beautiful highland country.

The road to Gondar was somewhat less than a hundred miles and meandered from Debra Tabor first to the west and then northward. Because of the uncertainty of the times and the presence of his wife and young family, Asfaw Yilma organized a large contingent of his militia to accompany them. Safety lay in numbers, but aside from the threat of shifta, which was readily managed by the size of their party, the trip would be pleasant and comfortable. At this time of the year the weather was dry, which made the roads passable and the rivers fordable.

Their first, and overwhelming, delight was their initial view of Abyssinia's great inland body of water named Lake Tsana. Stretching out for as far as the eye could see, and occasionally dotted with wooded islands, the lake was truly a delight. Waterfowl abounded in every direction including white pelicans, Egyptian geese and a great variety of ducks. To further enchant the children there was a small herd of hippopotamuses - most of them on a long shoal stretching out into the water, basking in the warm sun. Wishan decided that this was a good time to share some of the lake's stories.

"Do you know that there are thirty-seven islands in the lake," she asked, "and that perhaps a third of them contain lovely little churches or monasteries?"

"Mama," asked Giyorgis, "does the Ark of the Covenant live on the lake?" Giyorgis was two years younger than Worqenesh; a serious boy and interested in the Abyssinian Orthodox Church.

"No," replied Wishan. "We are told that the Hebrew Ark of the Covenant that was brought here at the time of Soloman's reign in Israel is now safely guarded at the Church of St Mary of Zion in Aksum; but you are, in a little way, right. There is a tradition that at some earlier time the Ark was hidden at the Tsana Cherkos, and that monastery is just a few miles from where we are standing."

Now Worqenesh had to chime in. "My favorite story about the lake is that the Nile River runs right through it. Is that true, Father?"

"Indeed it is," smiled Asfaw Yilma. "The source of the river is a spring in the mountains at Gish Abbey. That is south of Lake Tsana. The water bubbles up into a small stream that meanders through rural fields and soon turns into a real river. This river, that we call Tinish Abay, (little Nile River) enters Tsana at its southwest corner, flows right across the southern portion of the lake and exits across from the Zege peninsula."

The children sighed with thoughts of the grandeur of their country and its natural beauty. Today was a day to soak in the wonder of it all. The sky was cloudless, there were flowers blooming, brightly colored birds flitting through the air and thick stands of papyrus reeds waved along the shore as the lake water rippled against their long stems. Even the air seemed especially clear and invigorating. The family and their band of militia lingered by the side of the lake for the remainder of the day and camped that night just slightly inland, so as not to tempt a night-browsing hippo. The children dined on roasted guinea fowl that their father had shot, while the men shared a species of deer that they preferred to eat raw. The next morning the camp was struck early and the party headed north, keeping Lake Tsana on their left.

Within a couple of days, with the lake still over their left shoulders, the group approached the ruins of an ancient capital built by Sarsa Dengel nearly three hundred years earlier. Little now remained of this warrior king's castle, but there was still evidence of a two-storied, rectangular, stone building that had once commanded a grand view of Lake Tsana and had been surrounded by houses and gardens scattered over the hillside.

"Giyorgis," stated his father, "you will be interested to know that Sarsa Dengel stayed here with his troops not only during the rainy season when roads were impassable, but during the fasting days of Lent. Do you remember how long during the day it is necessary for us to fast?"

"Yes, it is until your shadow becomes nine times as long as your foot."

"Good. We shall need to remember that, for Lent will be with us before long. Here in Emfras it was easy to supply the court with fish from the lake as well as fruit and vegetables from the local gardens."

"I can see grapevines still," the little boy pointed out, and many of the group dismounted their mules to pluck and eat bits of the delicious fruit that were newly ripened in the February sunshine.

Worqenesh wondered why the court of Abyssinia would ever leave such a congenial place, but the vagaries of royalty were not always readily understood. The party continued along the well worn path toward the town that had eventually supplanted Emfras. Within another two days they were approaching Gondar.

It was, by the early nineteenth century, largely a city in ruin, but the people seemed not to notice and were still in awe of the royal compound that had been built by King Fasiladas and his successors. Gondar was the most important city in the country and served as the center of its political, commercial and ecclesiastical activities. Approaching it from the southeast, Gondar seemed to the travelers from Debra Tabor to be very large, wooded and widely scattered without any recognizable plan. Houses were scarcely visible until one came right upon them because of the extensive planting of the *wanza* tree. It was a common tree usually growing near rivers or planted near homes, easily reaching a height of eighty feet and garlanded with lightly scented white flowers.

From a distance the children could see the crenulated parapet of the old royal palace and its four domed towers. It was built of roughly hewn stone and, Wishan told the children, "the king would leave his palace and ride his mule along the top of a wall to church, so that he wouldn't have to touch the ground and soil his feet!"

The Gondar of 1838 was divided into a number of distinct sectors including the imperial quarter where the nominal King still resided, but certainly not in the royal buildings of the sixteenth and seventeenth centuries. Sahle Dengel inhabited a circular, straw-covered hut similar to that of many others of the city's inhabitants. Other parts of the city included an ecclesiastical section with homes for the Abun, the head of the Orthodox Church sent by the Patriarch of the Coptic Church in Cairo (the office was vacant in 1838), and for the *Ichege*, or highest ranking Abyssinian in the Church. As some of the churches provided sanctuary in times of turmoil, the most desirable neighborhoods were those close by. East of the *Ichege Bet*, or *Ichege's* house, and west of the royal palaces was the area known as *Qan Bet*, or right-hand quarter. This was where the aristocratic and mighty lived and it was toward this sector that Asfaw Yilma led his weary family and entourage. Here dwelt Welette Tekle and her hapless, but canny, brother, Welde. The house was two-storied with an outside stairway. Often, part of the lower story housed valued horses and other animals. The upper floor contained a reception hall, with sleeping areas distributed against the sides of the building. Meal preparation took place outside in the back of the house and, as was usual in Gondar, the whole was surrounded by shrubbery and the ubiquitous *wanza* trees. They were expected.

"Wishan, my dear child, how lovely to see you," trilled her grandmother, but her eyes were on Asfaw Yilma. It was her granddaughter's husband who must be evaluated as a potential component of any family power play. Both she and her brother were ambitious, constantly weighing their positions in the continuing political power struggles of their country. At the moment their places were secure because Welette's son, Kinfu, ruled Quarra and Dembea strongly, and with the implicit approval of Ras Ali.

In a moment her eyes shifted to the mule next to Asfaw Yilma where a gangling child sat, whose little slave clasped her around her waist. This time her surprise and pleasure were genuine. "This must be your eldest, Worqenesh. Why, she is quite beautiful – a little tall perhaps, but really beautiful," and she turned an unpretentious smile on the girl. "We must talk," she murmured. "I want to know you." Then her attention turned again and she called out, "everyone must come in and get ready to eat. I know you are all tired."

With Asfaw Yilma's militia to be fed, supper was planned as a *brendo*, or a feast of raw meat. A cow was thrown down in the back of the house and killed, skinned and cut up with impressive dispatch to be eaten raw. While the militia fed on well chosen pieces along with bread and various sauces, the family's meal in the reception room included a baked fowl as well as ribs and other choice pieces of the beef, grilled. There were sauces for the meat made of onions, butter and red pepper and dishes of vegetables, to be scooped up with pieces of the flat bread, *injera*. All sat on the floor with the food placed on low tables. Before the end of the meal the little boys and Issete had toppled over in sleep, but Worqenesh struggled to stay alert. She had been seated next to Welette Tekle, who was feeding her with her own hands, bestowing distinctive favor on the child.

"We must talk tomorrow, when you are rested. How long can you stay, Yilma," asked Welette.

"Leave them for now," enjoined her brother, Welde, who had said very little all evening. "There will be time for everything. I plan to take Wishan and the children to tour the royal enclosure tomorrow. They must be exposed to some history while they are here." And so the family dispersed for the evening, servants carrying the sleeping children to their mats and the adults wishing each other a restful night.

In the dark Asfaw Yilma whispered to his wife, "We must be careful of Welette. I do not want to be persuaded to do anything against my better judgment."

But the next morning brought an unseasonal storm, so after breakfast Welette gathered the adults in the reception room to explain her view of the country's government and her perception of where the family fit in and its future prospects. "We all know," she began, "that Ali Alula has been elected by the chiefs to serve as Ras, and that it is he who entirely directs the actions of that poor relict, Sahle Dengel. The person who prevents him from naming himself *Niguse Negest* (King of Kings) in Dengel's place is Ras Wube, who holds Simien and Tigre to the north. Wube is smart enough not to challenge Ali, but he is well organized and holds the most firearms. It is guns, not spears, which will decide the future."

"Yes," responded Yilma, "but Ras Ali's mother, Menen, is from the nobility of Galla, and they are Muslims."

"That does not matter," said Welette.

Here Wishan countered quietly, "It does matter. Our Christian people in the highlands hesitate to back Ali and Menen with enthusiasm, but she is very clever and knows that they retain power only by holding different factions in tension."

"My grand niece is right," noted Welde, and both he and Yilma nodded in agreement.

"That is just the point," continued Welette, who was somewhat annoyed at being interrupted but still pleased that everyone was attentive. "We are also part of the balance of power because Wishan's father has successfully repelled the Egyptians on our western border. Ras Ali has been grateful, and has approved of Kinfu's strong governance in Quarra and Dembea, but I sense a cooling of his approbation. Menen is leery of any exertive leader and is afraid that my son will join with Dejazmach Goshu and his son, Birru, in Gojjam, and topple him from power. I think our contingent is strong enough at the moment, and that includes you, Yilma, in Begemder; but if there is even a small change in our position I want to be sure that you will continue to stand with us."

It was not a difficult assurance to give. Asfaw Yilma knew that the happiness in his life was entirely tied up with Wishan and the children. Unlike many in his culture, he and Wishan were profoundly committed to their relationship. While his existence was dependent on his success as a warrior, his joy was his family and he would fight with all his being to keep them safe. "Of course, I stand with you and Kinfu," he declared, and Welette was convinced of his purpose.

"Now, there is another matter," Welette went on. "Worqenesh is growing up and we should see to a propitious marriage for her. It would be wise to strengthen our alliance with Goshu's family in Gojjam, I think."

Asfaw Yilma visibly blanched and his jaw set in a hard line, but Wishan replied smoothly, "Oh, there will be time for such thoughts next year. We are in no hurry."

Welde looked at his grand niece and slowly let one eyelid droop. "Do you know, I believe the storm has passed. If the roads are clear let's take the children to the royal enclosure."

## Chapter 4

The streets were still a little wet, but the family rode mules so they clopped along quite comfortably. Asfaw Yilma had gone to put in an appearance at Menen's house where people gathered throughout the day, so it was Welde and Wishan who took the children on their trip back in time.

"Let's enter through the Judges gate," directed Welde. "It is the one closest to Fasilidas' Palace. Do you children know who Fasilidas was?"

"He was Susneyos' son, and the first Emporer to make his home in Gondar and to build many different buildings there," replied Worqenesh, "but I don't know why he chose Gondar."

"There are some wonderful stories as to why, and I think that I can remember at least two of them," said Welde. "Gondar came into existence in the 1630's – that's two hundred years ago, children. It often happened that a sovereign's son abandoned his father's capital, and Fasilidas was no different. We all know how young people like to do things differently! There is an early legend that the Archangel, *Raqu'el,* had prophesized that a new capital would be built having a name beginning with "G". People assumed that this capital was Gondar, conveniently forgetting that in the interim there had been capitals at Guzara and Gorgora."

"The other story is more fanciful. It is told that the young Fasilidas was out hunting one day and saw a handsome buffalo. He chased it on his horse, and suddenly it ran into a pond and vanished. Then an old man rose out of the water in its place, as bright as the sun and royal as a lion, and told Fasilidas that God had guided him to this place where he should build his new city. The spot was called Gondar, meaning the paradise of Ezra and Enoch. Wherever the truth lies, and the choice of location probably had more to do with the accessibility of trade routes than to prophesy, Fasilidas built his palace here in 1636 and, while he spent many months of every year out in the countryside campaigning, he would usually come back to Gondar to sit out the rainy season in comfort."

Giyorgis, always the observant one, pointed out that the building reminded him of the castle at Emfras.

"Indeed," responded Welde. "People speak of this sort of architecture, with crenellated walls and domed towers, as Gondarine; but the style was in fashion many years before Fasilidas built his palace here."

As they approached the castle the little party dismounted their mules, handing their reins to their ever present servants. The building was in ruins, but the great staircase to the main doorway was still manageable. Welde pointed out the semi-circular arches over the doors and windows decorated with red tuff, and peeking inside he told the children to notice that the Star of David was worked over each of the doorways. "You see, Fasilidas wanted to be sure that his visitors recalled his exalted lineage going back directly to Solomon of Israel."

The next building they came to had been built by Fasilidas' son, Yohannes I. "Do I not remember," queried Wishan, "that he was imprisoned in the palace before he acceded to the thrown?"

"He was," agreed Welde, "and it seems a great shame as he is reputed to have been a pious and saintly soul, and a great lover of books and learning. See, the walls of this building are decorated with crosses made of red tuff. It was Yohannes' library, and he loved to be here."

Walking back toward their right, Welde led the family to the castle of Iyasu the Great, Yohannes' son. "Worqenesh, you will like to imagine this palace when it was new. Of all the buildings in the enclosure it is second in size only to Fasilidas' palace, but it had some really remarkable attributes. The ceiling of its second story was not flat, but vaulted, made with brick ribs and concrete. There were also cavities in the walls which may have carried air heated by fires below. When it was first built it was said to have been decorated with ivory and gold, and there were palm trees painted on the walls and ceiling."

"I can hardly imagine anything so grand," sighed Worqenesh.

Little Issete's eyes grew big with wonder. "Oh," she said, "I wish we might have seen it then."

"No one builds such beauty now," added Worqenesh. "All people do nowadays is fight. I wish we could always live peacefully and that my Father never had to summon the *negarete* and go off to war."

"Come," enjoined Welde. "I did not mean my description of an old palace to make you sad. Let's go and see the *Ambassa Bet*, or Lion house. You know that our rulers have always been known as the Lion of Judah, just like David and Solomon. Their royal seals have shown a lion, carrying a cross and wearing a beehive crown. They also have usually kept a few well-fed lions about their persons to remind their citizens of their royal position and power. There are still some in the *Ambassa Bet* today, Haylu," and now he addressed the youngest child. "Let's go see the lions," and Haylu raced to catch hold of this exciting great uncle's hand to see yet another wonder. The *bet*, or house, was a low structure made of stone with an arched doorway and wooden beams supporting its flat roof. The building was shaded by an enormous fig tree that kept the animals cool in the warm months of April and May before the rains. There were rumblings from within, and when Welde lifted Haylu up to look through the grill-covered window, the little boy could see a shaggy mane and enormous teeth exposed by a wide yawn. Haylu, who tended to be a vocal child, said not a word and held tightly to Welde's neck.

"There are two or three more buildings that I want to show you before we leave," Welde continued. "The first is just a few steps this way. It was constructed more than eighty years after Fasilidas' palace, when Dawit III came to the throne, and it is called the *Dabal Gemb*." Welde showed them a rectangular structure with two towers, one round and the other square, at opposite corners. "Here is where the court celebrated many religious ceremonies and also where many lavish entertainments took place."

"Dawit's successor was called Bakaffa, and was another of Iyasu's sons. His palace was built in 1726, near the northern wall of the enclosure. He seems to have been a paranoid soul, always worried about insurrections and plots against his life. When he would leave

Gondar to go campaigning, he would always make careful provision for the protection of the city in his absence. It is said that he became so anxious that one time he decided to test the people and he hid in his palace, pretending illness. When the governor of the city surrounded the building he suddenly emerged on horseback and innocently rode off to church. The next day he ordered the execution of the governor he had tricked."

"What a dreadfully cruel man," cried Wishan. "It is indecent and cowardly to trick people into doing wrong."

"Well one thing he did right, as did your husband, was to choose a wife who was both wise and able," said Welde. "Her name was Menteweb, and when Bakaffa died early leaving an infant to succeed him, she served as regent until the boy's accession and as a figure of political continuity for many years after that."

"Bakaffa was able to make use of many of the earlier structures in Gondar. His own palace was a long, low single-story affair. Outside of the palace gates were two large kettle drums designated the 'lion' and the 'lamb'. In times of war or violence the 'lion' was struck, but when there were occasions of joy, it was the 'lamb' that was sounded. The people knew the distinctive tone of each instrument."

"I wish I could have sounded the drums," shouted Haylu.

"You're too small, and I bet it was a dangerous job," retorted Giyorgis. "What if Bakaffa didn't like the way you beat them? You might have ended up like that governor."

"Oh, don't tease Haylu. Beating the 'lion' or the 'lamb' would have been great fun," their mother broke in. "What is this last building, Welde, another palace?"

"It is, and this one was Menteweb's. You can see that it is a two-storied, square and castellated building, and that it abuts an oblong structure. Both have terraced roofs and the towers are decorated with red tuff crosses, rather like Yohannes I's library. Menteweb had herself crowned *Itege* (Empress). During Iyasu II's childhood he and his mother remained in Gondar, but as he came of age and began to go on hunting expeditions and war campaigns, Menteweb remained behind in Gondar to assure its security, and the city continued in peace and prosperity for many years. Come, I know everyone is tired and hungry, and you have imbibed enough history for one day. You have visited all of these royal structures and not stepped inside a single church. Tomorrow I must take you to see a real wonder – the new replacement of Debre Berhan Selassie."

"I shall like that better than anything, Uncle Welde," said Giyorgis, and his uncle beckoned to the servants who were holding the mules nearby. Soon the sight-seers were clopping back down the hill to Welette's domain.

# Chapter 5

When the family met for dinner that night, each one was brimming with news of their day. Welde delineated the sight seeing itinerary while Haylu roared like a lion and Worqenesh carefully described one palace after another. Giyorgis filled in architectural details and reiterated his anticipation of seeing a newly rebuilt church in the morning. Wishan smiled encouragement to the recitations of each child and leaned back to enjoy their evident pleasure in the day. Welette seemed to enjoy the children's company too, but finally turned to Asfaw Yilma to ask, "And what about your day? How did you find Menen's court, and what did you learn of our Ras and his mother?"

"The day was revealing," responded Asfaw Yilma. "You know that when we were talking yesterday we assumed a grouping of our family coalescing with Goshu Zewde in Gojjam and Wube up north to balance the ambition of Ras Ali and his mother. Only a strong alliance can contain Ali's thinly diguised desire to get rid of our *de facto* king and usurp his position. Today at Menen's house I noticed several people I recognized as friends of Goshu's son, Birru, openly laughing and chatting with her, and enjoying her seeming interest and approval. You know Menen. She is avaricious, vain and violent; and she is constantly scheming to advance her son's position and her own."

Welette, who secretly admired Menen's single-minded ambition but found it beyond her own ability to be as ruthless, frowned at Yilma's news. "I must send a messenger to tell Kinfu. He is the only one of my sons still alive and able to protect the political status of the family along with our lands and income. He and his son, Mekwennin, and you, his son-in-law, are the ones still remaining to help us. I had hoped that our agreements with Goshu and Wube would hold, but it appears that Goshu's son is not to be trusted. I have always respected Dejazmach Goshu as a man of honor, but that does not guarantee the merit of his offspring. Yilma, do you have any knowledge of the fighting strength of his army?"

"I believe he has a few matchlocks, but no more than perhaps twenty. The Gojjamis rely most heavily on their warriors armed with lances, and most of them are well mounted and good riders. Of course, no one can match the Gallas for horsemanship, but Birru Goshu's men are quite good enough. I think they number about ten thousand, and that does not include his father's army." Yilma paused for a moment to further consider. "He is no match for my father-in-law, particularly not when Kassa Haylu is supporting him as he did on the border."

"Yes," answered Welette, "but one certainly never knows when Kassa might show up and when not. Right now, he is an unknown factor. I have a feeling that Kassa is only going to be for Kassa."

"Is there any country so complex as ours," observed Wishan who had moved over to sit next to Asfaw Yilma. "No one can really usurp the crown because there is no Abun in the country to anoint a new sovereign. Abune Qerlos died nearly ten years ago, and no one has sent to Alexandria to find his replacement."

"Yes," agreed Asfaw Yilma, "and now our church is disrupted by arguments between the Monophysite faction and those who support the doctrine of *Sost Ledet*. Internal quarrels do not demonstrate strength. There has been no resolute action to bring a new Abun to Abyssinia because of these schisms, and without a strong leader of the Church, we are fractured into weakness." By now Giyorgis had edged toward the adult conclave.

"Father, what does *Sost Ledet* mean?"

"I am a soldier, not a cleric, Giyorgis, but I think it refers to a belief in three births of Christ."

"But, Father, how can we believe in one devine nature of Christ, three births, and the message that Abba Guebra Barke at home has mentioned? He told me a foreign missionary had said that Christ's nature was both fully divine and fully human. These ideas don't match up."

"That is just the point, Giyorgis. Our opposing religious doctrines reflect the confusion in our government and in every aspect of our public lives, but I must not sound so glum. We do have strengths. Our shared history is a strength, as are our resilience and constant good humor. Let's all get to bed now, so that we can be ready for another adventure tomorrow."

\* \* \*

The next morning dawned crisp and clear, so that everyone hurried through breakfast to be ready for their outing. Even Welette was to join them. Their destination was built on raised ground to the north and west of the royal enclosure. Once again the family rode along the irregular, stony pathways of the city guarded by their retinue of well-armed soldiers.

This day Welette led the family, keeping Worqenesh at her side. "Gondar is a city full of churches," she began. "I have been told there are forty-four. The Emperor Iyasu I built at least two churches during his reign, and Debre Berhan Sellase was the second. It was a wonderful, circular building made of stone, and measured 100 cubits from its eastern to its western doors and from the northern to the southern. The roof is said to have resembled a rainbow and was topped by a splendid decorative piece made of gold. But all of that magnificence was destroyed, and what you shall see today is the church that has recently been built to replace it. I do believe that our new Berhan Sellase must be even more lovely than the structure that it has replaced. Look over there - it is surrounded by a large, stone wall with twelve rounded towers representing the twelve apostles."

Welde ventured to interrupt his sister's narrative. "The thirteenth tower is larger than the others, and serves as the entrance gate. It symbolizes Christ, and is shaped to represent the Lion of Judah, but the lion's tail is missing."

"Welde, you are always foolish."

"My dear sister, I am quite serious; and if you look very carefully over the grounds, you will find a lion's tail."

"In any case," continued Welette. "you see that the new structure is not a circle, but a rectangle. It is built of stone and mortar, with stone columns circling the building forming a sort of portico. We ladies will enter from the south, as is proper, and we will meet you inside."

As Worqenesh stepped through the doorway, she drew back in wonder. Every wall was covered with vibrant paintings of saints, martyrs and biblical stories. Looking at her brother, Giyorgis, entering from the opposite door, she relished his obvious delight in the miracle of this holy place. Then, as if drawn by a magnet, they both lifted their eyes to the ceiling.

"Oh, Worqenesh," breathed Giyorgis.

There, row upon row, were winged Ethiopian angels – at least a hundred of them – each seeming to have a different, questioning expression on its face. All three children leaned back to take in the wondrous sight. Worqenesh and Giyorgis were struck with awe, but little Haylu grinned back at the angels as if in perfect harmony with them.

"What remarkable artistry," murmured Wishan. "I am so glad that you brought us. This is a sight to be remembered in our hearts; one we can draw comfort from in years to come."

Giyorgis spotted a pile of prayer sticks in a corner. "Uncle Welde, do you think I could borrow one to walk around with?" But his Uncle was hurrying on.

"Come, Giyorgis. Those sticks are for the priests."

The family slowly moved about the church, examining one painting after another, and then walked back out into the sunshine to wander over the church grounds. Suddenly, Haylu shouted, "I've found it; I've found the lion's tail!" There, indeed, over an arched gate on the western side of the structure was a round stone medallion, and on it, carefully carved in a curve to fit the edge of the medallion, was a lion's tail.

By now the sun was overhead, but no one seemed to be overly tired so Welette suggested a little exploring of the city. "It has somewhat fallen from its original splendor, but Gondar is still the center of commerce for Abyssinia and there is much to see and understand. Let's head to the south of the palaces to what is called the *Addababy,* or main courtyard, which is where our Monday market is held. There are four more great churches in the area."

Going through the market area they passed the *Worq Gabaya*, or gold market. This is where gold is exchanged for salt," explained Welette. "And no one may measure out the gold except for licensed silversmiths."

Continuing to the southwest, they saw the *Faras Bet*, or place of horses where these animals were bought and sold. Even further to the south and to the southwest was an odd stretch of land filled with rocks where the main market was held every day of the week. Here the family wandered about looking at honey, salt, coffee beans, various sorts of cloth and even cattle. Also to the southwest of Gondar were the *Eslam Bet*, where Muslims lived, and several *Falasha*, or Jewish, villages.

"You must have noticed that in all our traveling about, we have seen no sources of water in Gondar itself," pointed out Welde. "All of the city's water must be hand carried from the Qaha and Angerab rivers here in the south to the residents above. There is a spring halfway up our neighboring mountain to the east, but it dries up this time of the year until the rains come again in June or July. Firewood must be carried too. The lack of these essentials can be a serious problem during times of conflict such as we have seen in recent years."

The sun was setting over the western plains of Dembea as the family turned their mules back uphill toward the *Qan Bet* and Welette's house. There would be one more day in Gondar to rest and prepare for their journey home.

Their last evening in the city Welette received a response to the message that she had sent Kinfu. It had caught up with him at Fenja, not many miles away. "We are strong," he had written, "and can thwart any mischief Menen may plan with Birru. Thanks for your vigilance."

# Chapter 6

The next morning Asfaw Yilma and his family began their trip back to Diddim. It was a quiet progression, as if each one was adjusting internally from days of adventure back to the pace of their normal routines. As usual, the family was surrounded by its protective militia. Lake Tsana was visible to their right, and again they camped above its shore so that they could enjoy its changing beauty until nightfall and as they broke camp in the morning. This time Asfaw Yilma did not stop at Emfras, but rather lingered for a little while at an early seventeenth century *katama*, or military headquarters, nearby called Qoga. It too had fallen into disuse, but still occupied a lovely situation high above the Lake.

At Qoga they turned to the east and began climbing the hills toward Debra Tabor. From here the animals seemed to sense their approach to home, and to quicken their pace. Worqenesh and Issete cut their mule in front of the boys in childish competition, but Wishan dropped behind, enjoying the sunshine and the cooler elevation.

"Are you tired?" asked Asfaw Yilma.

"No more so than with the other three," and she looked over at him with a smile. With his answering recognition she continued, "It is due at the end of August, and it will be another boy. What shall we call him? I rather like the name 'Welde' and I was really delighted to become reacquainted with my great uncle. He is a bit of an enigma, but an interesting and a kindly man."

"Then Welde Yilma he shall be," promised her husband, not dreaming to counter her prediction of the child's gender.

The family skirted past Debra Tabor, heading directly for their home high in the hills. As they climbed toward Diddim they were not slowed by the incline, but rather hastened their pace, as anxious as their mules to reach home. The villagers heard their approach, and Yilma's mother was standing at their main doorway with a warm welcome spread across her face. 'How different from Welette she is,' thought Worqenesh as she and Issete fell into the woman's arms. 'How good it is to be home.'

\* \* \*

Cognizant of a growing weight of responsibility upon his shoulders, particularly in his role as a defender of Wishan's family, Asfaw Yilma departed for Debra Tabor early the next morning. While he held his position as Dejazmach of Begemder at Ras Ali's pleasure, he was increasingly aware that he must first be able to take care of himself, and only after that, his larger family. Ras Ali's place in the delicate political balance was tenuous, and could change at any time. Riding down the path from his misty aerie, Yilma thought of the battles he had already fought and those that might soon come.

Surrounding him as he moved forward were the members of his military entourage. Just to his side was his *Bellata Gaeta*, or the person who had the power to act for Asfaw Yilma or issue orders in his stead – a highly trusted and capable officer. Behind him was the *Ajax*, or man whose duty it was to provide food and housing for Yilma's army when it was on the road. There was the *Fit-Aurari* who would lead the advanced guard into battle and who was Yilma's special friend, Fenta Tadese. There was also a person who tended the horses and saw to providing for their fodder, and two men who were responsible for guarding Yilma's camp – one at night and one in the daytime. The same contingent of his militia that accompanied the family to Gondar and back followed behind. Asfaw Yilma's appearance was daunting, sitting astride Selpha. In addition to his usual trousers and belt he had donned a thigh length shirt with slashed sleeves, and over this he had thrown a lion's pelt. The entire group made a formidable showing as they moved down the slopes of the mountain range.

Asfaw Yilma's purpose was to engage his forces in honing their warrior skills in the national game of *guks*. The meadows below Debra Tabor provided a large, flat space for field exercises and war games. Sides would be drawn, and would face each other across a shallow gully cut across the land in the rainy season. The mounted warriors would substitute blunt sticks for their metal-tipped lances, and would charge their opposites, hurling their improvised weapons to force their opponents back behind the gully. The game was exceptionally dangerous and there were frequent, and sometimes fatal, injuries.

Word had gone ahead of Yilma, and troops from the town had gathered, as well as bystanders, to ogle and cheer. Those who came to watch would need to be careful as they too, could be at risk. Sides were quickly chosen, all of the participants being members of Asfaw Yilma's fighting force. The ritual would have seemed almost chivalric if there were not so much noisy bragging and bravado. Men shouted taunts as the two sides backed away from each other and prepared to charge with blunted sticks in their right hands and shields in their left. A skilled rider would guard his mount's hind quarters as well as his own person with graceful twists and turns, moving his shield back and forth; and a good horse would be as well aware of the essence of the tournament and the flight of sticks as would his rider.

All eyes were on Dejazmach Yilma's raised arm, and as it dropped the riders on both sides accelerated across the field, shouting their horses' names as a war cry. Yilma could feel Selpha's speed beneath him and as they approached the opposite team, directed the horse with his body. To his utter joy the gelding obeyed each signal, and as they approached the onslaught of hurled sticks Selpha began his own pattern of dexterously shifting from side to side. Both horse and rider seemed to respond to the challenge of the field with matching enthusiasm. As he and Selpha maneuvered two opponents toward the back of the field, Yilma remembered his first sight of the horse at Worqenesh's direction. What a gift from his daughter this animal was. Yilma wondered if she would always be so perspicacious. Selpha would be a boon companion in the months to come. Yilma had a feeling they would not be easy ones.

When they tired of riding, Asfaw Yilma had the horses moved to the side of the field and the men began a good-hearted sham fight on foot. There were shouts of war cries as the brightly dressed soldiers shifted and fought across the field. Rushing at each other with wild yells, they fought hand to hand, with Yilma's team pushing their combatants continually back. He seemed to be everywhere. Of a slightly taller stature than many of his countrymen, lean and sinewy, Yilma was noticeable by the grace and dexterity of his movements and the expression of exhilaration on his face.

"Fenta," he called across to his friend. "I think we are ready for anyone!"

And Fenta, who was serving a heavy blow to a member of the opposing team, looked over at his friend with sheer joy. "We could roust the Gallas, or Ras Ali himself." Then, realizing the seditious nature of his outburst, he ducked and continued hacking away at his mock foe. Yilma grinned and shook his head. They would need to be more guarded with their tongues. Ras Ali, with his mother, was expected back in his capital at any time. Asfaw Yilma was always uneasy about the workings of Menen's mind. She had no loyalty, but to herself and her son.

Yilma decided to remain overnight in Debra Tabor and, as usual when he stayed, he sought Fenta's hospitality. The two men, with their entourages, made their way back up from the field to the town. The settlement was really a military town and would have felt transitory had it not been for the churches that Ras Ali had built. There were no stone houses, and only the two wattle palaces of Menen and Ali were buildings of any significance. As always, Yilma was glad to think of his own haven in Diddim. Still, it would be pleasant to visit his friend and talk over matters of mutual concern.

The town was spread out, with houses and huts sprawled indiscriminately. There were even tents set up for soldiers on duty. Fenta lived in a comfortable compound that included a sheltered stable for the horses. Yilma could feel secure about Selpha.

That night a cow was slaughtered and there was the customary raw beef, as well as *wat* (stew) to be soaked up with *injera*. Mead flowed, and when others in their party had eaten their fill and faded out into the dark, the two friends talked well into the night.

"You must be more guarded in your speech, Fenta. We are in a very delicate alliance with Ras Ali. I think he tolerates my family and my wife's, simply because her father has held the Egyptians at bay for the last few years. When I was in Gondar I picked up on some gossip at Menen's house. I believe that Ali, who has benefited from my father-in-law, Kinfu's, ruthlessness; now begins to fear it. Being back in Ras Ali's capital, and under his thumb, we must be very careful of an appearance of loyalty, as well as its reality."

His friend was quiet for some moments, and then looked up. "Do you think that Ali Alula will shift his allegiance away from your family?"

It was now Yilma's turn to pause and consider. "I believe that Ras Ali tries to be marginally loyal to his friends, but that his mother, Menen, has no such scruples. If she sees an opportunity to advance herself, she will push ahead, and old allies be damned!"

Fenta's eyebrows shot up, and then his face relaxed into a smile. "Yilma, my friend, know that I am not of that ilk. Come what may, I shall be with you and we will put up a good fight wherever we find ourselves."

The tension in the room dissipated, and the two friends talked on. For each, it was good to know that there was someone who would remain at his side, and who understood the exigencies of the seemingly endless quarrels leading to the merciless battles of their time. They agreed that they should arrange frequent bouts of *guks* until the seasonal rains began, probably in June. Their native soldiers were known for bravery, but not for discipline, and it would be wise to continue to hone their skills. It would also be politic to speak with Ras Ali about these games and to seek his approbation. It would be most expedient if he consented to join in.

The next day Asfaw Yilma rode back to Diddim, leading that portion of his militia and his *negarete* who lived in the area. What was somewhat unusual about his appearance that day was that he rode Selpha, and not one of the mules customarily used for his domestic travel.

# Chapter 7

The rains came. April and May had been hot, as always, but being able to retire to the mountains at Diddim after the numerous games conducted in the fields below Debra Tabor had eased the burden of rigorous training. Ras Ali had returned to his capital and, with no campaigns planned between the season of Easter and the rains; he had been delighted with Asfaw Yilma's idea for training, and had frequently joined him on the field. Even Menen had sometimes ridden down to the fields from her palace to watch the games and encourage the participants. 'Such a woman,' thought Yilma, 'would enjoy watching the violence of their efforts and would carefully analyze the strengths and weaknesses of each player.'

Asfaw Yilma was pleased with the energy and persistence of his soldiers. They were never easy to command, but their enthusiasm knew few bounds. His concern was that the field on which they practiced was flat and predictable. How would the men fare if the land was rolling or the enemy hidden? Still, Ras Ali was complimentary and the soldiers diligent. Yilma was content that he was actively working with his militia and not leaving fortune to chance.

In June the *guks* tournaments were curtailed because the fields became saturated with the annual deluge of rain. It did not rain all day, but on most days, beginning in the middle of the afternoon, dark clouds would roll overhead and the heavens would open. Sometimes in the mountainous area of Diddim there would be hail and, for a little while, the ground would be white. Then, in these upper reaches, the fields of barley that had been plowed by oxen and sown by hand would germinate and begin to grow. They would be carefully weeded by Asfaw Yilma's peasants and by the children. There were no fences to protect the crops, but while the grain was ripening young boys with slings would be stationed to guard against wild boar and other invading animals.

Worqenesh loved to help in the fields. She and Issete would move through the growing grain tenderly removing undesired, intruding plants and always careful not to tread on those that were being cultivated. When the barley was harvested it would feed both the people and their animals, and Worqenesh thought with pleasure how Selpha would enjoy his feed in the months to come. She knew how special the horse was to her father, and she was very fond of the animal herself. On a particular day late in August, Worqenesh had the feeling that the rainy season was drawing to a close. The fresh verdure of June was long gone. She sensed a change that would culminate in the golden days of Meskel when the fields would ripen for the harvest.

In the last few days her mother had deliberately kept close to the house. Wishan was hugely pregnant, and this time her daughter was very aware of the event about to take place. In Abyssinia, as a birth date drew near, women in the village began to congregate near the home to be available to assist the mother when called upon. Only women would be allowed in the house: it was not suitable for a man to be present. As this day was drawing to a close, Worqenesh and Issete were walking home from the grain fields when Worqenesh saw her father guiding her brothers down the path toward the center of the village and some of their neighboring women slip quietly into the house. The two girls hurried forward. Worqenesh was nine now, and quite old enough to know about the business of women. She hurried to her mother's side to hold her hand as the village women skillfully began to go about their work. There were no men in sight. The house was now considered, in the eyes of the church, unclean. If a man were to come in, he would not be allowed to enter his church for forty days.

Being the fourth child, Welde Yilma soon arrived, to be washed in cold water and have one of the women push on his head and different features to assure that he would be handsome. In some parts of the country a man would have reached through a window to poke a lance in his mouth to make him brave, but Asfaw Yilma did not countenance such superstitious behavior. Soon the village women emerged outside to fill the air with joyful ululations, repeated twelve times because the child was a boy. After eight days Welde was circumcised, and on the tenth day the priest came from the village church carrying the cross and incense, and sprinkling holy water throughout the house to purify it.

Worqenesh was enchanted with the baby. Whenever Wishan grew tired, Worqenesh would pick up the infant to cuddle it under the watchful eye of her grandmother. It was not long before she was judged quite reliable as a care giver and she, along with Issete, would carry little Welde outside to sit under one of the great fir trees in the yard and sing him to sleep. These were happy days, when the sun was shining all day again and the wonderful mountain air of Abyssinia was fresh and clear.

On exactly the fortieth day after his birth, which fell in the first week of October, Welde Yilma was christened. Because he was the son of a great Dejazmach, the affair was to be elaborate and planned with care. The family traveled to Debra Tabor the day before so that the ceremony could be held at the Church of Iyasus, and their beloved Abba Guebra Barhe would officiate. Asfaw Yilma's good friend, Fenta Tadese, would stand as godfather, and it would be a joyful day for both the family and the community. Even Ras Ali and Menen had been invited: one could not forget the niceties.

So on a glorious day in early October the family rode their mules from Fenta Tadese's house, up the hill to the southeast of the town along the path that led to the Church of Iyasus. A large crowd had gathered outside, and the highest ranking of the community were already inside the holy structure. The family dismounted, and as they approached the front of the church, Wishan handed little Welde to his godfather. Then the men and women separated, the women to enter the door on the right of the building and the men to carry the baby through the door on the left. Going inside, Fenta handed little Welde to Abba Guebra Barhe who placed his hand on the child's head and poured on a few drops of water. He next took oil and made the sign of the cross on the baby's head, hands, chest and knees. Finally he took the *mateb*, a light blue cord, which he tied gently around the little boy's neck to signify his Christian faith. The kindly priest then returned Welde to his godfather, admonishing Fenta Tadese to always concern himself with the child's education, and his spiritual and temporal welfare.

At the conclusion of the ceremony, Abba Barhe and the entire party returned to Fenta's house where he and Asfaw Yilma put on an enormous celebratory feast. As the day drew to a close the women and children gradually withdrew, but the men continued with their festivities long into the night.

Late the next morning, when Fenta and Yilma were eating bread and drinking mead preparatory to the family's departure, Fenta remembered Abba Barhe's advice concerning his new godson. "We must think about his education, Yilma."

"Don't you think it's a little early," grinned Yilma. "Perhaps he should first learn to walk!"

"*Isshi*," replied the new godfather, "and I know that he will learn his letters and the psalms with the other children and that you will be sure that he can shoot and ride as he grows older. He must learn to swim as well. But," he said looking directly at his friend, "I play a better game of chess than you do, and I can teach him to play the *bagana* (a ten-stringed harp). He will become a great warrior, but he will also be a man of some learning."

"You are very sanguine about the days ahead," said his friend. "I hope you and I are both here for many years. I sometimes worry that I will not be: our countrymen are so volatile, and who can say what the days ahead will bring. But I am much too gloomy. It is too fine a day to have dark thoughts. I am sure, though, that Ras Ali will have both of us on the road very soon. The rains are well gone, and he will want to begin his campaign against the Gallas. He has already said that this year we shall accompany him."

"That's all right, Yilma. It will keep us well practiced in our battle skills."

Asfaw Yilma looked at his friend with real affection. Here was a good man. The two men rose up together and walked outside where Wishan was already directing the servants and the children.

It was not long before Yilma, his family and their retainers clattered out of Fenta Tadese's large enclosure and began their ride back to Diddim. The family rode together, with guards before and behind and the militia straggled out in both directions. Giyorgis and Haylu shared one mule and Worqenesh with Issete another. Wishan rode next to her husband carrying little Welde in her arms. When the pathway began to grow steep Asfaw Yilma, knowing the climb to be tiring, reached over and lifted the sleeping baby into his own arms and moved a little ahead. While he could still be with them, he would happily ease the small burdens of daily life from his family.

When they reached their home in their mountain village there was a messenger from the Ras already waiting. On the day after the following Sunday, Ras Ali would gather his army together in Debra Tabor and ride in a southeasterly direction to sort out the continuing skirmishes between the area of Lasta and the country of the Yejju and Wello Gallas. Dejazmach Asfaw Yilma should summon his army and meet the Ras as he sallied forth from Debra Tabor to begin his dry season campaign of 1838-1839.

The few days for the family to be together quickly passed, and much of the time was spent in the arduous task of gathering and packing supplies for a campaign of undetermined length. In particular, there were cooking utensils to organize, grain for bread and grain to feed the animals, butter and honey, animals for slaughtering, tents, grindstones, hides for beds and enough mules to carry everything. Then there were camp followers, most of whom were women, who would grind grain into flour, prepare meals and herd animals. An Abyssinian army on the move was a spectacle of disorder, countered by the cheerful cohesion of its participants.

Well before dawn the next Monday morning, Yilma briefly held his sleepy family close, mounted Selpha and led his *negarete* and the militia who lived in Diddim down the mountains to enter Debra Tabor as the day began. The long train of supplies, herders and camp followers straggled along behind. He would assemble the rest of his militia and pick up Fenta Tadese upon arriving in the capital. A few trusted men were left behind to protect his village, and Wishan's household servants and the farm peasants were fully capable of doubling as fighters if the need arose. It was the way of life in Abyssinia.

# Chapter 8

The season's campaign was to be, very simply, a show of force. Menen's clever balance of the various Galla tribes against Gojjam, Dembea and the Simien mountain area still held, but it required a continuous display of strength. Ras Ali, essaying forth from his centrally located capital, commanded an impressive array of gunners, cavalry and foot soldiers – enough to give most would-be troublemaker's pause.

The army which, for this exercise, did not include all of the force that Ali might have assembled, moved slowly through the countryside of Begemder to attain a crossing point at the Bashilo River near its junction with the Nile. Its progression was spread out and in modest segments, with overnight encampments along the way. As each halt was called, the Ras' *Fit-Aurari* would mark the spot for his master's tent and then go forward to pitch his own. A large space around the Ras' designated spot, which was on the highest ground in the vicinity, was kept clear for his private retinue to encamp, and his tent was erected to face the direction of the next day's march. A few tents nearby were even set up for his favorite horses. To the right were his household, including his *negaretes*, and to the left were the guards. In like manner, each Dejazmach or important chief established his own area. Far to the rear, in a sort of half-circle, were those great chiefs who were part of the rear guard; and far in front of the forces were the most powerful *Fit-Auraris*. Throughout the campaign these positions would be maintained relative to each other, wherever the army might be, with the Ras, in his elevated position, able to oversee all. Asfaw Yilma was a part of the rear guard and situated in the semicircle at the back.

With each encampment the grass and wood cutters would be sent out, sometimes to a great distance. The animals, too, would be disbursed to feed and to be watered, and soldiers could be sent a fair distance for supplies, for after a week or two the army would run out of the supplies it had carried, and have to feed off the countryside. In the evening there would be a great banquet, and meat from the slaughtered animals would be distributed according to each person's rank, or position. Mead would flow, and then the *doomfata*, or tales of individual exploits, would begin. An Abyssinian warrior was notoriously reckless and brave, but also boastful; and loved to recite tales of his deeds of valor. There would be praise for the heroic, and bitter scorn for those deemed cowardly.

Approaching the Bashilo River, Asfaw Yilma was surprised to look across its channel to see that it was easily half a mile wide, but with the cessation of the rains the water was only ankle deep and easily forded. By the side of the river Fenta pointed out the huge footprints of hippopotamuses, noting that there must be deep pools just downstream where the behemoths would frolic. They would likely be sharing the space with their frequent cohorts, the Nile crocodile. The weather was pleasantly warm, and camping that afternoon was on the far side of the river. The next day the army began a gradual climb to the higher tableland of the Wello Gallas.

As they progressed upward the cold became bone-chilling and the mornings were foggy. Their way led through deep pine woods and along the sides of mountains. The land of the Wellos was at least a thousand feet above the place of the river crossing. At length their pathway led to grass and low shrubs alone, and to a great open space. They were in the land of the Galla. Ras Ali was, himself, of the Yejju tribe, and so they were welcome as long as they did not overstay the local resources.

The Ras did not propose to linger, but as he passed from the lands of the Wello Galla and the Were Himano to those of the Yejjus, it seemed to those around him that for him it was a homecoming. Then Ras Ali strung his army out into a line, rather than a mass, and gave strict orders against theft or vandalism. The punishment for an infraction would be the loss of a hand or a foot. He would not allow his show of force to disintegrate into profligacy. The land was sufficiently fruitful to support the army as it passed through, and that was all that was necessary. They moved across plains where there were fields of grain, and dotted between them magnificent horses were tethered and brood mares with their foals sedately grazed. Often, Asfaw Yilma thought of his children and how they would enjoy seeing such beauty. When the army reached the northern edges of the Yejju Galla's land that bordered on Lasta, Ras Ali made sure that these unruly subjects knew of his whereabouts, and then abruptly turned his army westward and back towards their own province of Begemder and his capital of Debra Tabor. They were home just before Christmas.

\* \* \*

Wishan and the children had enjoyed quiet days while Asfaw Yilma was gone – days filled with household chores, tending fields and the children's weekly lessons with Abba Barhe. The time had gone by quickly. In Yilma's absence Wishan was particularly vigilant to assure that the villagers were both secure and busy. While the nobility of Abyssinia was entirely military, the ordinary people of the mountains were industrious, and were generally independent and scornful of any restraint. They were also fiercely loyal to their lord and perfectly able to throw down their farming tools to defend the land. In Abyssinia there was a remarkable equality throughout society. A man who plowed the land was perfectly capable of taking up arms to lead his fellows into battle. Conversely, a powerful soldier was equally capable, having suffered defeat, to submit to another man's leadership.

Asfaw Yilma was welcomed home with joy. He returned to the assurance of another child, to be born at the end of *keremt*, the season of the big rains. This year Wishan was not claiming prescience of the child's gender. As part of his normal routine, Asfaw Yilma exchanged messages with Welette and Welde in Gondar, who both seemed unconcerned about any new political imbalance; and as he had the previous year, Yilma organized regular *guks* tournaments on the fields below Debra Tabor. This year Ras Ali was constantly traveling and was rarely in Debra Tabor long enough to participate in the games. Menen did not appear at all. Yilma did sometimes wonder if this change in behavior boded difficulty ahead, but he was too active to dwell on conjecture for very long.

Easter came and went. Worqenesh was now ten years old, and Issete probably just a little younger. Having been separated from her family at an early age, no one was quite certain how old she was. The two girls were always to be found together, and they were a striking pair to those unaccustomed to their company. Worqenesh seemed to grow taller every day; her complexion was fair, like her mother's, her smile ready and her wit keen. Issete was petite, her skin dark and her manner kindly, but shy. Together, they could usually be found playing with little Welde in the shade of the fir trees in the family compound, working in the barley fields with the village women or sitting with Giyorgis and Haylu in the company of the good Abba Barhe. Worqenesh was also beginning to learn the art of spinning from her mother, and Issete was privy to these lessons as well. In the night time, they still curled up together on the animal skins that Asfaw Yilma had brought home from hunting excursions, and they still emerged the next day with the wonder of a mountain morning in their eyes. But rural Abyssinian children grew up quickly, and they both knew that their lives would change before long.

"Worqenesh, do you think that your family will look for a husband for you soon? Is that what you would like? Do you remember your great aunt Welette talking about someone from Gojjam last year?" Issete's eyes were wide and sparkling with curiosity.

"I do not want to ever leave home," countered Worqenesh. "If I should marry, I want to stay here in Diddim, and I certainly don't know anyone near by that my parents would consider. I wish Father's friend, Fenta Tadese, had a son, but he doesn't."

Issete's eyelids dropped shyly, and then she lifted them to look straight at her friend. "You must marry someone as fine as you are," she stated with great emphasis. "It must be someone special and unusual."

Worqenesh smiled at this dear companion whom she thought of as a part of herself. "Thank goodness there is no talk of anyone right now, Issete. I think everyone is too interested in politics and war. Why is it that our countrymen do so love to fight? They think of nothing else. I wish that someday they would build us up instead of tearing us apart. I wish that Father could stay with us always, and never had to follow after Ras Ali, but I am afraid that that is too much to long for."

Wishan noticed the two girls deep in conversation and wondered what could so consume their attention. Issete was like a second daughter, and she was grateful that Worqenesh could have a close female companion in her family of brothers.

* * *

The rains came a little early in 1839, but they were always welcome in the highlands as the heavens daily unleashed the burden of their waterlogged clouds. One afternoon, soon after Meskel, Asfaw Yilma looked out from the doorway of one of his stables to see a messenger mounted on a mule and struggling up the pathway. He appeared exhausted, but he was urging his animal on in an extreme state of agitation. Yilma ran out to meet him and draw him into the quiet of the stable.

"I come from Gondar," the man gasped, "sent from Welette Tekle. Her son, Kinfu of Quarra, is dead."

# Chapter 9

With these few words, the delicate balance of power in Abyssinia was broken. Yilma handed the messenger's mule over to one of his servants, and guided the exhausted man toward the main structure in the compound. "You must rest and eat," he said, "and then tell us all that you know."

When the man had been served *tej* and a hastily assembled meal of *wat* with *injera*, and had been given a little time to recover his breath and rest before the small fire in the hearth, Asfaw Yilma said, "give us what details you know, or may have heard, as well as what Welette Tekle has sent you to tell us."

"It happened while Dejazmach Kinfu was campaigning on the western border," declared the messenger. "Welde Tekle was with him. They were in the area of Metemma checking for signs of Egyptian infiltration. You know the area. It is low lying and tends to be feverish, but Kinfu was not ill. He simply fell from his horse and was dead."

"Is this what Welette has said, or is this acknowledged news from the front?" Yilma was trying to adjust his mind to the enormity of what was happening.

"Both," assured the man. "No one is questioning the manner of his death, but all are surprised at its consequence. The Woisero Tekle has sent me to tell you that you must come to protect your inheritance. In Gondar, Ras Ali has declared that the lands of Dejazmach Kinfu will not be given to his sons, that is, to Mekwennin and to you, the husband of his daughter. He has handed them over to Birru Goshu of Gojjam. All of Dembea and Quarra, as well as Gojjam, are now to be held by Goshu. Welette begs you to waste no time in coming to join Mekwennin and Welde Tekle in Gondar to defend the family's land."

Yilma let his eyes glance around the circular room. Wishan was with him, as were Worqenesh and Giyorgis, his eldest son. Issete was crouched behind Worqenesh's shoulder, but he knew he could trust the child. "Is there anything else," he questioned. "You are hesitant, I think. What have you not said?"

"It is only hearsay," replied the messenger, "but you did say to give you details."

"Yes, I must understand all that has happened."

"Then I believe this to be true, although Welette Tekle has said nothing. On the evening of Kinfu's death his *Bellata Gaeta* called Dejazmach Kinfu's militia together and ordered his *Affa Dejachmach* (literally, the mouth of the Dejazmach) to read his will. In it he had given orders that his uncle, Welde Tekle, should be blinded so that he could not impede the succession of you and Mekwennin." At a nod from Yilma, he continued. "The word is that the man who was charged with the task of blinding Welde has, whether intentionally or not, only slightly injured one eye."

"Then what is happening now," demanded Yilma.

"Mekwennin and Welde Tekle are gathering their own forces and appealing to all of the men who served Dejazmach Kinfu. I am sent to tell you that you must come immediately, fully prepared to march down the western coastline of Lake Tsana to confront the family of Goshu."

"My good man, I thank you for your service. It is not an easy thing to be the bearer of bad news. Go now, and get some sleep. You must accompany us back to Gondar." With that, Asfaw Yilma beckoned to Giyorgis to escort the man to a servant and turned to Wishan. "I must leave before dawn tomorrow. Please organize the foodstuff, utensils and cooks for me. There is no time. I shall need only provisions sufficient for the march to Gondar, and will gather more supplies there." With that, he hastened to the doorway to summon his *negarete*. Within seconds the alarming timpani of the drums could be heard, and then shouted orders and the sound of footsteps rushing through the village.

Yilma sent word to Fenta Tadese to gather the remainder of their men and to quietly meet him, at early light, on the trail west of Debra Tabor. To his knowledge, Ras Ali was not in residence at his capital, but it would be foolish to risk an encounter.

When she had finished ordering the assembling of the militia's food Wishan hastened to her mother-in-law, who had begun to prepare a large family meal. Yilma must be well cared for and fed before being sent off to what was sure to be a savage and momentous battle. War was both an accustomed way of life for this family, and a rude disruption.

When they retired that night for a restless sleep, Issete threw her arm around Worqenesh and whispered in her ear, "It is as if you knew this was coming. Are you gifted with prophecy? Never mind, I am here with you. Your father is a great warlord and will surely prevail. You must not be afraid." And she reached for Worqenesh's hand to comfort her, and pulled the warm leopard skin up over her shoulder.

\* \* \*

The men left in the pre dawn, when only the slightest hint of gray could be seen behind the mountains. Asfaw Yilma's head was reeling with the strange tale the messenger had relayed. Indeed, he was aware that blinding and imprisonment were both used in the country to prevent siblings in the royal family from plotting regicide. He knew that his father-in-law had been a hard and a ruthless man. In the back of his mind he wondered if the Woisero Welette had been in collusion with him and back to her old tricks, but Welde had once more proved himself to be a survivor. Yilma grinned to himself in the darkness. He was fond of the canny, older man.

Fenta Tadese was waiting with the remainder of Yilma's men at the appointed fork in the trail. They had left the town quietly, but in any case, neither Ras Ali nor Menen had been in their capital. Fenta had heard that the Ras had left a few days earlier headed in the direction of the *Abbai* (the Blue Nile) and the crossing at the old Portuguese bridge. With the two groups of militia meeting in the early dawn, Yilma had close to eight thousand fighting men. In addition there were the usual essential wood and grass cutters as well as those responsible for providing *tej* (the passion of all those who fought) and the women who would grind the grain and cook. Asfaw Yilma's army was fairly modest as it had been assembled with such haste and must travel at a pace close to a forced march. It would rest briefly at night, but press on quickly during daylight hours.

"Tell me what has happened," enjoined Fenta. "How did Kinfu die, and why has Ras Ali gone back on his word?"

"That should be no surprise," answered Yilma. "His family's first distinction is duplicity. Dejazmach Kinfu died in the saddle, but it would seem that his great success on the western border has made Ras Ali nervous. My father-in-law was a ruthless warrior and the Ras has found his strength intimidating."

Asfaw Yilma did not elaborate, nor did he indulge in gossip about Kinfu's reach from the grave to nullify Welde Tekle. About that, the least said was best. Welde would be part of their league to wrest Quarra and Dembea back from the Goshus, father and son, and his good sense and experience would be invaluable.

The two men led Asfaw Yilma's forces along the same road that he had traveled with his family only twenty months ago. This time there was no leisurely stop at Sarsa Dengel's castle to sightsee, nor were there halts to enjoy the wildlife along Lake Tsana's shore. Both Asfaw Yilma and Fenta Tadese, as did many of their mounted warriors, rode mules and led their horses so as to preserve the stamina of these animals for battle. Within two days of their dawn departure from Debra Tabor, the army approached the land south of Gondar where the Qaha and Angerab rivers joined to flow into the lake. Here was the appointed rendezvous arranged with Mekwennin and Welde.

They were waiting. The combined army now numbered over twenty thousand fighting men, divided almost evenly between foot soldiers and cavalry. Their weapons were lances, with only a very few muskets. In Abyssinia, in the middle of the nineteenth century, guns were a rare commodity and the few that existed were almost entirely held by the Ras. He did not distribute them among his great chiefs, but rather held them for his own use to employ an independent group of between one and two thousand gunners. Welde Tekle, over a lifetime of wary, self preservation, had managed to ferret away five or six of these weapons, but they were only effective with proper maintenance and ammunition, and then only at short range. Artillery was almost unheard of.

Mekwennin shouted out the traditional greeting. "How are you, are you well?" Then with boyish enthusiasm he added, "thank God you are here!" He looked his youth, being younger than his sister, Wishan, and just short of his eighteenth birthday; and he was obviously relieved to have his older brother-in-law in his camp.

Yilma glanced about for the leaders, and there were only Mekwennin and Welde, whom he embraced with affection. "I do not see Kassa Haylu. Has he not come? In the name of all the saints, he is Kinfu's stepbrother!"

Welde gave a short, scornful snort. "Ha. We sent him word, but he is not here. I do not look for Kassa."

But barely were the words out of his mouth than they heard a shout from across the Qaha River and looked up to see a large band of cavalry bursting through the water in a nearby ford. Asfaw Yilma lept to his feet in an automatic motion of defense, only to realize that WeldeTekle had spoken too soon. Kassa Haylu had come. As the much younger step brother of Dejazmach Kinfu, his interests lay with the family. He would fight by the side of Mekwennin and Yilma. He was almost exactly the same age as Mekwennin, and Asfaw Yilma was struck by his energy and obvious traits of leadership.

As the day waned, the four family leaders, along with Fenta Tadese, sat down together to map out their plans. Their march must be quick and they would have to follow the coast of Lake Tsana until they reach Gojjam, unless Birru Goshu came to meet them. Welde had seen to gathering a minimum of provisions so that they could start at dawn. They would first pass north of the Gorgora Mountains that directly bordered and blocked the northern shore of the lake, and then drop down the western coastline, avoiding frequent barriers of rock formations. They must go as quickly and quietly as possible.

## Chapter 10

---

Before dawn the army of the late Dejazmach Kinfu's family was marching west toward the Gorgora Mountains. Asfaw Yilma rode beside Kassa Haylu, listening to his diatribe against Menen and her son. "The woman is dangerous. She has intrigued with her son to renege on his promise. Next, she will contrive to assume royal power. You see if I am not right."

Asfaw Yilma nodded. He had not really thought through what share of Kinfu's land Kassa might covet, and reasoned that the young man would at least expect to control Quarra. Kassa had spent a good bit of his young life in the province and had faught there at Kinfu's side against the Egyptians.

Yilma sent Fenta Tadese ahead with some of Kassa's guides who were more familiar with the terrain. They would scout out a course and look for any signs of Birru Goshu. Mekwennin and Welde Tekle pulled up parallel to the leaders and the army moved out in the early sunlight. The mountains ahead were painted in subdued grays and lilacs and the still waters of Lake Tsana reflected the soft colors of the morning sky. It was a glorious day in early October. The marchers moved behind the small mountain range, and the lake disappeared from their view. Steering their men along the base of the Gorgoras, they could see the vast range of the plains of Dembea to the north and the west, stretching on to Quarra. This great expanse of land supported a wealth of crops and grazing animals, and had been in the family's control for a number of years.

By mid day the forward part of the army had passed the lower foothills of the Gorgora range and turned to their left and back toward

Tsana's western shore. They continued only a little further along, to stop at the side of a river called Kemu where they watered their mounts and waited for the grass cutters, cooks and food supplies to catch up. The following day they marched on to the south, ever more careful as they felt their way toward the forces of Birru Goshu.

\* \* \*

The son of Dejazmach Goshu Zewde of Gojjam was indeed a soldier to approach with care. His father, still very active in the land bordering the great inner curve of the Blue Nile, was a man respected for his steadiness and honor. His son, Birru, was better known for cleverness and a relentless pursuit of power. He was tall, like his father, with striking features – a mouth that in anger could be savage and a nose somewhat Roman. Even in his mid twenties his hairline was backing away from his forehead, although on each side of his head his curls were thick and glossy. His eyes were piercing, seeming at the same time to see both everything and nothing. When angry, his speech would slow to become painfully deliberate and distinct.

When the armies of Dejazmach Kinfu's survivors had closed ranks to challenge the loss of their presumed inheritance, Birru Goshu persuaded his reluctant father to join in the defense of Ras Ali's gift to him of that legacy. Rallying their troops from Gojjam through Damot, south of Lake Tsana, they approached the western shore of the Lake where they expected to apprehend the Kinfu family's army before it could step foot into their own territory.

\* \* \*

In the middle of the fourth afternoon of the family's joint march along the coast of Lake Tsana, Fenta Tadese was seen hurrying north along the lake's shore. Galloping to Asfaw Yilma's side he reported, "I have seen them. They have stopped to camp just east of a huge rock formation in Alefa. If we could intercept them before they attain it, we could easily defend the narrow passage in the rock that controls access to your lands. The place is called Chenti Ber."

The leaders quickly drew together to confer with Fenta, both to understand the lay of the land where they would fight and the strength of their enemy. "Chenti Ber is in a line with Dek Island out in Lake Tsana. The great rock is on the shore of the lake. If you are coming from Gojjam to try to usurp power in Dembea and Quarra, as are the Goshus, there is only a narrow passage through which to proceed," explained Fenta. "I do estimate that Birru Goshu's fighting force may exceed ours by about five thousand. His men are well rested as they have barely left their homes, and they appear to be well mounted. But if we can reach Chenti Ber first, we will be at an advantage and can block their way."

Word was spread throughout the troops, and their pace doubled to meet the challenge. The support forces dropped further behind. Welde Tekle, trotting along on his mule just behind Yilma and Kassa, leaned forward to offer a caution. "Even though a narrow passage can easily be blocked, we need to remember that it might be skirted by the enemy. A long detour around to the west of Chenti Ber might well serve the Goshus."

Yilma acknowledged the wisdom of Welde's comment with a curt nod. "What if we split our men, with the lesser number to guard the passage at Chenti Ber and the greater to be held back at the ready to attack a potential feint to the left?"

So it was decided. Welde Tekle, with a small group of his own men, would guard the passage at Chenti Ber. The assignment was straight forward and would be less rigorous for the older man. Asfaw Yilma, with Kassa and Mekwennin, would hang back and tentatively draw to the west. As twilight settled Welde, with a limited number of his infantry and the few muskets he had hoarded and maintained over the years, took up their positions at the tall rock shielding the narrow opening next to the Lake. It was in such a situation that the firearms would be most useful. The greatest part of the family's forces found uncomfortable rest on rough ground a little to the west. Yilma had ordered no cooking fires and silence. If any of his army had been detected by the enemy, it was hoped that they were thought to be only an advanced scouting party.

Soon after dawn there was a rush by Goshu's infantry toward Chenti Ber, but Welde's men and muskats were primed and easily effected a flensing of the attackers. The first rush of infantry was followed by horsemen, who were just as soon vanquished. There was simply no room for more than one or two riders to charge the narrow passage at once, allowing sufficient time to reload, aim and fire the few muskats. Welde recognized the horses as a larger and easier target, and the Goshu cavalry had no chance. Yilma looking on from a great distance detected a noticeable reduction of attackers. Wishan's clever great uncle had been right: Goshu's approach to Chenti Ber was a diversionary probe. The main battle would take place west of the rocks on the lakeshore, and he must hasten to move his army into battle position. Yilma could already see Kassa Haylu and his horsemen racing west, and could feel a tightening in the middle of his chest. Only a fool would not acknowledge to himself that there was fear, but a leader's duty was to show a gay heedlessness – a careless lack of concern. Now was not the time to think of either fate or family. After days of riding on a mule, he was finally mounted on his prized horse. He could feel Selpha's tension and knew that the horse was as ready as he to throw himself into the fight.

As *Fit-Aurari*, Fenta Tadese would lead the advanced guard into battle, only preceded by the drums of the *negarete*. Yilma was responsible for the main charge. The great wall of rock was on his left flank, and Kassa Haylu would be to his right. Mekwennin was behind to act as a reserve and to throw the weight of his horsemen where it was most needed. Before they were even in sight, Yilma could feel the rumble of the earth as thousands of horses approached around a wall of rocks. He raised his right hand for his men to watch, and dropped it as Goshu's army came into sight. There were approximately five hundred yards of stony ground between the two armies, and the enemy was approaching at full speed. With a cacophony of voices shouting a battle cry of their horse's names, and the wild tattoo of the *negarete's* drums, the two armies collided.

An Abyssinian battle was an uncontrolled medley of bravery and frenzied fighting, with very little strategy. Yilma could hear shouts of "*Ayzore!*", the comradely call to "be strong!" and rushed into the battle only a few yards behind Fenta. He became aware of a deadly calm within himself as he was surrounded by the shouts of men fighting, the screams of those wounded or slain and the terrible noise of horses struck in the melee. He felt the enormous jolt as the two armies met at full charge and the sudden stop to meet an opponent and lunge with his lance while guarding his own body. He caught his first man in the neck with blood splashing from the great vein, threw Selpha back on his haunches and wheeled to the left, throwing his shield behind to guard the horse's hind quarters. As quickly, he knocked a second man from his mount, drew his shield forward to protect Selpha's forehead and leaned far to his right to pierce a third man in the chest. He could feel himself surge with the jubilance of doing what he had long trained to do, and doing it well. His body seemed to merge with Selpha's to become a powerful fighting force. The ground was uneven and studded with small rocks, but he unconsciously trusted his horse to carry him safely and concentrated on shielding the animal and using his lance. Selpha was obedient to the bit, wheeling and turning with precision. It took raw nerve to ride with speed over the difficult terrain, and Yilma charged through the enemy lunging, piercing and slashing.

Knowing he needed to assess the condition of his force and its progress, Yilma began to slow a little and work his way to the side. He was suddenly aware of the awful noise of the terrible conflict. He could see the men surrounding Fenta ahead beginning to slow and fall back, and turned back toward Mekwennin to wave the reserves into action. Kassa was locked in what appeared to be a terrible struggle over toward some open land. The *negarete* had stopped the beat of their drums which, for an instant, made Asfaw Yilma hesitate.

The next moment he was guiding Selpha back into the contest and lunging forward. Now there were foot soldiers running among the horsemen, and Yilma reached far to his right to strike a man, who fell under the feet of an attacking horse that shied to avoid the body. Feinting in the other direction he thrust his lance into the face of a horseman, blinding the man with his own spurting blood; and then wheeled tightly to catch another under the ribs. Both he and Selpha were spattered with the butchery of battle, but they themselves were untouched. Gradually, he began to feel himself being pushed back. The very weight of the numbers of Goshu's army was beginning to have its way.

Slowly, Yilma realized that his *negarete-match*, or chief drummer, had been slain – a sure sign of impending disaster. The two armies struggled in close combat, but the direction of his force was backward, toward the lake. He knew that the pursuit of his family's cause had become futile; the defendants of the Kinfu lands were overwhelmed. Catching sight of Fenta, he waved him away, hoping to convey to his friend a message of escape. Asfaw Yilma and Mekwennin were being moved closer and closer together and he had lost sight of Kassa Haylu. He and Mekwennin were soon surrounded by Birru Goshu's most powerful chiefs. In short order they were escorted back through the narrow passage of rock at Chenti Ber and toward the Goshus' encampment. The battle was over. He had failed.

Approaching the Goshus' field tent, Asfaw Yilma was forced to dismount and his beloved Selpha was led away. Almost simultaneously Birru Goshu rode up to his tent, the open-cut sleeves of his battle shirt flying and the drops of metal on his *kalicha*, a kind of coronet, twinkling in the bright sunlight. His famous mount Dampto, the leveler, stopped and reared in seeming triumph. A guard threw open the tent flaps, the few guns that had been captured were thrown in and piled together and Yilma and Mekwennin were shoved forward and put in chains. Mead began to flow and the inevitable *doomfatas* were performed while the minstrels began their impromptu praises of the warring Goshus. Yilma and his brother-in-law could only clench their jaws and strive for a little dignity. They would not be killed, but they were prisoners, and would remain so as far into the future as they could see. As they were led out Asfaw Yilma suddenly remembered that he had not seen Welde Tekle. Had the older man been killed, or had he managed to escape with Fenta? Yilma could only hope for his safety and for Fenta's quick return to Begemder to protect his family. Kassa's fate was also a mystery, but Yilma expected that he had faded into the countryside of Alefa where he would have contacts and protection. In the devastation of his defeat, he had no way of knowing that the fickle atmosphere of politics in Abyssinia would sustain the Goshus' victory for only six months. Then Ras Ali would take back his gift of Dembea and Quarra from Birru Goshu and give the two provinces to his own mother. Birru Goshu's triumph would be very short lived, and Kassa Haylu's assessment of Menen would prove clairvoyant.

## Chapter 11

Worqenesh was filled with grief. That her proud father should be in chains was beyond her capacity to comprehend. True to his friendship, Fenta Tadese had raced back up the western shore of Lake Tsana, Welde Teckle by his side. Welde, from his post at Chenti Ber, had seen the impetus of the battle reverse and then noticed Fenta Tadese fleeing to the north. He had rushed to intercept him. The two warriors parted on the northern shore of the lake near Gondar, and Fenta had hastened from there directly to Diddim.

Wishan heard his news almost with relief. Yilma was alive. People in their culture were used both to sudden advancement and to precipitous falls. There was hardly a man in Abyssinia who did not recognize a master, either willingly or in chains. Yilma had survived the battle and she knew he would be able to manage its aftermath. Her job was to remain calm and protect Diddim. Worqenesh and Giyorgis were standing with her as she spoke to Fenta. She knew they were both old enough now to support her.

Christmas came and went and then the feast day of Saint John the Baptist. Worqenesh was now eleven. The baby that had been born just before the battle of Chenti Ber was a girl and, as a female, she was not christened until eighty days after her birth. Father Berhe performed the ceremony and all was done quietly in the little church in Diddim at the end of December. The baby was named Ribka, to honor Asfaw Yilma's mother. Worqenesh was pleased to have a sister at long last, but Ribka could not ease the ache in her heart for her absent father. While it had been she, with Issete, who had taken such delight in caring for little Welde, it was her grandmother who bonded with

Ribka.

The season of Lent, with its perpetual fasting, began. Father Berhe doubled his instruction time with the children, both to give them their annual lessons in the Easter message and to provide comfort to them in their father's absence. One day when he appeared his eyes were sparkling in anticipation of telling the children about someone new he had met. "I have seen and spoken with a *ferenji* (foreigner) – a man like Gobat," he began, "but he is tall, with light brown hair and blue eyes. He says he is not a missionary, but an explorer. He had come to Debra Tabor to ask Ras Ali's permission to travel in the country, and he was about to head toward the eastern shore of Lake Tsana, and then down to Korata."

It was Giyorgis who pursued the good Abba's information. "If he is an explorer, what is he looking for," asked the youngster.

"He said he wanted to see for himself the source of the *Abbai,* which he calls the Blue Nile."

"But we all know where that is. How long has he been looking?"

Father Berhe smiled. "He only arrived at Christmas time, so he has not been here very long. I know we are familiar with the little springs at Gish Abbai that feed the great river, but very few Europeans have seen them – only a man from a small country called Scotland about sixty years ago, and one of the Portuguese Catholic Fathers even earlier."

Little Issete ventured to ask if it was frightening to see a tall, pale person, but Father Berhe hastened to assure her that she would like the man. "He is young, and seemed to me to be a good person - kindly, and filled with good will. He has already acquired a great liking for our lovely land."

Worqenesh smiled politely, but said nothing. She had little room in her mind to think about an Englishman. Father Berhe went on with his cheerful chatter and she began to pay closer attention.

"There are also interesting political rumors in Debra Tabor. I have been speaking with your mother and telling her that Ras Ali's mother, Menen, plans to marry again. We shall watch closely for this news, for it may affect your father's status."

"Oh, might he be freed," exclaimed Worqenesh. Her face had come alive. "Oh, if only Father could come home."

"I believe it is likely, or I would not mention these things. I would not want to raise your hopes carelessly. You must think positively, Worqenesh. Your father would not want you to mope."

This time Worqenesh smiled back with warmth. What joy it would be if Asfaw Yilma was back with them in Diddim soon. Would his career as a great warlord be over? What would it be like if he no longer held power? Could he live happily in a quiet retirement? She began to let her mind drift; then suddenly turned directly to Father Berhe and asked, "What is the Englishman's name?"

"I call him Yohannes, but he would say John Bell."

\* \* \*

Events began to transpire much as Father Berhe had predicted. Very soon after his chat with the children, and well before Easter, Ras Ali was at war with the Goshus, father and son, and retracted his gift of the Kinfu family's inheritance. Instead, he gave Dembea and Quarra to his mother. With this affront, Birru Goshu relinquished his residence at Gondar and returned to Gojjam, where he quickly released Asfaw Yilma and Mekwennin from their chains. The political fortunes in Abyssinia were once more in an uproar. Not only did Menen acquire Kinfu's lands; she also contrived to marry a son of a former emperor. Yohannis III was much younger than she, and said to be not overly intelligent, but Ras Ali now forced Sahle Dengel from the throne and Menen reentered Gondar on the arm of her new husband as Empress, or *Itege*. The year was 1840. Political power in Abyssinia would remain in flux for another fifteen years.

\* \* \*

To his astonishment, Birru Goshu returned Yilma's horse, Selpha. The Gojjami chief spoke briefly of Ras Ali's duplicity which he now had experienced, as had Yilma. While Mekwennin retraced their invasion route back to his home in Gondar, Asfaw Yilma struck out in an easterly direction along Tsana's southern shore and then across the Blue Nile at the famous Portuguese Bridge below the *Tis Isat* (water that smokes) falls. From there he turned north to Korata and then east to his beloved mountain home. He had traveled in the company of a few itinerant merchants – it was never prudent to traverse the countryside alone – but he and Selpha had separated from their company when they climbed the path to Diddim. A sudden cry from the villagers brought the family from their compound. The people of Diddim paid little attention to the vagaries of power, but they rejoiced at the return of their well respected chief. His family could barely contain their joy. Wishan and Yilma's mother greeted him with requisite decorum, but Worqenesh flew into his arms.

That evening, after an elaborate family meal prepared by Wishan and his mother, Yilma sat in deep contentment with his family around him to recount his experiences. He did not dwell on the battle, although Giyorgis and Haylu both pressed him, but rather told the children about the Gorgora Mountains, the rocky western shore of Lake Tsana and the vast plain of Gojjam with its belt of high mountains. He described the ambitious Birru Goshu to them and explained how he had at first been treated at least decently, but finally, as a potential ally. He tried to paint the grandeur of the *Tis Isat* falls with its great plumes of mist rising from the depths, its myriad birds and the little vervet monkeys that scampered about.

He then continued by describing his visit to the holy city of Korata on the eastern shore of Lake Tsana. Its streets had been crowded with priests of the Abyssinian Orthodox Church and with an abundance of merchants passing to and fro. "Actually, that's how I happened to come to Korata – because the merchants with whom I traveled were headed there. As a matter of fact, I was taken to the home of one of their friends, one Ayto Cassai, and there I met an Englishman who has recently come to our country."

"Oh, Father," shouted Haylu, "Father Berhe has told us about him: he is an explorer."

"Well, I hope he meets with better success than he has enjoyed so far. On his way from Debra Tabor to Korata, he and three of his men were attacked by bandits and the Englishman was severely wounded in the face."

"How horrible," demurred Worqenesh. "He will despise us as barbarians."

"Not at all," replied Yilma. "He seems to have a good opinion of the country and blames himself for traveling without adequate protection. He says he knew better, but had missed a meeting with a small caravan."

"Father Barhe told us his name," Haylu interrupted. "It is John Bell."

"Yes, that is what he said. The night before I left Korata for home we sat and talked. I liked the man. He appeared to me to be both intelligent and resourceful. We had heard earlier that evening of the imminent arrival of Dejazmach Goshu Zewde – Birru Goshu's father. Bell was hoping to join Goshu on his return to Gojjam so that he might beg an escort to Gish Abbai. He said the sole object of his life's ambition was to see the source of the Nile."

"Then I truly hope he achieves his ambition," declared Worqenesh. "It is grand to really know what you want to do."

"Time for bed," broke in Wishan. "Isn't it lovely to know that your father is here and that we can talk with him whenever we like. We must thank God for his safe return in our prayers tonight."

Later, when they were alone together she questioned Yilma, "What shall you do now – are you in enmity with the Ras?"

"I am certainly no trusted friend," he chuckled. "For now I shall remain here and care for the people of the village. I have lost a great deal and, indeed, I am lucky to be alive. Certainly I am no longer part of Ras Ali's power structure, and I cannot say that I care; but we live too close to his capital to make ourselves noticeable. I have lost my *negarete* and many of my men: I shall remain quietly in Diddim. Fortunately, I am like Worqenesh. This is the place on earth where I most like to be. Do you know, Wishan, the one thing I am sure of is that the present government will soon change. I have learned that after Chenti Ber, Kassa Haylu escaped to the west. Birru Goshu never caught up with him and by now he will be surrounded by friends in Quarra. I am impressed by the young man, although I have not developed any great liking for him. I am sure that he will soon be visible in Abyssinia. Our future will remain uncertain for a long time to come." And with an overwhelming sense of gratitude for his homecoming, Asfaw Yilma drew his wife close in his embrace.

# Chapter 12

In the aftermath of the battle of Chenti Ber, there were such a multitude of changes of alliance in Abyssinia as to turn the political landscape into a morass. To his great disappointment, Yilma learned that when his brother-in-law, Mekwennin, returned to Gondar, Welde Tekle immediately challenged and defeated him, and took control of the city. In his turn, Welde was almost immediately overcome and imprisoned by the new Empress, Menen.

Kassa, as Yilma had supposed, safely reached the province of Quarra where he soon quarreled with Menen's people and adopted the role of outlaw, raiding caravans and sharing the booty with his soldiers. He also shared with the local peasants, and began to build a large, loyal following. Quarra might be on the western frontier of Abyssinia, but it was not insignificant. In years past its governors had been strong allies of the Gondarine kings, and the only governors to be permitted to have their *negarete* beat their drums through the streets of the old capital and to the very steps of the king's palace.

The Egyptians continued to threaten the western border, and there were rumors that Ras Ali was prepared to seek an alliance with that country at the expense of the Christian highlands. To counter this threat Ras Wube, of the Simien Mountain area of Tigre, took it upon himself to fill the long empty position of the head of the country's Orthodox Church, and sent to Cairo for a new Abun. The new man, Abune Salama, arrived in 1841 and was received with great fanfare in Gondar.

With the Abun at long last in residence, Wube felt confident that he could march on Gondar. He was joined by Birru Goshu with his massive army of Gojjam, and in February of 1842 their combined forces continued on to Debra Tabor. Ras Ali met them outside of his capitol with a large army made up of his trusted Yejju Gallas. They were roundly defeated and fled.

What happened next was beyond belief. One of Ras Ali's Yejju allies returned to Debra Tabor in the evening to make his obeisance to Ras Wube, and found him sitting alone. Instead of groveling to the mountain chief, he captured him; and Ras Ali was able to claim a most improbable victory. Upon hearing of Wube's capture, Birru Goshu escaped to Gojjam. Eventually there was a reconciliation between Ali and Wube, but never between Ali and Birru Goshu, who had managed to steal Ali's wife. So the tables kept turning: first one great chief would realize power, only to be overthrown by another.

These were, perhaps, the most tumultuous years of the *Zemina Mesafint*. Ras Ali made peace with Ras Wube, and even helped Wube recapture the Simien area from where he could control Tigre and attend to the Red Sea coast, but Ras Ali was never able to bring peace to the Highlands. For a while his mother and her imperial husband, who came to be known as Yohannis the Fool, held sway in Gondar and lent their forces to Ali during his annual campaigns. Birru Goshu continued as a feverish thorn in Ali's side. Each year the Ras would set out from Debra Tabor across the Nile to flush Goshu out from the plains of Gojjam; and each year, whether with the assistance of his father or not, Goshu would cannily retreat to the mountains where it was impossible to rout him out. Ras Ali would then establish proxies to implement his rule and leave. Immediately, Birru Goshu would descend from his amba heights, murder the proxies and reestablish his dominance.

While these antics persisted, in Quarra Kassa Haylu was gaining strength and drawing attention. He sometimes acted as a bandit and sometimes provided military service to local chiefs and even to Ras Ali. His fortunes varied, but the predominance of his successes augured recognition and the assumption of governance. Kassa managed to serve the Ras for a number of years while increasingly threatening his supremacy.

\* \* \*

In their remote mountain village, Asfaw Yilma's family was able to avoid the throes of the country's feudal struggles. Their claims to power and position had ended. Yilma supposed that he might be forced to support Ras Ali at some point, but for now the Ras seemed more comfortable with his Galla warriors. Yilma was still recognized as part of the country's nobility, but he had left the scene of active political maneuvering. He continued to provide tax revenue from Diddim to the Ras, as required, but otherwise he lived quietly.

The children were growing quickly. Worqenesh was thirteen now, and a young lady. She was fair and willowy, with curling dark hair and golden eyes. The people of the village often smiled their admiration at her, but she seldom noticed. It was happiness to her to live among them; to share their good times and to help ease their burdens. With her father's fall from the centers of power, she no longer worried very much about being married off for political advantage. She and Issete continued to study with her brothers and, to her delight, Father Berhe would sometimes find an extra poem or narrative to pique her interest.

Giyorgis was specifically studying for the church. In spite of being the eldest son, his bent had always been in this direction, and Asfaw Yilma saw no reason to interfere. He knew that Haylu and little Welde would grow into fine soldiers, and so he let his eldest son seek his own way. Sometimes when his friend, Fenta, climbed the path to Diddim, he and Yilma would oversee the younger boys' riding and teach them the proper technique for holding a shield while throwing a lance.

One more child had followed Ribca into the family – a fourth son, who had arrived toward the end of 1841 and who was named Haile. The family was complete and, compared with many in Abyssinia during this unsettled time, it was secure and stable.

\* \* \*

Amid the turmoil of the early forties the English explorer, John Bell, pursued his dream. He was annoyed at Ras Ali's refusal to punish the bandits who had attacked him and at the Ras' peculiar reasoning that Bell himself, in fighting back, had grievously wounded his assailants; but he was not one to be daunted by the peculiarities of the local system of justice. Bell soon found himself marching through Gojjam and Damot with Birru Goshu's father, who occasionally ingratiated himself with Ras Ali and Menen by providing a few thousand militias for their support. Bell thought the elder Goshu a fine looking man of noble conduct, deeming him the most princely of all the chiefs he had met. It was at Goshu Zewde's side that he first witnessed the ravages of war on the fertile countryside; it was through Goshu Zewde's kindness that he saw the little Blue Nile, just fifteen feet wide, enter Lake Tsana and it was thanks to him that he was finally escorted south to the springs at Gish Abbai to see the modest beginnings of the mighty river.

Bell had formerly been employed by the British Foreign Office and was a highly competent linguist. He quickly learned Amharic, the prevalent language in Abyssinia, and it was not very long before he mastered its subtle idioms and nuances. By the time he and the soldiers of his escort had sprinkled a little of the spring water from the Gish Abbai on their heads for luck, he was thoroughly immersed in the country and its culture. He had come to explore, and he would remain as a willing captive of the lovely, turbulent land.

When Bell left Gish Abbai he returned first to Korata to the home of his good friend Ayto Cassai, and then went back to Debra Tabor. By this time, as a foreigner in the country but one who planned to stay indefinitely, he aligned himself with the ruling power who was currently Ras Ali. Eventually he would need a home, or a town or village that would support him and that he would be responsible for. To Ras Ali, Diddim immediately presented itself. It was true that the mountain village was the family home of Asfaw Yilma, but certainly it could support Ali's new English attendant as well.

\* \* \*

It was after Meskel in 1842, when the countryside was bright with ripening grain and burgeoning with flowers, that John Bell first rode his mule up the mountain path to Diddim. In Debra Tabor, Ras Ali had singled out Fenta Tadese and instructed him to accompany Bell to Asfaw Yilma's home and explain his presence. The Ras courteously, but allowing no room for refusal, sent his instruction to Asfaw Yilma to share the revenue from his village with John Bell for the duration of his stay in their country. Bell was free to take up residence there, in Debra Tabor or almost anywhere else; but Diddim should provide him with an income adequate to his needs.

A messenger from the Ras had preceded the two men to the village so that Asfaw Yilma was standing out in the sunshine to receive them. He remembered having spent an evening with Bell in Korata the previous year, his terrible face wound and his agreeable company; and he smiled a greeting to the young man. Ras Ali's request was neither unusual nor demeaning. It might be diverting to have the Englishman living in Diddim off and on.

Bowing low and touching his right hand to the ground, then bringing it to his lips he queried, "How are you? How have you passed the time since we met?"

Bell had long ago assimilated the manners of the country and replied, "Thanks be to God, I am well. How are you," and he thought to himself that the famous Dejazmach had noticeably aged in the last year.

So they greeted each other in easy friendship and, with Fenta, began to walk along the path that bordered the village. The local children raced about, curious to see the foreigner, and some of the men came out to bow a courteous greeting, which Bell was careful to return. Asfaw Yilma noticed, and was grateful for, Bell's gentle civility. These men of Diddim were his loyal warriors and tribesmen, his grave responsibility and his friends.

Completing their circumnavigation of the village, which took some time because of frequent stops for conversation, Asfaw Yilma invited Bell and Fenta to share a meal, and led them back toward his compound where his family was standing outside, waiting to greet their guests.

"My wife, the Woisero Wishan," he pronounced, as John Bell bowed low and touched his left hand to his right elbow, "and my daughter, the Woisero Worqenesh."

Worqenesh caught her breath. Her father had never before thus indicated her rank or maturity to anyone. John Bell turned from Wishan to her daughter, and lost his heart.

# Chapter 13

John Bell was a tallish young man, but the golden eyes now engaging his were nearly on a level with his own. He saw a luminous face in front of him, brimming with intelligence and curiosity. "How are you? I hope you are well," he managed to recite.

"I am well." Worqenesh completed the litany and smiled at the bemused Englishman.

By now the boys were jumping in anticipation of meeting a newcomer, and little Ribca had come tottering into view holding on to her grandmother's hand. It was an animated group that sat down to share a *misir wat,* a stew made with lentils - it was another saint's day, so there was no meat. They shared the local gossip as well. Yilma asked Fenta and John Bell of news from Debra Tabor. "Where is the Ras? Has he again set off to campaign in Gojjam? He will never capture Birru Goshu."

"Yes, he has gone," returned Bell. "I should be with him because I have pledged my support, but he wanted me to be settled first, and sent me here. It would be strange to oppose Birru Goshu as last year I fought along side of his father."

"You must take a little time with us," was Yilma's hospitable response. "We shall build you a *gojo* (a circular hut), and lend you guides so that you can explore our mountains. A man needs to be familiar with the outlay of his surroundings. We should not want you to become lost in our vast woods."

The children's inquisitiveness was bubbling over. Barely able to contain himself, Haylu questioned Bell about Gish Abbai. "We have been told that you traveled to the mountains where the great River

Abbai begins. Tell us what you saw, please."

So Bell described the wooded, rolling countryside, the hill sloping down to the marshy ground, the springs – about two feet in diameter – and the small stream that cut away to the east for about two hundred yards and then turned north. Looking toward Giyorgis he added, "I am told that you are studying for the church. At the hill above the springs there is a church called Gish Kuddes Michael. It is a quaint building nestled among the trees at the crest of the hill. Perhaps you may see it someday."

Worqenesh was touched that Bell had noted her eldest brother's passion. The conversation continued around her with talk of the abundant local harvest, of the unpredictable outcome of the recent battle of Debra Tabor and of Kassa Haylu's latest challenges against the Ras. "Kassa is our kinsman," her father pointed out. "He is the much younger half brother of my wife's late father."

"We are not close to him," Wishan demurred, "but undeniably, there is a relationship."

Well after dark, Asfaw Yilma and the two older boys escorted Fenta and Bell to a small, circular hut made of bound tree branches topped by a thatched roof. Happily, it contained two *alga*, couch-like pieces of furniture, that could be used as beds. Fenta would stay overnight and then return to Debra Tabor. John Bell would remain in Diddim long enough to establish a tenuous home. Fenta would send Bell's few serving men from the capital and Bell would find a woman in the village to grind his corn and cook for him.

\* \* \*

John Bell always said that his home in Diddim made him think of Scotland. When he awoke the next morning there was a thin, cold fog hovering along the tops of the fir trees, and when he looked out for a short distance under the fog he could see fields of barley. He hurried to dress and follow Fenta Tadese to Asfaw Yilma's compound for a hot breakfast.

The day would be a busy one, and he was anxious to begin. He and Asfaw Yilma must decide upon a location for his *gojo*. They agreed that there should be ample space near the little building to add a stable and any other structure that might be needed in the future, and they chose a spot on the opposite side of the village from Yilma's compound. There were loose rocks on the side of the mountain to construct a little stone hut, and they would use tree limbs and grasses to thatch the roof. Bell's view would be to the southeast - out over the village's barley fields, and the northern side of the *gojo* would be sheltered by fir trees. It would be a haven to which a man could happily retreat from the roiling political disorder of Abyssinia.

By early afternoon Asfaw Yilma had organized a small work force to collect rocks and dig a circular trench in which to lay foundation stones. Bell remained at the site to oversee the work and join in the heavy lifting; but late in the day, as the workers returned to their own hearths, he strolled back to Asfaw Yilma's compound. Father Barhe was sitting outside with the boys, hearing their lessons, and he saw Worqenesh nearby with a small parchment in her hands.

He first approached the boys to see what sort of work Quebra Barhe set for them, and then turned toward Worqenesh. "What about you – what are you reading?"

"Father Barhe has given me some more psalms," she answered. "He knows that I am always looking for something to read, and that I love poetry."

Bell was almost afraid that in traveling the world to see various wonders, he might just have found one that he had not planned for. He did not know which he loved most – the adventure of travel or language. His one companion in all his wanderings was a well thumbed copy of Shakespeare. Was it possible that here, in the highlands of Abyssinia, he had stumbled across a girl who shared at least one of his passions. "Why poetry?" he asked.

"Because it gives the things we cannot understand, a name."

Bell could think of nothing to say. She had just said everything that could be said. Instead, he began to tell her about the little *gojo* and the wonderful view of mountains, mist and grain fields. "But you are used to this village," he observed. "I suppose that to you it is ordinary."

"No," answered Worqenesh. "I always feel lucky to be here, in Diddim. My country is filled with war and the possibility of war. I believe that my countrymen love nothing so much as to fight. I am happy to be here, where the battles seem to pass us by. I do not take any of this for granted, or think it ordinary. Now, may I ask you what puzzles me? Why are you so far from home?"

John Bell took in a deep breath. "I have been away for a long while. My father served in the British navy, so we were seldom in one place for very long. Our roots are in England, but I was born in Malta." Bell found himself blurting out family history and telling this young woman surrounded by her siblings about his own. "I have a younger brother, William, and a sister, Susan, and I do enjoy being with them; but I love traveling to new places – just the very freedom of it." Then, not wanting to sound irresponsible, he added, "I do plan to see William in Malta soon, but just for a visit. In truth, I have found your country to be a wondrous place. Its history is unique on this continent, its people are cheerful and clever, the climate is temperate and the land lovely. I hope to settle and become a part of it. That is why I have come here, to Diddim. I have pledged my support to Ras Ali, and I am here to stay." Then, amazed at his courage, he went on, "And you, Worqenesh, do you have plans?"

"I shall marry whenever my father decides, but I think he is content to have me at home for a while longer. I am grateful that I no longer have to think of myself as a pawn in Abyssinian politics. Since my father's defeat at Chenti Ber I am not in very high demand, and I am happy to be able to stay at home."

"Do you not like to venture off on journeys at all?" asked Bell.

"Oh, I do. I used to love it when I was younger and Father would take us on trips, but then I always loved to come back here."

Wishan came outside then and noticed the two young people with their heads together. Issete was nowhere to be seen. "Come everyone, it's time for supper," she called, and the little tete a tete was broken apart.

When Worqenesh crawled into the fur covers that evening, Issete whispered into her ear, "Do you like him? I am not at all afraid of him even though he is a *ferenji*. He is older, but not so very much."

Worqenesh hesitated for just a moment, and then quickly hugged her friend. "I think he is a man I could love, Issete. He is kindly and intelligent. I believe that he doesn't just do things, but thinks through what he does. And he loves to read. I must ask Father Barhe if he knows the name, Shakespeare. Issete, do you think that my father thinks well of him?" Then, suddenly realizing an overwhelming weariness, she closed her eyes and was instantly asleep. Issete beamed in the dark. Here, she thought, was indeed someone who might almost be unusual and special enough; and he was going to live, at least part of the time, in their village.

In fading light John Bell walked back to his newly acquired home place. He had traveled throughout the near East and as far as India; but now, in a way he could not explain but certainly recognized, he felt at home. He would sleep outside of his unfinished hut, wrapped in an old blanket and absorbing the clarity of the African sky lit by a legion of stars and a sickle moon. He had planned a trip back to Malta to visit his family, but it would be brief. Before he left he would speak to Asfaw Yilma. Bell heard the rumble of a lion in the valley below and nearby, the brief snicker of a hyena. He pulled his rifle closer and set his mind adrift in the enchantment of the night.

# Chapter 14

John Bell did travel to Malta to visit his family early in 1843. Before leaving, he had reached an understanding with Asfaw Yilma. Because of his intended absence from the country their agreement was tenuous, but Asfaw Yilma had said that Bell might speak to his daughter upon his return. Yilma would not commit himself further, nor would he permit Bell to speak to Worqenesh of his hopes and plans before his departure. Young men were often unpredictable and sometimes unreliable. He would wait for Bell to prove himself.

Bell, himself, looked upon his trip as a sort of farewell. He had made up his mind to cast his lot with the Abyssinians. William Bell received his brother's gift of the black leopard skin John had hunted knowing full well that it would be years, if ever, before he saw him again.

In July, on his way south, John Bell stopped at the Red Sea coastal town of Suez, where he was conspicuous to other Europeans by his dress in the white, draped attire of an Abyssinian. Always one whose curiosity prompted conversation with those around him, he was chatting with a small group of Arabs on the beach when he noticed a young Englishman observing him. Interrupting his conversation in Arabic, he smiled and beckoned to his fellow traveler, who introduced himself as Walter Plowden. "I am returning home from India," he explained. "I had gone out to join a mercantile establishment and had hoped to find adventure, but I have only discovered that credit ratings and balance sheets are unbearably dull wherever they are. I was foolish not to understand how sedentary life in an office is, even if that office is in the near East."

Plowden was all of twenty-three when he introduced himself to his tall, fellow countryman. They agreed to have dinner together, and by evening's end he had thrown off all trappings of his civilized life and was investing what small resources he still owned to return with Bell to Abyssinia.

"But, Walter," remonstrated Bell, "I am going back to make a life for myself there. I have fallen in love, and I shall make my home in the highlands."

"Don't worry about me," replied Plowden. "I confess I should like your company to reach the land that you have described, but I shall not be a burden. If you make exploratory trips, you might like to have me with you, but I shall also strike out on my own. As you describe Abyssinia, I already have thoughts of becoming an emissary between England and the Ras. First, I shall need to form my own impressions as to the possibility of trade and such, and I am excited at the prospect."

His enthusiasm was a pleasant reinforcement of Bell's own fascination with his adopted homeland. "Then we shall take ship down the Red Sea to the port of Massawa off the coast of the general area known as Ethiopia. From there we shall strike inland across the hills to Adwa and Aksum, and on through the province of Tigre, across the Simien mountains and then drop down to Debra Tabor. I hope that the Ras will be in residence in his capital and, as the rainy season will have just ended, it is likely that he still may be. My home is just a couple of hours from there."

They talked late into the night, Bell describing the mountains, the inland lakes, the unusual equality of the people throughout society and their cheerfulness, wit and love of linguistic complexities. It would be pleasant to have a fellow Englishman so nearly his own age with whom he could share impressions and compare ideas.

Within just a few days they had found places on a dhow headed first south across the Red Sea to Jiddah, and then south again and back across the water to the west coast port of Massawa. Walter Plowden felt almost a reckless joy in parting from Suez. For John Bell, it was his second venture to the land of the Habesh (from which the word, Abyssinia, was derived) and his feelings were tempered by the challenge of persuading Worqenesh to accept him as her husband.

He was not absolutely sure of her feelings toward him.

The dhow, with its lateen sail and small jigger, sailed along in a warm, light breeze. The two Englishmen shared a small cabin that was about nine feet by six, and less than four feet high, so they stowed their gear there and spent their time, sleeping and waking, on the deck. Eventually, the distant mountains of Abyssinia came into view, strongly back lighted by the setting sun, and the ship anchored in the harbor of Massawa a little after a summer midnight in a stupefying heat.

They remained three days in the appalling climate of Massawa, arranging for mules and a guide to convey them as far as Adwa, and on the fourth day they struck out due south. They soon left behind the inflated temperatures and humidity of the coast to pass through country that was rough and wild, gradually climbing the rocky foothills. They shot guinea fowl to eat and camped near a small, rippling stream. Plowden was delighted. Here, nature shone in its brightest colors. Wild ducks and geese sported brilliant plumage and the bright green of the foliage was framed by the clear, deep blue of a cloudless sky.

Within days the two men were consumed with fever, undoubtedly contracted in the miasma of the coast. They were forced to seek shelter at a small village north of Adwa, and only reached their first milestone after long days of illness. They arrived in a driving rain and found the capital of Tigre to be little more than a large village of shoddy huts. Being soaked by the downpour the place had a most dreary appearance and, crossing a small brook; they slipped and slid in muck. Their intent was to pay a call on Ras Wube who happened not to be in residence; and so they rode on the next day, continuing to be hampered by recurrent bouts of fever. Plowden, in particular, found traveling painful. Stumbling on for two more days, they arrived late one afternoon, during yet another heavy rain, at Wube's camp.

Bell and Plowden had to wait until the next day to visit the court – a hut measuring perhaps thirty feet in diameter. They gained entrance at last; bowing in what they hoped was the general direction of the famous chief, being blinded by the strong sunlight outside. When their eyes adjusted to the dimly lit interior, they saw the great man reclining on an *alga* and being warmed by a blazing wood fire.

They exchanged gifts, presenting Wube with a Turkish rug and two light cavalry swords and receiving, in return, an emaciated cow. When the unfortunate animal was delivered to their campsite that evening, she was immediately slaughtered by their attendants, and not a morsel remained by the next morning. Plowden was impressed by the ruler of Tigre. He was small and lithe, with a reputation for truthfulness, capable leadership in battle and good governance.

John Bell found Walter Plowden to be a boon companion on the road. Even when suffering with a raging fever he never complained, but was simply grateful for the least assistance. Soon after leaving Ras Wube and returning to Adwa, Plowden began to recover his health, and his enthusiasm for all that he saw matched Bell's own. They passed through Aksum, beautifully situated on a wide plain sheltered by high hills; and admired the ancient stealae and huge sycamore trees. Their journey continued south and west until a gentle slope brought them to the banks of the great Takaze River, which they crossed with some difficulty as it was only just beginning to recede after the rains. Close by was a unique area where the ground was covered with huge rocks. Lions frequented the place and loved to sleep in the cool shade of the stones. Plowden shot and killed a young boa constrictor.

At last they gained the high mountains of Simien and, with their party of guides and attendants, passed through the narrow opening at Lemalmon in Wagera to descend to the central province of Begemder and Debra Tabor. Their trip was nearly at an end. John Bell took just enough time to present Walter Plowden at Ras Ali's court, and hurried on up the mountain path to Diddim.

\* \* \*

He found the village in mourning: Asfaw Yilma was dead. Those who had known him well had detected a decline in the years following Chenti Ber, but no one had taken it seriously. He was only aging in his retirement. Then, very quietly one morning late in the rainy season, he had slumped over and was gone.

According to local custom he was buried the same afternoon before his family could even begin to assimilate their loss. Guns had been fired as his body was carried to the village church, and the requisite seven halts had been observed along the way as prayers and psalms were recited. At the village church a long service was performed and Asfaw Yilma's body had been wrapped in a cover woven of palm leaves suggesting the analogy between Christ's entrance into Jerusalem and Yilma's spiritual entrance there. He was buried in a hastily dug grave in the churchyard that had been scented with incense. Now the forty days of mourning were drawing to a close.

On hearing the news, Bell hurried to Asfaw Yilma's compound where Wishan and the children were preparing to walk to church on the fortieth, and last, official day of mourning. She bowed to John Bell, and then beckoned him to join the family in their walk to the village church.

Wishan was flanked by Worqenesh and Giyorgis, so Bell hastened to fall in with Haylu and Welde. Yilma's mother held the hands of the two youngest, Ribca and Haile, and they proceeded to walk along the path that circled the village. An instant later Bell was struck with the significance of what Wishan had done. Very quietly, deliberately and publicly, she had acted to include him, an outsider, into her family group. At the church, as always, the women separated from the men and entered the door on the south side. Haile's grandmother handed the little boy over to Bell and followed Ribca through the women's door. Holding on to the toddler, Bell followed the other boys inside where he saw Fenta Tadese reach out and put his arm around his godson. He looked across at Worqenesh and their eyes met briefly. Then the deep drum sounded and the priest began to intone the words of the sacrament.

When the service was over the family reconvened in the sunshine outside. Their grief was palpable, but once again Wishan took charge. This time she drew John Bell to her side and began a more informal walk back to her home. A large contingent of the village followed them and, when they reached the compound, there was a generous feast in preparation for the crowd. The season of mourning was at an end.

Sometime in the late afternoon, when their neighbors were beginning to drift away, John Bell approached Wishan. "Your loss is great," he said in a low voice. "I grieve with you."

"I must talk with you," she answered, drawing him aside. "Yilma spoke with me after your departure from us. He said to me that you had told him of your love for our daughter and that, if you returned to us and still wished to marry, he would give his consent. In his stead, I give you mine. Worqenesh was her father's joy. Perhaps now, she will be yours."

Tears came to John Bell's eyes as he bowed to this remarkable woman. "You do me great honor," he replied.

She nodded and turned away. Bell looked around for Worqenesh and saw her standing just a little way off, smiling at his happiness.

# Chapter 15

Wishan asked that they wait another few weeks before they married so that a more suitable time had elapsed after Asfaw Yilma's death. It would be a civil marriage. At that time in Abyssinia, very few couples chose the sanction of the church until, perhaps, in their latter years. Worqenesh and Bell were content to oblige Wishan, and spent the days in happy companionship and anticipation. The first evening, when Wishan had given her blessing, Bell had taken Worqenesh's hand and led her along the outer path circling the village. "You know I have come back to ask you to marry me. I hope you can begin to love me as I love you."

Worqenesh had returned the pressure of his hand and with her usual directness responded, "I already love you, John." When Bell left Worqenesh that evening he held her close. Life scarcely had greater adventure than this.

In the ensuing weeks John Bell worked hard at his home place to prepare it for Worqenesh. Sometimes she and Wishan would come by with one or two of the children to compliment his efforts and offer ideas; and sometimes she and Issete would come to oversee and arrange what would become the cooking area. Issete would eventually join the new household to help Worqenesh direct its management. Always, toward the middle of each afternoon, Bell would stop what he was doing and go to spend the rest of the day with Worqenesh.

Often they would sit under a great fir tree near her home. "Tell me about the book you always carry," she would demand. So Bell would tell her about the greatest poet of his language and attempt to translate bits of the sonnets for her. He particularly liked to regale her

with lines from the eighteenth because it contained her name, "worq."
…Sometimes too hot the eye of heaven shines,
And often his gold complexion dimmed…
But thy eternal summer shall not fade,
Nor lose possession of that fair thou owest…

Worqenesh loved to hear him read and translate, and began her own ventures into his language. To her family he was Yohannes, but to Worqenesh he was, from the very first, John.

The villagers grew used to seeing the two of them together. Bell's friendly manner and willingness to help his neighbors earned their respect. They knew that his relationship with the Ras would demand their loyalty as well. Asfaw Yilma was dead, but his village still owed feudal loyalty to the king who, for the moment, was represented by Ras Ali. Their allegiance would now be channeled through the leadership of John Bell. His sporadic trips down the mountain to Debra Tabor testified to his emerging position. Worqenesh accepted his growing influence and was proud of him. Now, in the waning days of 1843, there was relative peace, but she also understood the timbre of her countrymen. "John," she would counsel, "the men of my country love nothing so much as to fight. I think it is a part of our culture: I do not know if we shall ever be at peace. I do sometimes fear that you will become entangled or injured in our animosities."

"It is a risk I shall take," he would reply. "I have thrown my lot in with your people, and I must share the bad with the good. I do promise you that I shall never deliberately court danger. I do not want to quickly lose what I have only just found." Bell was fully aware of both his happiness and his responsibility, and would not risk either lightly. He also recognized the immense loyalty to each other that Worqenesh's family displayed. It was one of the characteristics that had drawn him in.

The weeks of waiting that Wishan had imposed fostered a deepening understanding between Worqenesh and John Bell. After the crushing experience of her Father's death, her youthful gaiety reblossomed in answer to Bell's delight in her company. They walked together, read together and laughed together. The people of Diddim seldom saw one without the other, and approved the pending alliance between their beloved Dejazmach's daughter and their new village leader. John Bell was certainly not a tribal chief, but he had become their trusted link with Ras Ali.

\* \* \*

Worqenesh Asfaw Yilma and John Bell were married in December of 1843 on a day that began in a deep, foggy mist and ended in a glorious sunset of gold with clouds cascading in various shades of rose and purple. The event took place in the compound where Worqenesh had lived since her birth, and it occupied most of the day. The actual brief ceremony was preceded, as were most such significant occasions, by a generous *brendo*. It was hosted by the bride's family, with Fenta Tadese helping Wishan to oversee the slaughter of the cows, and her mother-in-law presiding over the preparation of the numerous, necessary breads and sauces. The affair was, perhaps, a little subdued because of Asfaw Yilma's recent demise; but still, it was a happy time and it was largely attended by the citizens of Diddim.

John Bell was accompanied by Ayto Cassai, from Korata, who had made a special effort to be with his English friend on this auspicious occasion. They arrived together on horseback attended by Bell's faithful servant, Gabriote; with a large group of the village's warriors at their side. Walter Plowden was off campaigning with Ras Ali and not able to be present, and Bell was sorry that his new friend missed the joy of the occasion. All were dressed in their finest. Bell wore tight-fitting, thigh-length pants and a white over-tunic with slit sleeves, but rather than an animal skin draped over his shoulders he had slung on the native *shamma* (a shawl wrapped like a Roman toga).

After Bell's entourage entered the compound and settled to one side; Worqenesh, with her family, appeared on the opposite side and the festivities began. When, over a period of some hours, large quantities of food and drink had been consumed by all attending, an area in the center of the compound was cleared and John Bell was seated there in state. Next, Worqenesh was brought forward. She was dressed in heavily embroidered white trousers and tunic, and shone with the simplicity of her manner and warmth of her demeanor. All of the early portents of beauty in the gangling youngster had materialized: she was lovely. Bell gazed in delight as she was seated on a low stool in front of him and a large cloth, like a canopy, was held above them somewhat shielding them from the general view. He was then asked if, indeed, it was his intention to marry this daughter of the house, and hastened to respond in the affirmative.

When they were next instructed to crook their little fingers together, both John Bell and Worqenesh looked at each other in sheer amazement. How great a distance they had both come to reach this moment, and with what joy. Suddenly, they were smiling broadly at each other as Father Barhe offered a few wise admonitions and their friends and family gathered around to conclude the ceremony.

There followed a brief spate of war dances, with the men of the village carrying their shields and lances – leaping, charging and feinting; performing mock attacks and withdrawals. A very few possessed guns that they flourished in similar demonstrations and then fired off into the air. Normally, at this time, the bridegroom would have been presented with gifts from his father-in-law, but John Bell had begged Wishan to forego this tradition. The gift of her daughter and the family's acceptance of him as a son and brother was fortune enough for any man. As the evening sun began to paint the clouds in the west, Bell lifted Worqenesh onto a new mule, the color of ripe coffee beans; and, mounting his horse beside her, they set off for the path on the perimeter of Diddim, followed by some of the village warriors. Gradually, their local escort peeled away into the evening shadows, and they were left alone to approach their new home.

Their side of the mountain caught the last rays of the evening sun, and Worqenesh hurried inside to locate tapers to assure a soft light. Then, arms linked, they strolled the walkways of their own newly constructed compound. Bell had put up the horse and mule in the stable, and the soft noises of their munching and exhaled breath were sounds of peace and home. "Come," whispered Worqenesh, "I have ached for you. Show me why."

## Chapter 16

They had seventeen years – seventeen years to hold each other, raise a family and witness the end of the *Zemina Mesafint* and a return to a strong, centralized monarchy. These were among the most tumultuous years in the country's history, and they were both fully embroiled in them. Life in mid nineteenth century Abyssinia was not for the weak, and both John and Worqenesh were enmeshed in the struggles at the highest level; but as the year 1843 drew to an end, the country seemed to catch its breath and hold still for just a little while.

\* \* \*

On the first morning after the wedding, Issete came humming along the village pathway bearing the makings of breakfast, only to set them down quietly and steal away. Worqenesh had woken early, to curl tighter against John and enjoy again the wonder of their bodies together. When she did emerge from the *gojo*, she laughed to see the package sitting discreetly on the front stoop. "Look, John, we have breakfast," she called with delight. "Mother has sent grilled beef from yesterday, along with mead, fresh bread and honey."

Bell, suddenly realizing an enormous appetite, helped her to set out the dishes. "Everyone has been so good to us, Worqenesh," and he proceeded to bolt down a fair share of the impromptu picnic. Then, pulling Worqenesh to her feet, he insisted that they walk to her Mother's home to reiterate their gratitude and greet the villagers on the way.

Their early days together were a time of pure happiness. Bell would glance at Worqenesh, seeing a lovely young woman of the nobility with her direct honesty, lively intuition and innocent passion; and she, in turn, reveled in his tall strength and ranging mind. They quickly settled into their life together as leaders in the village, deferring gently to Wishan, but carefully carrying the weight of their own responsibility to the community.

\* \* \*

Abyssinia, as one of the oldest civilizations on the continent of Africa, still followed the Julian calendar and so, some weeks after their marriage, on the 7$^{th}$ of January, Worqenesh and Bell celebrated *Ganna*, or Christmas. It was a day, not of gift giving, but to be in church. Bell had long decided that his old Anglican affinities could give way to the Orthodox Church of his adopted country. He and Worqenesh joined the family in their long fast on the day before the celebration of Christ's birth. Then, very early the next morning, they all dressed in white and wrapped their thin, cotton *shammas* around their shoulders for warmth. Stars twinkled brightly in the clear, dark sky as the family, joined by neighbors along the way, progressed to the village church. They heard the deep strum of the *kebbero* (large church drum) summoning them to the mass, and hurried so as not to be late. Standing during the long service of the Eucharist, Worqenesh looked across to the men's side of the church to see Bell, and they both breathed a sigh of contentment. Worqenesh, remembering being in Gondar and looking at the angels across the roof of the Debre Berhan Selassie Church, decided that this was another such perfect moment. Later in the day there was a large family feast, and afterwards the children played with friends in the compound. Fenta Tadese had joined the family, and while the children ran and shouted, the adults sat under the trees to talk.

"Ras Ali has set off for Gojjam again, Yohannes. Will you be coming with me to join him?" Fenta asked.

"I have promised," returned John Bell, "but sometimes I wish he would stop pursuing Birru Goshu, as he never seems to finish the job. How many seasons has he chased the man away and positioned his own governors, only to have Goshu descend from his amba and murder them as soon as he leaves?"

"At least three years – maybe more," returned Fenta.

Then Worqenesh chimed in, picking up on her constant theme. "Why can our people not move beyond violence as a solution to their problems? Why do they so love to fight?"

Wishan smiled at her daughter who had grown up so much in the few years since Chenti Ber. "It does seem to be part of our tribal culture."

"If there were a true monarchy, it would not be like this," suggested Fenta.

"Indeed," continued Bell, thinking along the same lines. "There are many cohesive elements in the country including the historic monarchy and the church, but since the time when the Scotsman, James Bruce, visited Abyssinia in the 1770's, the powerful Rases have jockeyed continuously to control the king."

Giyorgis had come to sit near the adults, and now spoke up. "Nowadays the church is not such a cohesive influence. My Father made that clear to me. I wonder if the new Abun that Ras Wube brought here two years ago will begin to make a difference."

"I think he may be helpful in matters of the church. He has certainly spoken against the upstart belief in the three births of Christ and is trying to force the *Ichege* back to a more traditional position," Fenta answered. "Still the problem remains, as Giyorgis has just said, that the divisions in the church reflect the fractures in our governance."

"Fenta," asked Bell, "do you know anything about this fellow in Quarra? Sometimes he sounds like the English Robin Hood, robbing the rich to help the poor; and sometimes he seems like a legitimate supporter of Ali. I think he is expected to fight against Goshu this year."

"He is my Uncle," enjoined Wishan, "but I do not know him. I think he must be just about your age, Yohannes. Yilma never really approved of Kassa Haylu. He believed that any of his positive attributes were obscured by a vaulting ambition. I might feel a vague family loyalty to him, but I mistrust him."

The men went on discussing politics while Wishan turned to her daughter. "Shall I send Issete to you soon so that you can begin to organize your own household? I know she is longing to be with you and, if Yohannes is leaving to campaign with Ali, she will be a comfort to you."

"Yes, I'll go and find her now and tell her. I have missed Issete. John has said that he will leave before *Timket*, and I shall welcome her company."

Before he and Worqenesh walked home that evening, John Bell sought out his young brother-in-law. "I am leaving with Fenta in just a couple of days, Giyorgis, and shall count on you to look out for Worqenesh."

"Haylu and I shall always be here for our sister," the boy replied, but Bell could tell that he was pleased by his trust. Many times, in the years to come, John Bell would commit those dearest to him to Giyorgis' care.

* * *

When John Bell left to join Ras Ali, Worqenesh and Issete set about organizing her compound so that the area could operate as a productive household. By now there were a number of buildings which included the original *gojo*; a stable; a small hut for Bell's man, Gabriote; a larger one for Issete and any other women needed on a permanent basis and a kitchen area with a small storage building and an oven. This last item was an oblong structure containing a concave, circular slab made of pottery with a conical cover in which the daily *injera* would be baked. The storage room was a place where grain was kept before it was ground to make bread. Grinding was a daily task, and a woman from the village would come each day to perform this basic chore. Likewise, another village woman was hired to make the treks part way down the mountain to the spring and little stream where the village enjoyed a continuous supply of water. There were various vessels to store various supplies – large mud jars in which to keep grain, and jars with long necks and narrow mouths for carrying water. There were earthen dishes for the preparation of meat and vegetable *wats* and for cooking sauces, and there were small containers for storing honey. Finally, there was the all important grinding-stone and the grinder.

Worqenesh and Issete took great pride in collecting and arranging the essentials. Some of the items were contributed from Wishan's kitchen and others purchased at the market place in Debra Tabor. It was a delight for them both to be working together.

"You are very happy, aren't you," Issete said, more as a statement than as a question.

And Worqenesh beamed her assent. "You were right, Issete. John is someone very special, as you said he should be – kind, intelligent and, I think, brave."

*Timket*, which commemorates the baptism of Christ, arrived twelve days after *Gamma* and lasted for three days. Fenta Tadese had offered his home in Debra Tabor to the family, even though he and John Bell were campaigning in Gojjam. Wishan decided that they all should go and celebrate the holiday in the capital. It was a festive time to see old friends, and so they descended the mountain together on the family mules to join in the celebration. Wishan rode the lovely cream colored animal that Yilma had given her years ago and Worqenesh was on her new, coffee colored mount. Issete followed close behind holding Haile while the other children rode two by two. As always, they traveled with an armed escort made up of young warriors from Diddim who had been left in the village specifically to guard its people.

Their celebration was somewhat tempered by the absence of Yilma and of Yohannes, but the children were able to parade with friends to church, dressed in their finest; and the women followed, wrapped in *shammas*. The priests were splendid in their red and white robes, carrying embroidered, fringed umbrellas; and the *sistra* tinkled their metal disks in time with the deep percussion of the drums. Worqenesh remembered the Meskel celebration when she and Issete had seen the little dikdik, and was grateful for a sense of continuity.

John Bell returned home late in *Hudaddie*, the fifty-six day Lenten fast. Ras Ali had confirmed to him his ownership of Diddim, and he ascended the mountain path to the village in the company of his fighting men. Once again, Birru Goshu had been pushed back to the heights of his wilderness amba, but once again the wily nobleman had not been captured even though his father had, this year, fought on the side of Ali. It remained to be seen what would transpire next; but when Bell had parted from the Ras, the noble was beginning to rant less against Birru Goshu and much more against the upstart, Kassa.

"I am glad to be home and away from it for a while," he told Worqenesh. "Ras Ali certainly tries, but he seems incapable of bringing peace to the country. You know that I am sworn to him as part of the agreement that I receive income from Diddim and, in turn, I am responsible for the people's safety, but I sometimes doubt his ability. Now this fellow, Kassa, your Mother's Uncle – he is someone to watch."

"Why do you say that, John?" she asked.

"It is not just that he shares any earned booty with his men and makes them happy. It seems that he also cares for the people around him. He has shared food with the hungry in Quarra, and even helped them to acquire tools, clear land and plant. There is something about the way he interacts with people. In English, we would say that he is charismatic."

"Then I expect that we shall see Ras Ali trying to negotiate with him," observed Worqenesh. "But if I were Kassa, I should be even more wary of Menen, who calls herself the *Itege* (Empress). She is a woman with no compunctions."

Easter came and went, then the warm days of May followed by the heavy rains beginning early in June. There were never maneuvers or campaigns when each afternoon brought darkening skies followed by torrents, with the water making deep cuts down mountains and hills. Life came almost to a halt then, but there was a sense of both relief and expectation. The season of *Meskel* would follow with its deep blue skies, yellow flowers and ripening fields; and this year, as *Meskel* approached, Worqenesh told John that she was expecting their first child.

# Chapter 17

Early in 1845 John Bell was sitting in his mother-in-law's compound one day visiting with Fenta Tadese. The two had become good friends and trusted each other's observations on the political front of the country. For a moment Bell interrupted his thoughts to look out over the mountain side to the west. It was one of those heart stopping days in the highlands when the air is absolutely clear, the sky a deep, intense blue and the surrounding hills amazing in their cover of greens and occasional bursts of color. He sipped slowly on a horn of mead marveling again at his fortune, and slowly brought his mind back to his companion.

"He is a popular commander, Yohannes. Queen Menen is growing edgy. Have you heard the latest?"

"You're talking about Kassa, I suppose," answered Bell. "I have heard that Menen has asked him to come to her in Gondar and join Ali's government, as it were. I think they have offered him Quarra. He has so many devoted followers that he is an embarrassment."

"Yes, and that is not enough for him. They will also offer him the means of marrying into the family."

"How is that?" asked Bell.

"Ras Ali is said to have an exceptionally lovely daughter. This Tewabach will marry Kassa in return for his cooperation. I really think that Kassa has fallen for her beauty, but you know as well as I do that a peace will not hold. Kassa will be quiet for a little while, and then break lose again."

Worqenesh appeared from the side of her mother's hut, largely pregnant and carrying a platter of cooked meat, whey and bread.

"What you men cannot seem to understand," she interrupted, "is that Ali and his mother will never be accepted here in the highlands. They profess Christianity, but they come from the Muslim tribes of Yejju. Basically, our people do not trust them."

"She's right," echoed Fenta, "and Kassa also carries with him an aura of invincibility. The last time Menen sent troops against him, they fled the field before his reputation! By the way, Worqenesh, when is the baby due?"

"In a matter of weeks, now; it cannot be too soon." She smiled, and then continued. "There is another thing that indirectly helps Kassa. Ras Ali's relationship with the new Abun is deteriorating. Abune Salama has quarreled with the *Ichege*, particularly about the fringe doctrine of *Sost Ledet*, and Ali has always supported the *Ichege*. It will not help Ras Ali if the Abun excommunicates him."

"You realize your wife's subtlety, Yohannes, I assume," mused Fenta. "She well understands our people. Who knows where it will all end? I shall head back home now, before it grows dark. There will, no doubt, be more news circulating in Debra Tabor. Will you be coming to the capital soon?"

"I shall probably come down overnight next week, and then I plan to stay here until after the baby comes. These are busy times," and he grinned at Fenta. His life was teeming with challenges and activity: he would not have it any other way.

When Bell rode down to Debra Tabor the following week there was news that Walter Plowden was nearby. He had been roaming the highlands, having visited such diverse communities as the camp of one Toko Brillay in the lofty mountains of Wello, Birru Goshu's headquarters in Gojjam and Queen Menen's palace in Gondar. Nor had he neglected attending upon Ras Ali, who had allotted a lovely site just northwest of the capital for Plowden's maintenance. "You must come out to Gaffat," he urged Bell when they met at Ali's palace. "It does not enjoy your lofty view from Diddim, but it is one of the loveliest pastoral scenes you will ever encounter."

Indeed, it was so. Bell rode out the next morning with his man, Gabriote, to discover a rural idyll. Set in an open, flat valley; Gaffat boasted fields of ripening *teff* with a stream running through the middle. To the west was a small hill on which Plowden had built a group of huts to house himself, his men, and their mounts. Local cattle wandered down to the stream for their morning drink, and there were three or four women with their little hand scythes sitting back on their haunches and cutting the early grain crop. All was green, gold and tranquil.

"It is almost like on of those bucolic watercolors of rural England," Bell observed. "Walter, you do always seem to land on your feet. However did you manage this?"

"Well, in spite of my wandering, I do try to keep in the way of the Ras," answered his friend. "This is an amazing country with a nearly perfect climate. The government should be encouraging farming and trading abroad. The way I see it, I shall stay here another year or so and then go home to England to try to arrange a trade agreement between the two countries. If only the government here would stabilize a bit, these people could do very well economically and England would profit as well. I am trying to gain the trust of the Ras so that he will be receptive to such an arrangement. John, I can see myself as British Consul here, overseeing trade."

John Bell shook his head in disbelief. "I grant you that the climate is temperate and the land fertile, and that there should be endless opportunities; but do you not forget the annual campaigns? Fields are planted only to be ground to dust or pillaged by marching armies. I have never known a country to be so at war with itself. You need to recognize realities, Walter. I am not even sure that, in the long run, Ras Ali is the man you should be courting."

"But John, do you not see this country as nearly paradisal?" Plowden could barely contain his enthusiasm. Bell could only nod mutely. He, too, had early come to love it.

Walter Plowden joined John Bell and Gabriote in the short ride back to town, and the three men went with Fenta Tadese to attend a *brendo* on the grounds of Ras Ali's palace. The company here, as was usual, was almost entirely made up of military men. Along with the raw beef and spicy sauces there was a constant bandying of wit and repartee that was the very core of the Abyssinian culture. Plowden reveled in the easy joking and camaraderie as Bell marveled at the gaiety juxtaposed against the constant violence.

* * *

About four weeks later, on an early March morning floating in mist, Susan Bell made her appearance right on schedule. Known to the villagers as Jewubdar (the limit of beauty), she was named for John Bell's sister, Susan. It was her Mother's secret hope that the little girl could one day meet her English aunt, but for now she was more than welcome to her family in Diddim. John Bell was beside himself with delight and Wishan was vastly relieved at the easy delivery. Through her early weeks of life Susan Bell proved herself to be a boisterous new member of the family, and her parents properly interpreted her noisy bursts of indignation as a sign of strength and good health, and were grateful.

By now Issete was an expert in tending the infants of the family and was happy to relieve Worqenesh of the care of her daughter whenever she needed some rest. "I think she is the most energetic of the babies I have known," she remarked one afternoon, "and she certainly is a long child. She will be tall like you and Yohannes."

So the days passed happily, and another rainy season came and went. John Bell frequently made the trip down the mountain to Ras Ali's palace in Debra Tabor where he learned, with a grimace, of *Itege* Menen's latest antic. Having leaned over backward to buy *Lij* Kassa's loyalty with the province of Quarra and the hand of her granddaughter, Tewabach, Menen came right back up to insult him. Declaring that only a man with at least the title of *Dejazmach* could rule in the western province, she sent a superior along with him to humiliate him in front of the people. Bell learned the story at the palace, and could not understand a pride so overweening as to court calamity. Even a fool could understand that Kassa was not a man to play games with.

Bell shared the news with Worqenesh when he returned home. They were sitting in their compound watching little Susan pull herself up against a tree stump and then working her way around it. Now that she was becoming mobile, the child was cheerful and inquisitive, and often had to be rescued from her explorations.

"You need to understand, John, that Menen is not of the people," observed his wife. "She is clever in a crafty, manipulative way; but not in an empathetic way. She would much prefer to hurt than to help."

"She does Ras Ali a great disservice," replied John. "I can see the coming year or two shaping up to be extremely active in the field. How does she expect her son to balance Wube of Tigre, Birru Goshu of Gojjam and now Kassa of Quarra; and still command the country?"

# Chapter 18

By 1846 the ingredients of disorder were rubbing against each other and setting off small sparks of revolt in every part of the Highlands. The Abune Salama losing patience, excommunicated both Ras Ali and Menen for their support of the *Sost Ledet* doctrine and its chief proponent, the *Ichege*. He then hastily retired from the intrigues of Gondar to the more agreeable atmosphere of Wube's Tigre. Lending protection to Salama, Wube declined Ras Ali's invitation to join his annual campaign against Birru Goshu in Gojjam and remained in the unapproachable heights of Simien.

Once again John Bell gathered the fighting men of Diddim, rendezvoused with Fenta Tadese in Debra Tabor and marched off with Ras Ali to Gojjam. "This is becoming an aggravating habit," he remarked to Fenta. "How many more years shall we make this same sortie? Still, the sight of our river crossing near the Portugese Bridge is a never ending entertainment. There is enough laughter and commotion to frighten every living crocodile clear to Sinnar."

Fenta laughed. "You must admit, Yohannes, that in the face of trials and tumult, we remain a cheerful race."

Bell nodded his agreement. Indeed, the bravery, stamina and good humor of the Abyssinians were remarkable. He knew of no other people who could ford the mighty Nile or race up the side of a mountain while maintaining a constant repartee interspersed with bursts of laughter.

The year's operation in Gojjam followed the usual pattern. Birru Goshu was successfully forced to retreat to his amba heights, Ras Ali and his forces retired back to Begemder and the rebel warrior reemerged as strong as ever. But late in October there was a new and different threat. Kassa Haylu, thoroughly annoyed with *Itege* Menen's insults and snubs, invaded Dembea. Twice Menen sent troops to deal with him, and twice he defeated them. While the engagements were relatively small, Kassa began the assaults with spearmen and about twenty rifles. He emerged with one hundred rifles captured from the Queen's men. It was a notable success.

Toward the end of the year an outbreak of hostilities was expected between Ras Ali and Wube in Tigre, so Menen marched her army east, to be able to support her son in Wagera (the province just south of the tall Simien Mountains). As soon as she left the ancient capital of Gondar, Kassa Haylu pounced. In early January of 1847 he advanced to occupy Gondar and had the audacity to demand and collect the annual taxes due to be paid to Ali and Menen. Furthermore, the people complied. Then, putting his own men in charge of the city, he moved east and south to occupy the towns bordering on the shores of Lake Tsana.

At the time, John Bell was with Ras Ali fighting in Wagera. They were able to defeat some of Wube's men, but Wube himself never left his mountains. It was impossible to use mounted forces to fight in the Simien heights, and so he remained unchallenged.

By June of 1847, Queen Menen marched back to Gondar to deal with Lij Kassa, and their two armies met at the northwestern corner of Lake Tsana near a small village called Iloha. The outcome of the battle astonished conventional expectations, for Menen was captured along with her husband Yohannes III. Ras Ali was not with his mother at the time, but pursuing his conflict with Wube, and so he sent high ranking allies in Gondar to negotiate her release. Kassa's demand was simple. He wanted all of the lands that had once belonged to Kinfu Haylu – the lands that he, Asfaw Yilma, Mekwinnen and Welde Tekle had fought for at Chenti Ber in 1839. The Ras was dumbfounded and, at first, refused; but Menen sent word that Kassa should be appeased peacefully as he could not be persuaded by force of arms. So Lij Kassa became Dejazmach Kassa and controlled Quarra, Dembea, and considerable land to the north of those provinces.

\* \* \*

While Kassa and Ali negotiated through the rainy season, John Bell had returned home to the joyous news of a second child, a son. John Aligaz Bell was born shortly after Easter in 1847, and was already two months old when his father first saw him. Father Barhe had quietly christened Aligaz in the village church, on the prescribed fortieth day after his birth; and Worqenesh had sent for Ayto Cassai, John Bell's friend in Korata, to serve as godfather. By the time Bell led his contingent of warriors home to Diddim, his growing family was already settled back into its well-ordered routines.

At about the same time that Aligaz was making his first appearance, Walter Plowden had set sail on the Red Sea bound for England. He was gone long before Menen's debacle and Ras Ali's fretful bargaining for her release. Plowden had decided to approach the British Foreign Office with his thoughts about a trade agreement. He had traveled in Abyssinia for four years, and he had convinced Ras Ali that if his country was to be thought of as a modern state, it should have a treaty with Great Britain. He carried with him gifts from the Ras To Queen Victoria – some samples of fighting lances, a bolt of hand-woven cotton and three little gazelles that were being fed by a nanny goat. While still in the Red Sea, the dhow on which he sailed wrecked on a reef off the coast of Egypt and he barely survived, to continue home empty-handed.

John Bell and Worqenesh had no way of knowing of Plowden's ill luck. Bell had seen Walter at Ali's palace earlier in the year and knew he was leaving. "You know, Worqenesh, Ras Ali is curious about Walter's mission, but I do not think he puts much faith in treaties with European nations. For him, Walter's ideas are a fleeting thought. His domestic problems are much more compelling and consume all of his time and attention."

"But Walter is so enthusiastic, and he is ambitious," she noted. "He is not like you – content to be one of us. I wouldn't be surprised to see him back soon with an executed document waiting for the Ras's signature. Walter's zeal is hard to resist."

Bell smiled. His friend was indeed one of life's enthusiasts. He and Worqenesh walked over to what had been Issete's hut, but was now thought of as the nursery. Issete was holding the baby and watching Susan playing with pebbles and a small pile of dried needles from a fir tree. The little girl was dressed in a long white shirt, carefully embroidered around the neck and the hem, and covering knee-length trousers. She was chattering to herself in a juvenile babble of Amharic, occasionally addressing her comments to her infant brother. Bell picked her up to hold her close for a moment and then set her back on her sturdy little legs. "She is interested in everything she touches," he observed. "I do wonder what her life will hold, but she is alive to everything around her, so she should manage well enough. At least you and I shall never force her into one of those alignments that you so dreaded when you were growing up."

\* \* \*

While John Bell was relishing a rainy season furlough at home, and Ras Ali was bargaining with Dejazmach Kassa, Walter Plowden reached London where he wrote a letter to the Foreign Office presenting his arguments regarding a trade agreement with Abyssinia. Now his luck held. A presence on the coast of the Red Sea made a great deal of sense, both to balance the energy of the French in the region and to foster trade. Carefully checking the character of their young correspondent, Lord Palmerston decided to send Plowden back as the British Consul to Massawa with both a salary and an allowance for dealing with Ras Ali. Plowden carried with him a nineteen-point treaty and returned to Abyssinia early in 1848. Thrilled to once more traverse the land between the port of Massawa and Wube's Tigre, he climbed the heights of the Simien Mountains and, with Lake Tsana on his right, descended to the capital city of Debra Tabor. Outside of the palace he caught sight of John Bell, who he embraced with enthusiasm, and then entered the dark interior of the building to begin his assault on Ras Ali. A few days later, much subdued, he retired to Bell's home where he described the encounter.

"I should have expected it," he mused. "At least I was well received. There he was, the Ras, surrounded by horses, courtiers, children and flies. I simply greeted him, told him that I bore gifts and a treaty, and retired. I was warned not to present all of the gifts at once, but I thought to overwhelm him with England's generosity. The next day I lay all before him and began to read the treaty."

"Oh," grimaced Bell. "I can well picture it. Did he pay you any mind?"

"Barely. While I explained the concept of exchanging representatives, he stroked the flank of a horse and examined its teeth! He finally declared that he saw no harm in any of the words, but did not really see the point in such a document. When I suggested that he might like to think about signing it he simply smiled, said he would consider it and waved me out. Then each day he sent to me requesting more gifts. I have come up here to remove myself from his cupidity; and hope that, in time, he becomes more receptive."

Worqenesh almost giggled. "Oh, Walter, you should know our people better by now. They may not be worldly wise, but they are clever. You have let him see how important this treaty is to you. Now he will string you along and try to bleed you dry. Oh, poor Walter," and she reached out to assure him of her concern.

"I am afraid she is right," added Bell. You have left yourself wide open. Why don't you stay out of the way with us for a few weeks? He will eventually grow tired of teasing you."

Plowden looked at them both, and then laughed. "I have been a fool, but I can be stubborn too. We shall see."

He remained with John and Worqenesh for about a week and then went back to his place at Gaffat . From there he would often go to Debra Tabor to discuss the treaty while Ras Ali sought to strip him of all his personal property including his pistols and a rifle. When an elderly relative died, Ras Ali pretended overwhelming grief and retired to the hot springs at Goramba where he refused to see anyone. Finally, he abruptly left for yet another campaign in Gojjam.

Plowden consulted Bell, who was to follow, and decided that with the expectations of the British Foreign Office sitting heavily on his shoulders, there was nothing left but to follow along. Worqenesh ordered the preparation of supplies for the two friends, and off they went. The next day they rested at a lovely camp where there were trees for shade, grass for grazing and fish for supper; and Plowden fell prey to his old nemesis, the fever. He was hardly able to sit his horse as they crossed the old Portuguese Bridge over the Nile along with a large group of men, horses, women and children pressing forward in their usual cheerful confusion.

So the days followed, with Ras Ali moving to battle and Walter Plowden struggling to keep up. Weeks later, as they returned to Begemder, Ras Ali at last condescended to hear the treaty read once again. Plowden went to Ali's tent where the Ras was talking to his servant about a horse that was tied up inside the tent. He begged for Ali's attention as his scribe read, the Ras yawned; the scribe continued, the Ras stroked the horse and said that really, the document was excellent, if useless. Then he bent over, signed two copies and walked out of the door.

# Chapter 19

Worqenesh could only sigh in sympathy when her husband returned and related Plowden's saga of frustration. "You know, John, Ras Ali will be overbearing when he can, and have you heard the latest about Dejazmach Kassa? He has suffered a defeat. This will surely embolden the Ras."

John Bell looked up in surprise. "Are you sure? Where have you heard this?"

"Fenta Tadese was visiting Mother yesterday, and told us. Do you remember we related to you the story of my grandfather's impressive victory defending the border against the Egyptians, and how it made Ras Ali really nervous? At the time, Kassa Haylu was fairly young, but he fought by Kinfu's side. Well, this time Dejazmach Kassa took on the Egyptians and lost."

Bell raised his brows. "That is news. I wish I could talk to Fenta."

"I'm sure he'll be back soon. He checks on the family almost every week. He said that Kassa and his men had attacked a small, but well fortified, Egyptian position west of Matemma, and that they were thoroughly trounced. It was Kassa who was the aggressor, not the Egyptians. Fenta said the attack was wildly uncoordinated and that all of the men in the front lines were killed by field guns. Kassa had to retreat."

This was indeed a turn of events. Bell had long admired the extraordinary bravery of Abyssinians in battle, and deplored their total lack of tactics. He wondered how Kassa would recoup. Then, remembering to complete his news of Plowden, he added, "but wait, I didn't finish my story. Walter has left Gaffat and gone to the coast.

His consulate is officially located at Massawa, and he will stay a little inland from there for now."

"You will miss him I expect, John. He will be a piece of home gone from you."

"He will come back. If I know Walter, he will not be able to resist the highlands. I think Ras Ali outwitted him. He nearly didn't let Walter go back to the coast where he is supposed to be stationed. Walter had to give up his last decent personal weapon to gain permission to return to Massawa. But I need to talk to Fenta about your news. Do you think we can ask Wishan to send us a message the next time Fenta visits?"

\* \* \*

Within the week John Bell caught up with Fenta Tadese across the path from Wishan's compound, coaching Haylu and Welde to throw themselves onto the backs of their mules while carrying a short stick "It would be too dangerous for them to hold a lance yet," he said in an aside to Bell. "I cannot let them injure themselves; or the mules either, for that matter!"

Haylu called a greeting to his brother-in-law and trotted back to Fenta. "Could we try it holding a shield? That could not hurt anything." And he dropped from his mule in front of the two men.

"Perhaps. We'll begin with something small - maybe a round lid. Do the exercise one more time, and we'll stop for today."

Bell looked with admiration as the two youngsters began to push their animals forward, and leapt onto their backs. "Their father would approve, Fenta. I wish he could see them. How old is Haylu now – nearly fourteen?"

"Yes. He will soon be coming with us on our annual campaigns. The responsibility of it all sometimes overwhelms me, but I know it is what Yilma wanted. I am glad that you and I are often together during these operations and can both look out for him; and I only wish the campaigns were more of an exercise, as they were a few years ago, and less like real warfare. Are you walking back to Wishan's compound, or to your own?"

"Worqenesh and the children are with her mother, so I am going there. I really came to ask you about Dejazmach Kassa's recent attack against the Egyptians. Worqenesh implies that it was unprovoked."

"Indeed, that is so. I believe that Kassa's success against Menen last year meant that many of her army drifted away from her and gravitated to him. He began to feel invincible. Even though Goshu, the elder, had just been named a Ras by our newly restored Emporer, Sahle Dengel, Kassa had sense enough not to challenge him. Instead, he drew his growing army around himself and went west."

"Why did he avoid the Goshus?" asked Bell.

"I think he realized that Goshu's promotion was a slap at Ras Ali, and had nothing to do with himself. Anyway, in March, he took his forces into Sudan to a place called Dabarki, east of Sinnar. It was a disaster. The Egyptians hid behind their fortifications, and when Kassa's men attacked, they gunned them down with cannon."

By now the two men had strolled into the compound where the family was gathered, and now listening to Fenta. "But Uncle Fenta," observed his godson, "Dejazmach Kassa is considered such a clever fighter. He never loses."

"Well, Welde, until now all of his battles have been out in the open. He has had no experience of storming a fort, and I don't think he has ever faced guns such as those at Dabarki."

"He will need to rethink some of his strategy," piped in Worqenesh.

"That's just the point," said her husband. "The thing is that up until now, he has not really had any. You are right, Worqenesh. If he is as intelligent as we all seem to suspect, he will be rethinking a lot of things. You know, I've just been wondering; have any of you ever met this conspicuous relative of yours?"

"No," answered Wishan. "Yilma was the only one who ever saw him. From what he told us, I had the feeling that Yilma was not really comfortable with him, even though he was grateful that Kassa came with the family to Chenti Ber. He did say that Kassa fought well."

"Perhaps this recent loss of his will be his undoing," suggested Haylu.

"No," countered Worqenesh. "I have the feeling that he will lay low for a little while, mull over his options and then come on stronger than ever"

"I think she is right," agreed Bell. "My wife has an uncanny knack for understanding her countrymen."

Walking home after Fenta Tadese headed back to Debra Tabor, Worqenesh began to think out loud. "You know, John, Kassa is well educated, whether or not that makes him intelligent. And his early years cannot have been easy – his father died young and I think he was brought up in Dejazmach Kinfu's household as a poor relative. Sometimes that makes a person excessively ambitious."

"I'm not sure if I want to know him or not," replied her husband. "For now it is just good to be home," and they walked on companionably in the fading light, with Susan trotting happily between them. The evening was humid, or as close to humid as it ever seemed to be in the airy heights of their mountain. The warmest days of April and May were nearly over, and the rains would soon be lending their relief. Worqenesh had come to look forward to this time of the year with her growing family when John was home with them. Their lives had taken on a rhythm dictated by nature, with the family gathered during the darker days of rain, and then separated by political necessity soon after the golden days of Meskel.

\* \* \*

But this year John Bell was not immediately called back to the Ras's camp. Instead, he had time to pay attention to the agricultural pursuits of the village; consult with the elders and, with their advice, act as a judge in local disputes. Just after the celebration of Christmas, he was sitting outside near the *gojo* on a lazy afternoon, when he saw Fenta Tadese with Haylu and Welde trotting by on their mules. He stood as they turned in and called Worqenesh, who quickly appeared carrying a tray of cooling drinks.

"You were right, Worqenesh, as you usually are," Fenta began, and sat down to share the latest from the capital with the young couple. "The only thing that I would add to your predictions is that Dajazmach Kassa has shown a violent streak that we should all be aware of. By the way, Yohannes, we haven't been called up to campaign because Ras Ali has been too busy trying to control his son-in-law."

What followed was a tale both of horror and adroit political skill. When Dejazmach Kassa had retreated from Dabarki back to Alefa and Dembea he, himself, suffered the embarrassment of deserting subordinates. Instead of quietly allowing disgruntled men to slip away, he captured them and had their hands and feet cut off. When Ras Ali ordered him to Debra Tabor he demurred, blaming his absence on the rains. In truth, he feared reprisals because of his earlier treatment of Menen. Ali then sent an army to Dembea, and the province suffered from the marauding activity of both armies for more than four months. The two sides had only just been reconciled.

Worqenesh listened to the story quietly and reached out to John to hold his hand. She so hated the violence that sometimes erupted in her homeland, and feared that her husband would be drawn in and injured.

"Anyway," Fenta concluded, "we are now ordered to join Ras Ali. Everyone will be campaigning in Gojjam against Birru Goshu this year. Dejazmach Kassa is trying to prove his loyalty to Ras Ali and has joined him; and Ras Goshu Zewde has, for the moment, abandoned his son and will also support Ali."

When Fenta and the boys had gone on, Worqenesh and John sat still and looked at each other in dismay. "John," she whispered, "what a people you have joined."

"Never mind," he answered and drew her close. "We are in this together and we shall both manage. Tomorrow I need to alert my men in the village and begin to pack. We must be in Debra Tabor by the end of the week. You know, I may even see this distant uncle of yours this season, and I am glad that I am not in Birru Goshu's shoes."

# Chapter 20

A few weeks later Worqenesh and Issete were walking along the path that circled Diddim, leading the two children. Aligaz was rapidly approaching his second birthday, and was happy to walk with his family, but was frequently distracted by a bug crawling on the ground or the cattle grazing in the nearby fields. Susan skipped back and forth around her little brother, singing to herself and laughing at his antics. She was a noticeably merry child, and old enough to anticipate the approach of Easter when she knew that Father Barhe would come to bless the family's home and the villagers would bring flowers. It had been another long day during *hudaddie,* and the four of them were on their way to Wishan's compound to break their fast with an early dinner.

"You know, Issete," said Worqenesh, "I never stop being grateful that we live so close to my mother's home. I think she finds it helpful too. This fighting season is once again an anxious time for her, with Haylu gone on his first campaign. I worry about him almost as much as she does, but we knew he would have to go."

"The men will watch over him, and he has Selpha," Issete reminded her. "I believe that horse is quite capable of protecting Haylu."

Worqenesh smiled. "I do think it is a comfort to Mother that he rides Father's horse. He always maintained that the animal never took a false step and invariably knew what to do."

They moved on slowly, to keep pace with Aligaz and his constant diversions. "Worqenesh, do you think that your John will meet Dejazmach Kassa? I should like to meet his wife. You know, she is said to be very beautiful, and she is of my people."

Worqenesh looked at her friend in surprise. Issete never mentioned her Galla origins.

"What puzzles me is that she seems to urge her husband against her own family. How can she do that? What have you heard?"

Worqenesh paused for a moment to gather her thoughts. "Perhaps, Issete, if this is true it is because her family, especially her grandmother, has behaved badly and has been distinctly unkind to her husband. People say that Tewabach and Kassa actually care for each other and are good friends. What began as a political marriage has become a real love. Tewabach is said to take great care of Kassa, but what really convinces me is that he consults with her. I have heard that when Kassa is not off fighting, he and Tewabach are often seen just sitting together and talking. We all know of his dreadful temper, but I think she takes the edge from it. He is lucky to have her, and when you think about it, we are probably lucky she is with him too."

Issete thought for a minute, and then nodded. "Well, when you put it that way, I do understand loyalty to those who care for you," and she hurried to pick up Aligaz and swing him over a pile of dirt. It wouldn't do to have the children arrive at their grandmother's house covered with dust.

"And what about you, Issete," continued Worqenesh. "This talk suddenly makes me feel very selfish. Wouldn't you like to marry? John's man, Gabriote, is older, but I do think he admires you."

Her friend smiled and shook her head. "You must believe me, Worqenesh. I have everything I want."

\* \* \*

John Bell was back with his family in Diddim just toward the end of the long fasting period of *hudaddie* in time for Easter of 1849, to stay through the rains until the golden days of *Meskel*. The reconciliation between Ras Ali and Dejazmach Kassa was holding, and would continue to do so for three more years. Kassa joined Ali's campaigns in Gojjam, and when his services were not required Ali would send him off to Agewmidir, which was just west of Gojjam and south of Alefa, and now served as Kassa's base. During this same period,

Wube, up in Tigre, was busy in his own territory and toward the Red Sea coast, where he was in constant conflict with the Turks to restrict their expansion inland from Massawa. So for about three years the areas surrounding Lake Tsana, which included Gondar, enjoyed peace; and were able to recover from the destruction of the fighting between Kassa and Ali.

During this three year period Worqenesh watched her brothers and sister approach maturity. They were all nurtured in the stable environment that had been provided by their father and Wishan, and that was augmented by their paternal grandmother, Ribca. John Bell now provided them security in the political environment of the highlands, with Wishan and Ribca creating the loving warmth of their home.

By 1851, Haylu was an experienced warrior, serving with either Fenta Tadese or John Bell, or both. Welde was thirteen, and pushing at the remaining familial impediments to his own military career. Both Haylu and Welde were recognized as young men of noble birth, loyal to Ras Ali. Their grandmother Ribca's namesake was twelve and, in their culture, marriageable. Not so tall and striking as her older sister, she was nevertheless quite pretty, with a warm and generous nature.

And Giyorgis, the brother Worqenesh was closest to both in age and in affection, was now twenty and about to enter the priesthood. Giyorgis had enjoyed the tutelage of the good Abba Guebra Barhe from the time he was a little boy. Thanks to the generosity of Asfaw Yilma, he had been freed from all but the most rudimentary military training to study music, theology and Ge'ez – the language of the Orthodox Abyssinian Church. He had served officially, first as a *debtera* to perform music and dance within church services and to learn astrology and the traditions of church history. Later, he was consecrated as a deacon by Abune Salama and able to lead some services. Now he was about to travel with Father Barhe to Gondar, where the Abun would ordain him as a priest. Giyorgis had not married. If he had done so before his ordination, the church would have accepted the alliance; but as he had not, he would be required to remain celibate. Worqenesh believed in and accepted his decision understanding that his goal, since early childhood, had been the priesthood.

"Giyorgis, I do wish I could be with you in Gondar. I would love to share what is so important to you, but I don't suppose I could come close enough to see you anyway."

"No, the ordination ceremony is only for men. Frankly, I think that is foolish, and I also object that our family has to pay the Abun so that he will ordain me. Somehow, that even seems sacrilegious to me. I suppose I have always had an idyllic view of our church which sometimes does not mesh with reality. Still, this is what I want to do. Father Barhe has taught me that a priest should be a servant, both of God and men. That is a view not generally held in our country. Even so, I believe there is still a place for me."

Worqenesh looked at him with great affection. "I am terribly proud of you, and I know Father would be too. Somehow, I think that he understood what you wanted, and approved."

Giyorgis thought of his sister when he stood in the crowd of candidates for ordination that had gathered on the grounds of the Debre Berhan Selassie Church in Gondar. Fifteen years had passed since his father had taken the family to Gondar and they had seen the new rectangular stone building with a portico surrounding its exterior and the lovely winged angels watching over the space inside. He remembered the moment when he and Worqenesh had entered the church from opposite sides and their eyes had met in wonder.

He and Guebra Barhe had traveled the well-remembered route from Diddim to Gondar on family mules and accompanied by guards John Bell had insisted upon. While there was relative peace, it was never wise to travel without protection. Today his mentor and good friend stood off to the side in a crowd of observers. The approach of the Abun was announced first by *debteras* shaking their *sistra.* They were followed by a group of men beating the deep sounding *kebbero,* and *ambilta* playing reeds of various sizes and sounds. Next marched priests in joyful progression, and then a man in a long, silk robe and carrying a large silver cross. He made way for the *Ichege,* who wore a purple velvet robe and a white turban from which was draped a piece of white muslin, gracefully hanging to the ground. The *Ichege* was shielded from the sun by a large, fringed umbrella; and carried a little silver cross with which he waved blessings to the crowd.

At last, Giyorgis saw the Abun, dressed as a Coptic priest, but with a grand cashmere shawl which nearly covered him from head to toe. He was thus properly protected from any random glance from a woman.

When the panoply of dignity was all suitably in place, a brief ceremony ensued, followed by the Abun's pronouncement of a blessing that he blew across the assembled crowd. Giyorgis was reminded of God blowing breath into newly created man. Somehow, it seemed appropriate.

Riding home with Abba Barhe they discussed a future division of responsibility. Barhe was growing older and would welcome quieter days. He would give up his duties in Debra Tabor in favor of the new Abba Giyorgis Yilma, who would now spend most of his time in Ras Ali's capital. Barhe looked forward to shepherding the little church in Diddim on a full time basis. Giyorgis would serve as one of the priests of the Church of Iyasus, but make weekly sojourns up the mountainside to Diddim to spend a little time with his mentor and to take over some of the tutoring of his sister's children.

The year of 1851 continued in relative peace. Giyorgis entered happily into the quiet routine of the church at Debra Tabor. He still occasionally performed music at the church, but now he was usually a full participant in conducting the liturgical services in Ge'ez, even preaching a rare sermon. In Diddim, Susan and Aligaz looked forward to his weekly visits and their lessons with him, and Giyorgis enjoyed staying overnight with his sister and her husband whenever he could eke out a little extra time. He and Worqenesh were close friends, and her husband was relieved that Giyorgis was a regular visitor – especially when he had to be away. After Meskel, John Bell joined Ras Ali, as usual, to campaign in Gojjam.

But by the beginning of 1852, the reconciliation between Ras Ali and Dejazmach Kassa began to wear thin. Kassa refused to obey a summons to join Ali, and the Ras dispatched a large army to Agewmidir to enforce his orders. Kassa retired to the familiar rock formations of Chenti Ber. This time he made sure that his position was too strong to challenge.

## Chapter 21

Dejazmach Kassa's position at Chenti Ber may have proved impregnable, but Ras Ali's army made a rapid feint to the west, bypassed the narrow passage through the rocks and marched quickly to Dembea. Gondar, which in the last three years had only just recovered from the rapacious onslaught of Kassa's and Ali's armies in 1848, was once again subjected to the violent deprivations of war. While Ras Ali's forces hovered near the old capital, Kassa's men retired to his former stomping grounds of Quarra to build up their strength.

John Bell and Fenta Tadese, along with Haylu, were with Ali's army as it dodged Chenti Ber, and both Bell and Haylu listened in fascination to Fenta Tadese as he described the battle there in 1839. As they rode west of the great rocks; Haylu, on Selpha, wondered if the nimble horse remembered fighting across the uneven terrain, but there was no battle this time. Upon reaching Gondar, Ali sent many of his closely loyal fighters back to Begemder. As he had when he broke his promise to Asfaw Yilma and Mekwennin, he called on the now aging Ras Goshu Zewde to do his work for him.

"I saw him before we left," Bell confided in his wife. "I have admired the elder Goshu since I first met him and he helped me on my way to see the source of the Nile. He is a princely looking man, and conducts himself nobly as well. I shall always be grateful for his care of me – I joined him just days after the *shifta* did this," and he pointed to the long scar running down his nose and across his cheek. "He seemed to understand the urgency I felt to reach Gish Abbai."

"I think my father thought well of him too, but certainly not of his son. Birru Goshu is a brutal man. It is telling that as often as not, the father refuses to support the son." It was still difficult for Worqenesh to think of the duplicity that had eventually led to her father's early demise.

"You know, Worqenesh, it was really Ras Ali's double-dealing, and not Goshu's, that was responsible. Birru Goshu was simply Ali's tool. I'm afraid he is using the father now in the same way he used the son then."

"Yet you support Ali, John."

"As did your father. It has simply worked out that way. Ali is the one who still calls the shots, and he is the one who set me up here, in Diddim, with your father. In this country one is almost forced to choose sides. I do not feel any great love for the man. Worqenesh, you do cut to the core!" He knew that her directness was what he trusted in her. In the tugs and pulls of the politics in their lives it was Worqenesh, of all those with whom he came in contact, whose thoughts and insights unerringly honed in on the truth.

The rains of 1852 began early, and John Bell was happy to have extended time with his family. At least once or twice a week, he and Worqenesh would stroll the circular path that skirted Diddim to visit her family, enjoy a meal and hash out the latest news from the capital. Issete would bring Susan, now seven, and Aligaz, four; and frequently Fenta Tadese or Giyorgis rode up from Debra Tabor and joined the companionable gatherings.

Late in the season, on a rare afternoon when the dark clouds forgot to gather and the children were able to lose themselves in play; the adult conversation turned, as usual, to the approaching time for campaigning. There was a general consensus that the days ahead would bring both challenge and change.

"Ras Goshu is said to be gathering his troops in preparation for his fight against Dejazmach Kassa whenever and wherever he may find him," observed Fenta. "We, on the other hand, will be ordered to join Ras Ali in Gojjam. Do you notice how Ali has split the Goshus this year?"

"It looks as if Ras Ali is deliberately pitting Goshu Zewde against Kassa. I heard that he had induced Goshu to fight by promising him the governorship of Kassa's land. That is the strategy he used against

Kinfu's family that devastated you people. He really doesn't mind who destroys who," observed John Bell.

"Why should he care? The defeat of either one of those powerhouses will equally serve his purpose," chimed in Worqenesh.

Haylu looked puzzled for a moment, and then spoke up. "What I see is that he has broken up everyone. Birru Goshu is split away from his father, who is savaged on Kassa. The man is clever."

"And so are you," smiled his sister, "more so than I thought."

Wishan looked at the dear ones around her. Only their loyal friend, Fenta, was of her generation, with John Bell somewhere between them and the next. Most of her children were now adults, or soon would be. Haylu, who looked so much like his father, was already a seasoned warrior and was planning to marry sometime between *Ganna* and *Timket* in January. His chosen bride was the daughter of one of Fenta Tadese's tribesmen in Debra Tabor, and Wishan was content with the match. After the wedding Sossina would come to live at the family's compound which was now the titular responsibility of Asfaw Yilma's second son. Welde was four years behind his brother, but would join Haylu, Fenta Tadese and John Bell for the fighting season the following year. She sighed quietly. At least he would be home for a little while longer.

Worqenesh, sitting next to her mother, could feel her emotion. Wishan was the solid rock of the family to whom they all turned, and she reached out to touch the woman's hand and speak her love. "Thank heaven for you and this place," she whispered.

Worqenesh and Bell walked home in the warm, soft night. Issete had gone ahead earlier to put the children to bed. The air was still and there were few stars and little light, but the path was familiar and Worqenesh and John chatted together companionably.

"It is a complicated time. I do feel that change is coming, but I cannot quite put my finger on the reason. It is just that Ras Ali never seems to be able to solve anything," and John reached for Worqenesh's hand.

Worqenesh leaned her head on his shoulder and smiled. "Then I don't suppose, with the uncertainty of the times, that you will think it wise to have another child."

John looked at her in surprise, and then laughed. "So that is what you are up to. You are wrong – I think it's grand. When is this one due?"

"In April, I should think. Actually, John, I'm rather excited. Somehow, I am really looking forward to this child. I expect you will be away, but we shall be fine. Mother is close by, I have Issete, and the village is well protected," and they walked on, arm in arm, in the dark.

\* \* \*

Within a month, and just after Meskel, the men of the family were back in Gojjam with Ras Ali, trying to intercept Birru Goshu. 'Surely,' thought John Bell, 'there has to be a better way.' He remembered his boyhood lessons about the Napoleonic wars and the masterful strategies of Lord Wellington. Here, Ali's army could chase their opponent all day, but Birru Goshu was always forewarned by his clansmen and always disappeared to a lofty amba. There was no plan, no forced march, no surprise. As soon as Ali's forces crossed the Nile from Begemder into Gojjam, Goshu was gone. It was more of a sporting event than a war. Their only accomplishment was to keep Birru Goshu occupied and out of the way.

But to the north, Ras Goshu Zewde's pursuit of Dejazmach Kassa was no game. In October, Kassa began maneuvering in the territory with which he was most familiar. He moved from Alefa along the western banks of Lake Tsana north to a little area known as Chilga. With each move, he adopted a position deemed by Ras Goshu to be too strong to attack. Then suddenly, in November, he marched away from his strongholds out onto the plains of Dembea, stopping at an open position at Gur Amba. Goshu's men were puzzled by the move. Why in the world, with so few men, would Kassa camp in the middle of a plain? On November 27, 1852, Ras Goshu's army attacked, and in a full day's battle they were completely routed. There were heavy casualties on both sides and Ras Goshu Zewde was killed. What was left of his army hurried back to Gojjam.

Even now, the clever Kassa did not directly challenge Ali. Instead, he asked members of the clergy in Gondar to seek out the Ras and express his wish for another reconciliation. This time, Ras Ali refused. Now the forces were in motion for change. In March of 1853, Ras Ali was able to acquire some assistance from Wube in Tigre, who sent men to join Ali's generals in Dembea to face Dejazmach Kassa. Kassa knew his own men possessed far fewer firearms than this coalition, and withdrew to the western border of the province; but there, in mid April, he took his stand and gained a second victory. After this success, there was no question that he would confront Ras Ali in person with the purpose of overthrowing his government.

John Bell had a few days at home before he was called urgently to join Ras Ali in Debra Tabor. Worqenesh was hugely pregnant, and both she and Bell knew that a crisis was at hand. "Any rational mind must know that we now have a gifted commander challenging a very ordinary fighter. I think there cannot be much doubt as to the outcome," Bell remarked. "I rather wish now that sometime in these last years I had had an opportunity to meet this imposing uncle of your mother's."

"John, do not risk your life foolishly. There is simply no point in that."

"I do have to join Ali and fight with him. You know that. I hate leaving you now. At least I will be with Fenta and Haylu and we shall look out for each other. I cannot renege on my sworn allegiance, but I do promise you that I shall be careful." He and Worqenesh looked long at one another as if to memorize each other's face. This time the prospects ahead indeed looked bleak.

When John Bell left Diddim it was Welde, along with a part of the village militia, who was left to protect the family. He was only fifteen, but well instructed by Fenta Tadese and Haylu. Added to those now under his protection was Sossina, Haylu's new wife. He took his new duties very seriously. Bell thought well of the youngster, but placed his chief hope in Diddim's remote and mountainous situation.

After his April success against the combined forces of Ras Ali's allies, Kassa had marched southwest to Debra Tabor and, in early May, he burned Ali's capital. Fenta Tadese had escaped the conflagration to join Bell and Haylu rushing to catch up with the Ras's army, now retired to Gojjam. On the 29$^{th}$ of June Dejazmach Kassa at last caught up with his father-in-law on the plain near Ayshal and a terrible battle was joined. By now, Kassa had accumulated nearly as many firearms as Ras Ali. Bell, who was expert in the use of his rifle, was briefly successful in rallying his men to protect the Ras's left flank, but a rifle is only good when firing at a distance. In close fighting it is better used as a bludgeon, and so he adapted it as the enemy closed. As the noon hour passed, Bell slowly realized that Ras Ali had disappeared and that he was almost alone in a bloodthirsty horde of strangers. Gradually moving backwards, he was able to break away and, with no friend in sight, ducked through the door of a church. He knew by the markings on the lintel that he had happened upon a *Geddam* (a sanctuary), and would be safe as long as he remained inside.

He was, however, trapped. If he had managed to enter the church undetected, he might hope to escape after sundown in the dark. He could hear the noise of the battle subside and was sure that the fight had been lost and that Ras Ali had escaped in the confusion. There was a lone priest in the building who nodded, and went on about his business. John Bell sat on the floor to wait. As daylight began to fade his hope for escape surged, when suddenly he heard voices outside.

"I saw him enter, sire. I believe it was a *ferengi*. His skin was as white as a European's."

"A European, you say?" and with that, the second voice called out, "I respect your sanctuary – you, in there. This is Kassa Haylu. Come out – I shall not harm you."

There was nothing for John Bell to do, but to emerge into the dusk and bow low to his wife's great uncle. He knew the man's history, his successes in battle and his reputation for violence.

"Your Ras has fled the field. At least I presume you were fighting with Ras Ali." Kassa stared piercingly at the tall, well formed fighter before him. He looked to be about his own age. Then he broke out in what could only be described as a smile of great charm. "I'm not sure who you are, but why don't you join me? You'd better, anyway, as I have won."

Bell returned the direct look of the intelligent, dark eyes. "I think you are right. I shall do that. My name is John Bell." With this quiet exchange of trust the two young men left the church.

"You will want to return to your home and tell them that you are safe," advised the leader of the day's triumphant army. "We must find you a horse. Then meet me in Debra Tabor at the end of the rains. I shall be on my way to Tigre."

Bell bowed his assent. He had just been a witness to the demise of the *Zemina Mesafint,* and cast his lot with a future king.

# Chapter 22

---

John Bell's journey home was fraught with peril. He was alone, with a mediocre mount for transport and his rifle, his sole protection. Kassa's men knew he went with their leader's blessing, but beyond the immediate vicinity of Ayshal he needed to rely on his own wits. He rode in the open during the day, so that he could not be ambushed from a cover, and at dark he sought whatever shelter was at hand. After riding east to cross the Nile at the old, stone Portuguese Bridge, he turned north to follow the shore of Lake Tsana to the city of Korata. There he knew he could rely on his friend, Ayto Cassai, to supply him with an escort. From Korata, he continued north until the road intersected the mountain path to Diddim.

As he approached the village he saw an old woman stop, stare, and rush back along the path. The pulsing song of her ululations thrust before her to be picked up by first one voice and then another. By the time he had gained Wishan's compound, she was rushing toward the path followed by the two Ribcas. Wishan reached up to grasp his hand and wave him on. He turned his horse to trot toward the back of the village and his own home, surrounded by the gay chorus of women's voices. Suddenly, there was Worqenesh racing to meet him, and he slipped down the side of his mount to run toward her. There were no words – only breathless tears of joy.

Soon she grabbed his hand to pull him toward their compound. "The baby," she cried. "You must see Mary Belletech," and they raced to the *gojo* together. Issete was standing in the courtyard with Susan and Aligaz on either side, holding a tiny baby and smiling.

Bell first knelt to hold his two older children and then stood to lift the baby and there, in her tiny face, were his own two light blue eyes looking back at him. Worqenesh saw his surprise and nodded. "Every time I looked at her, I saw you; so I could not give up hope."

Little by little, through the next few days, all of the stories were told. Fenta and Haylu had been forced to flee Ayshal after losing track of Bell. They told of the Ras who had looked at defeat and deserted the field. The rumor was that Ras Ali had retreated to the land of the Yejju Galla – his birth place – and was in hiding. Sitting in Wishan's compound, Bell told his story.

"I have met your Uncle, Wishan. For whatever reason, he was enormously kind to me. We are about the same age, and I think he sees me as someone he can talk to. I had lost track of my men and was lucky to stumble upon a church of sanctuary. I had planned to find my way back to Ras Ali after dark, but someone had seen me enter the church and had told Dejazmach Kassa. It was Kassa, himself, who told me that Ras Ali was gone, and offered me protection."

"What now," asked Haylu. "Does his protection of you extend to us? Does he know who we are?"

"Yes, and yes," answered Bell. "I think he is actually pleased that in finding me he has found a bit of family. Goodness knows he has little enough, although I think his mother is still alive. He well remembers Asfaw Yilma and is glad to know of his people. He has already assured me of my continued right to Diddim, which I share with you. I am obliged to join him after the rains, and I think that he will center his resources in Debra Tabor for now."

"But Yohannes, do you trust him?"

"I do, Haylu. He is an enormously capable, maybe even a brilliant, fighter, and he seems to be modest in his needs and to share his spoils. I think he genuinely wants to improve the country. On the other hand, I think he is complex, and balances certain extremes in his personality in a kind of tension. And I have never seen anyone with so much energy – he barely sleeps."

"It seems odd, doesn't it, that my mother's uncle is so young?"

"Actually, you must remember that he was Dejazmach Kinfu's half brother, and much younger. They had the same father, but different mothers. He is certainly well educated – he speaks Arabic as well as Amharic – and he often quotes from scripture."

"Well," sighed Haylu, "I don't know what lies ahead, but it will be different. I think, perhaps, that we are all very lucky that he has taken such a liking to you."

Later, walking home together, Bell asked Worqenesh about the children. "Does Giyorgis still come to give lessons, or do they study with Abba Barhe? I have not seen your eldest brother since I returned."

"A little of both. Giyorgis did escape the fires of May when Dejazmach Kassa burned the capital, but he has since been terribly busy trying to oversee the repairs at the Church of Iyasus. I feel fortunate when he can take the time to stop and check on us."

"And Mary. You have given her my sister's middle name, but I am not familiar with the Belletech part."

"In Amharic it means, beyond the limit of beauty. Perhaps you feel that it is overdone, but truly, with her dark curls and pale blue eyes, I think she is the loveliest child I have ever seen. Indeed, she is striking. She is quieter than Susan was, and seems to be content within herself. I cannot tell you what a joy it is to me to have her. Aligaz is five now, and Susan will be a young lady before we know it. It is somehow a comfort to have a baby to care for again."

"I hate to leave you so soon after I have come back," continued Bell. "Kassa said at the end of the rains, but I feel I need to reach him as soon as I can. I will stay for a few days, but then I must go on."

Worqenesh nodded in reluctant understanding. Until now, John had just been another useful face to the Ras, whose close associates had been from his own tribe in Galla. She had a vague premonition that her distant relative had singled her husband out to be a friend. It was unnerving.

*  *  *

John Bell left Diddim a week later accompanied by his man, Gabriote, and a fair sized contingent of militia from the village. Kassa had indicated that there was imminent work to be done in Tigre, and Bell was determined to be part of that effort. He was directed to the northwest side of Debra Tabor by a member of Kassa's forces, to the leader's encampment. Kassa, who was unaware of his approach, turned in surprise and an expression of delight lit his comely face.

"You are early. Good. We plan a lightning strike on Wube. You must be with me." With that he drew Bell into his tent, indicated a place to sit, flung himself onto an *alga* and swept his arm around to show a small group of men. There, for the first time, Bell met the intimates of Dejazmach Kassa – the well trusted Ingida; Barak, of Kassa's own region of Quarra; Ingida Worq; the older Abiye and Kassa's gun bearer, Welde Gabie.

"We must move quickly and catch him off balance," Kassa continued what must have been an earlier strategy session. "Speed is our best ally. Here, at the beginning, there are two men we must nullify – Ras Wube and Birru Goshu. We shall begin with Wube in Wagera, and head northward tomorrow."

Bell could feel the strength of the man spilling out over his cohorts. The air was alive with his energy. That evening Bell was asked to eat with the leaders of the army, and was seated next to Kassa. He was aware of an affinity for the man building within himself. Here was a warrior with vision. He would sweep away his competitors using his remarkable military talent, but he cared about more than battles. He dreamed of uniting his country and moving it forward. The question in Bell's mind was whether Kassa would take corruption from his enormous ambition? Maybe it was here that Bell could find his place. Perhaps his role was to counsel and guide, lending Kassa steadiness through his friendship.

The next morning saw the beginning of their rapid advance to the north. Kassa kept John Bell near his side, and Bell was amazed by the speed with which the army traveled. The fighting men kept well ahead of their support groups, halts for rest were severely limited and night time stops were brief. Wube, who in the last decade had fought against Ras Ali at least twice, was taken by surprise by Ali's sudden defeat and was still in the eastern part of Tigre dealing with the Turks. Hoping to gain time he sent his son to assure Kassa that he would accept him as Ali's successor. He even sent tribute. Kassa decided that, for the moment, he would be placated. That was not difficult. In catching Wube off guard, Kassa had managed to scoop up the Abun and assimilate him into his own camp. Abune Salama was not a reluctant captive. He shared Kassa's vision of a united country by including in that dream a church unified in orthodox doctrine. The heretical teaching of *Sost Ledet* was losing official ecclesiastical support. All that remained was to effect a reconciliation between the Abun and the *Ichege*.

Now, turning quickly to the south, and with the Abun literally by his side, Kassa marched toward Gojjam and Birru Goshu. Even before he reached that formidable force, his victory was assured. As rumors of his approach preceded him, Birru Goshu's men refused to fight and melted away. It was one thing to face the ordinary Yejju Galla, Ras Ali; a predictable fighter and a presumed Muslim: it was something else to defend against a man now thought of as invincible, who was attended by a Christian bishop.

With his men, and even his wife, deserting his side, Birru Goshu stumbled into Kassa's presence with a heavy rock tied about his neck. It was the custom, when begging for mercy. John Bell stared in amazement at the scene.

"I believe that were our places reversed you would execute me, would you not," Kassa observed with deadly quiet.

"*Jan Hoi*, Your Majesty," Goshu nodded agreement.

"At least you are honest," observed the victor, and sent him in chains to prison.

# Chapter 23

The rainy season of 1854 was approaching, and Kassa decided to leave Gojjam for Dembea and march to the heights of Amba Chera, near Gondar. Here he would sit out the wet weather. The Abun had been sent on to Gondar, and there were matters of the church to consider.

"Return to your home for now, Yohannes, but join me at Amba Chera well before Meskel. First I must work on the reconciliation between Abune Salama and the *Ichege*. Later in the year we will check on Wube. I have learned that he has applied to your friend at the coast, Plowden, for imported rifles. No matter. We will attend to one thing at a time. For now we all need to pause and reorder our resources."

As it was on his way, Bell stopped one night in Korata to catch up with Ayto Cassai. He loved the old city with its abundance of merchants and clerymen strolling the streets and the sound of the waves from Lake Tsana striking the shore.

"It is something like being inside a whirlwind," he told his old friend. "The man has enormous energy and seldom sleeps, but he does seem to energize the rest of us as well. There is always much to be done, and it must be done well."

"I hear he is kindly to ordinary people," observed Cassai.

"Indeed, he is simple in his own wants and generous to others. He will stop when fording a river to help women or children to cross. But he is exacting too. There is so much he wants to do, and it is exciting to think that one can be a part of it all."

As always, reaching the mountains to climb up to Diddim was

sheer joy. 'I know how she feels,' thought Bell. 'Worqenesh is right: the village is a welcoming haven.' Now, as he approached, he mused on how well removed Diddim was from the changes abroad in the country. It would assimilate them eventually, but it was not threatened by them. And then he and Gabriote were trotting their horses along the familiar path that circled his neighbor's huts; and there, up ahead, was his growing family spilling out of their compound to greet him.

Later, still holding Worqenesh close, but not yet asleep; he whispered with a sigh of contentment, "I have two whole months – the rest of June, all of July and the beginning of August. I am so glad to be home."

And she, buried happily in his embrace, suddenly realized the ephemeral nature of their days together, and held him a little closer.

His days on leave were busy. While the rains came every day, it was only the afternoons that were awash. Then the sky would darken, the lightening streak across the sky and the water pour down the mountainsides in flash floods; to find its way to streams, rivers and eventually the mighty Nile.

The mornings were usually clear so that Bell found time to enjoy his children, mingle with his neighbors and begin to arrange for the coming campaign. In years past it had been Fenta Tadese who would come up from Debra Tabor and share in the military preparations. Now, he held back, and even shielded Yilma's sons from fighting. "If we are not specifically required, I think the boys should stay here to help the villagers and learn their responsibilities as land owners. There will be other times to fight. I prefer to keep Haylu and Welde here until we get a better sense of the direction Kassa will take."

Bell could hardly argue. "We'll leave it for now, and I'll cover the family's military responsibilities, but you may want to rethink your position. I believe Dejazmach Kassa represents the direction of the future, and I know it is his intention to unify the country. He expects that in a year or so all opposition will cease and he will be able to get on with the business of initiating reforms and governing."

"It cannot be too soon," replied Fenta. "We can all support that."

One evening in mid August, Worqenesh and John sat in their compound watching the children play as the light faded from a well-washed sky. "John," observed Worqenesh, "you are more involved now, aren't you? With my great uncle Kassa, I think that you will begin to be part of the inner circle. You were never intimately connected with Ras Ali, nor did you believe in his activities or strategies."

"He really didn't have any, Worqenesh. He was more reactive than a strategist, and he was usually manipulated either by his mother or whatever force was pressing at the time. You will not see Dejazmach Kassa managed by anyone but himself."

"It frightens me a little. I do not want to lose you to his vanity."

Bell leaned toward her in his intensity. "No, Worqenesh. This will be an adventure we can share. We are living in an amazing time which holds great promise but no certainty. As soon as it is safe, I want you to travel with me. I think that in one more season most opposition to Kassa will fade away and the country will enter into a new era of peace. Kassa wants to end slavery, reorganize the army into a paid, professional entity and unite the country. It will be grand for us both to be a part of that. Kassa listens to me. I think I can be a positive influence in his governance, and you are the one who keeps me strong. We need to be in this together."

She nodded and smiled. "I do want to be with you. What comes next?"

"Wube," he answered. "He appears to be the last obstacle. After his submission Kassa can implement the reforms he plans and begin to govern."

\* \* \*

John Bell reached the heights of Amba Chera toward the end of August, with Gabriote by his side and accompanied by his militia. By the time he arrived, Kassa had arranged the expected reconciliation between the Abun and the *Ichege* which was soon followed by a proclamation ordering obedience to the Abun's faith and rule. The following month, standing between these two highest clerics, Kassa issued a proclamation naming himself *Nigus*, or King.

Sitting with Bell outside on an evening when the army was gathered and moving north, Kassa explained his hopes concerning Ras Wube. "He is a clever fellow and a good administrator. If he will accept my suzerainty, I shall retain him in Tigre. Where is your book? What would it say to that?"

Bell chuckled. Kassa was referring to the compact copy of Shakespeare that he usually carried with him. "I do not remember any particular admonition, but as to kingship, it requires a man. Taken for all in all, it says, it is a noble manliness that is needed. That is sufficient."

"You help me, Yohannes. You give me perspective and keep my feet on the ground. I beg you, do not leave me."

Bell nodded. He usually was close by, and had even taken to sleeping across the doorway of Kassa's tent when they were campaigning. Kassa had sent the Abun and the *Ichege* on ahead to persuade Ras Wube to submit to Kassa's newly pronounced royalty, but Wube had spent the last decade successfully vying with Ras Ali, and was not in the least willing to bow to his successor.

Kassa's army marched through Wagera and, in January of 1855, it began its assault on the mountains of Simien. He pushed his men without rest, hoping to catch Wube off guard a second time. Until now, these heights had always discouraged invasion and assured Wube protection. It was to these mountains that he retired to watch his enemies struggle to climb ascents of thousands of feet while their cavalries collapsed, and here that he kept a stash of considerable wealth. For the first time in Kassa's experience he saw his men hesitate, and then falter. The army was exhausted, and looking about saw nothing but more mammoth peaks to scale. Off in the distance was a group of white tents which Bell, looking through his telescope, confirmed were Wube's. Kassa's men were rallied with difficulty, and the ensuing battle was long and hard fought. Only when Ras Wube was accidentally discovered resting and was captured was the fight over. Two of his sons had been killed and a third was forced to disclose the storehouse of money.

Kassa had succeeded: he had vanquished his immediate opposition. He now controlled the highlands and most of the major provinces except Shoa; and here, in the mountains of Simien, he had acquired a treasury of gold and silver, a hoard of rifles and even two cannons. Suddenly Kassa had ample means to effect what he hoped would be the centerpiece of the changes he was proposing. In the morning, with John Bell and the newly appointed Ras Ingida at his side, he began to hand out coins to the individual men in his army. No longer would they be allowed to live off the countryside and terrorize the peasants: they would earn a salary and pay for their keep.

On February 11, 1855, in the Deresge Maryam church that Ras Wube had built in expectation of his own coronation; Kassa Haylu was anointed and crowned *Niguse Negest*, King of Kings. The ceremony was conducted by Abune Salama; the same man whom Wube had brought, at his own expense, from Alexandria. Kassa took the throne name, Tewodros (Theodore), aligning himself with a long standing prophesy predicting a glorious, thousand year reign. Kassa, the former shifta, had become Tewodros, the elect of God.

Soon after the coronation the new King, properly Tewodros II, marched south to the territory of the Gallas to overcome their opposition and capture their fortress-like Amba Meqdela. It was a significant conquest. While Debra Tabor would serve as a capital, it was Meqdela that became his stronghold. Here he would maintain his treasury and store anything of value. Here was his place of retreat and here he could safely hold political prisoners. In time, Birru Goshu was sent to Amba Meqdela, as was Ras Wube. The resolution of the status of Shoa was left for a later date.

# Chapter 24

"Do you notice he does not claim descent from King Solomon? Certainly our previous Kings have made a point of this distinction." Worqenesh was sitting under the tall fir tree in her mother's compound, and the whole family had gathered to listen to her husband's account of the coronation.

"Is that significant?" asked Haylu. "He appears to me to be just one more of the *Mesafint;* howbeit, a very gifted one. He is a near genius on the battlefield."

"Yes, I think it is important. It suggests that he does not want his name associated with the Rases, like Ali. He wants to intimate that he surpasses them. From what John tells me, he really believes that God has chosen him."

"She is right," agreed Bell, "and I would go even further. Not only does he not want to be thought of in the same way as the Rases of the last eighty years; he does not want even to be thought of as part of the Solomonic dynasty that the Rases managed. These kings were nothing but puppets. King Tewodros' failures have been very few. From his earliest years he has enjoyed amazing escapes and brilliant victories. He believes God has guided him."

"You know," added Wishan in her quiet way. "He is a rebel."

Worqenesh smiled at her mother. "You might say a revolutionary. John, you were reading to me of one such in your book of Shakespeare the other afternoon."

"Macbeth," John shuddered, "but there is a difference. With Tewodros it is not simply a lust for power. He does believe that he has a mission from God to unify the country and lead it into its proper place in the modern world. Oh, but there is so much he does not know about the rest of the world – so much he must learn."

Fenta Tadese was standing nearby between Haylu and Welde, and seemed to be deep in thought. "Then I am glad he has you as a friend. Certainly, none of us could help him there. We have seen that his wife, Tewabach, helps to calm him and to diffuse his anger. Now he has you to instruct him in world politics and other practical matters."

"Yohannes, tell us again about the coronation. What do you think was important?" asked Welde, who was now seventeen and old enough to consider the new direction of his country.

"Aside from what we have already said, it was important that he had both the Abun and the *Ichege* there to demonstrate the sanction of the church and, thus, the legitimacy of the occasion. And I cannot over-emphasize the importance of associating himself with Tewodros I. You people know your history lessons better than I do, but there seems to be a national memory of a brilliant, if brief, reign in the early fifteenth century. For many years there has been an expectation of a successor, which I would almost compare to the Biblical, Hebrew expectation of a Messiah."

Wishan was looking uncomfortable. "Do you think he is such?"

"It does not matter what John thinks," Worqenesh interrupted. "If the new king can bring in a period of tranquility and prosperity, the people will believe that he is the reincarnation of that first Tewodros."

"And he will try," continued Bell. "He has already begun to issue proclamations. There will be no more slavery, and what slaves there are must be sold off, baptized and their sale price given to charity. Murderers will no longer be handed over to the victim's relatives for reprisal. There will be roads. The military will be paid. Tewodros is appointing governors loyal to himself to replace tribal chiefs. Some of these changes are already underway."

"He may well be moving too quickly," noted Fenta. "Such things will take time."

"There is more," continued Bell. "Up until now, clothing covering the upper part of the body has been a prerogative of the privileged. He has introduced the fashion of a lose cotton shirt for all. And he wants to promote the formalization of marriages in churches. He has set an example himself by submitting to such a ceremony with

Tewabach, and is encouraging those about him to do the same."

At this pronouncement a conspicuous silence fell over the gathering. Slowly, the various members of the family turned toward Wishan, whose usually calm countenance had turned to stone. "Yilma was opposed to this custom." She spoke very quietly, and those around her knew that she would be adamantly opposed to such a marriage in her family. Wishan was usually forward looking with an inquiring and open mind; but if an idea transgressed her memory of Asfaw Yilma, it was anathema.

Only gradually did the discussion resume, with brief remarks and nervous laughter. Giyorgis, who had been standing to the side, now spoke up. "You mentioned slaves, Yohannes, and at first I did not think Tewodros's proclamation would apply to us, but there is Issete. What about her? She would be devastated if she had to be, as it were, sold into freedom."

Worqenesh cast an anxious look at her husband. It was becoming unbearably clear that entrance into the modern world would not be easy, as it had at first seemed.

Bell hesitated. "She has been with your family for so long. I am sure that we can refer to her as one of the family. Indeed, that is how we all think of her. Let us not look for difficulties if we do not need to. As to the household servants, we shall simply pay them wages."

After that, the tension in the compound eased, and the usual family banter returned. Worqenesh and her sister-in-law, Sossina, walked to the kitchen area to help Wishan bring out bread and whey, while servants passed around horns of *tej*.

\* \* \*

In October, after the rains of his coronation year, the King marched on Shoa. The province lay well to the south and east and had enjoyed years of stability under one family, avoiding the bickering of the *Mesafint*; but the old king was ill, and died just before Tewodros's attack. Victory was easy. The Shoan chiefs surrendered and quickly handed over the young heir to their throne, Menelick. In Tewodros's early generosity, the boy became a favorite and was educated at court. His uncle was left behind as the King's representative and governor. It would now appear that Tewodros had a sound hold over most of the country and could concentrate on his dreams of modernization and creating a central government, but rebellion had become a habit with the Abyssinians and, even as the King returned through Gojjam to Gondar, there were challenges to his authority.

\* \* \*

For the moment, pleased with prospects for the future, Tewodros contemplated the institutions of his own country and pondered, with puzzlement, the outside world. A continuing source of perplexity was the Crimea, and the battle between Europeans and the Russians.

"But, Yohannes, the Russians are Christians. How can England, that is a Christian country, befriend the Turks, who are Muslims, and fight against the Russians?"

Bell could provide no answer to satisfy him. For this King the situation was an imponderable enigma - even more difficult to accept because the Russian church was Orthodox, as was his own.

Concerning his church, Tewodros hoped to correct what he thought of as its deficiencies and difficulties. Services were conducted in Ge'ez, an ancient language that only the clergy was trained to understand. It held its people in thrall with their ignorance and consequent superstitions. The Abyssinian Church also controlled perhaps a third of the wealth of the country in land and tithes, and had an annoying proclivity for dictating to the government. And Tewodros was having difficulty in persuading even his closest cohorts to follow his example of choosing a marriage conducted by the church.

Dining with Tewodros late one afternoon, Bell was startled by the monarch's sudden statement of a directive. Tewodros had been passing food from his own plate to his friend, the mark of distinct honor, when he paused for a moment and then announced in his most persuasive voice, "I shall see you married at the Church of Iyasus in Debra Tabor. It is not so far from your home, and should be convenient. I shall stand up with you and ask Tewabach to stand with your wife."

Bell felt his stomach contract, and said nothing. He knew he should have prepared for this moment, but with foolish rationalization he had avoided thinking of his own involvement is this controversy. Somehow he had persuaded himself that, as a European, he could stay clear of church issues.

"Yohannes, this is important to me. I must insist."

Slowly, Bell gathered his thoughts. "Sire, I long to help you in all things, but I know my wife's family is opposed. For them it is a matter of loyalty to her father's memory."

"Then you must marry someone else. Usually, when we talk, I seek your advice. This is not one of those consultations. I order you."

For the first time in their relationship Bell felt the King's fiery anger bubble to the surface and knew there was no escape. "I ask leave to speak with Worqenesh," he replied steadily.

"So be it," and the King turned aside.

\* \* \*

"I knew this would be coming, John. You are too close to the King for the luxury of evasion." Worqenesh and John were lying in the dark together with Tewodros's order hanging over their heads. "We really should have talked before you left for Shoa, but I have been mulling over this dilemma for weeks."

Her husband groaned. "I have no solution. Tewodros wants me to find a woman who will agree to a marriage conducted in a church and including the celebration of the Eucharist. As someone who thinks he is advocating monogamy, the King is forcing me into bigamy. It makes no sense."

"But there is a solution," Worqenesh replied. "I would not think to suggest it if the King were not being irrational."

Bell looked at his wife in astonishment. Worqenesh was calm while he was beside himself with anxiety. "What are you suggesting?" he asked.

"Issete."

"Issete?"

"Yes. She and I have talked. I am not sure which of us first thought of it, but Issete is willing to go with you to Debra Tabor and go through this ceremony in the church. She is my sister at heart. She will never consummate the marriage."

"But Worqenesh, this means that she will not be free to marry a man of her own choice."

"You know, John, she has never really wanted to. That is the reason I can suggest this in good conscience. Her loyalty is entirely to me and to the family, and it always has been. I have asked her in times passed if she did not want to marry. Each time she has said no."

John looked at his wife. She never ceased to amaze him with her agile mind and good sense. "I am very grateful. You know how involved with Tewodros my life has become, but it is only you that I love. I never thought to harm us. I have learned to care about your country and what becomes of its people, but it is you that ties me to this place."

In the end the subterfuge was not necessary. King Tewodros had been unable to force his position on marriage on any of his other courtiers. When Bell was next in his company the subject was not brought up, and soon it was an issue of the past that was never mentioned. But John Bell's family did not forget. Each year, toward the end of the rainy season, the King would bring Queen Tewabach and the court to a site at the base of the mountains in Begemder to rest and enjoy the local hot springs. Then John Bell would take his children – Susan, Aligaz and Mary – to visit the royal couple, and Tewodros learned to know the children, and became fond of them. Worqenesh never joined these outings, nor did Issete.

## Chapter 25

"As I see it, he's got at least two major areas of difficulties." John Bell and Fenta Tadese were at Bell's home in Diddim, and Worqenesh was haranguing them both on the challenges of the new reign. "Tewodros must confront the Church and he must reorganize the army."

"John, your wife never minces her words," remarked Fenta, "but we both know that what she says is true. And I would point out a third area for the King to consider. He is trying to supplant the weaknesses of the *Mesafint*, but he is lost in the mire of their administrative structure. He wants to move beyond tribal loyalties to centralizing all loyalty in the monarch, but he is stuck with entrusting responsibility to local remnants of the tribal system. We have not had a powerful king here for almost a century, and Tewodros cannot be everywhere at once."

Bell groaned audibly. "Of course, you are both right. We had no sooner conquered Shoa, leaving it in the hands of the old ruler's brother, than we were faced with a rebellion on our way back through Gojjam. I confess I shuddered at my realization of déjà vu. I have been told that Tedla Gwalu is a member of one of the old local ruling families of Gojjam. We beat his forces roundly, but he disappeared into the mountains just as Birru Goshu used to do. I don't know if the King noticed the parallel, but I was horrified. And when we finally reached Gondar, Ras Wube's two grandsons had just vacated the city. I have a feeling we shall hear the names, Neguse and Tesemma, again."

It was late in June of 1856, the early days of another rainy season, and John Bell was on leave for a few brief weeks. It was a time to embrace his family and gather emotional strength for another year. Walter Plowden had observed the previous month that Tewodros had only to fight one more battle in which he should obliterate Wube's progeny, and order would prevail in the new kingdom. Bell was hopeful, but not convinced.

"Come, let's not be so gloomy." Worqenesh recognized the slump in her husband's shoulders and decided to change the tone of their talk. "Surely the King is aware of the obstacles surrounding him and has plans. He is a man of learning and intelligence. What will he tackle first, John?" and she nodded to her brother Giyorgis, who had just arrived to tutor the children.

"He has already begun to appoint his own governors and judges, and to pay them salaries. He will make them his men rather than advocates of their own inheritance. He has even made himself into a sort of final court of appeals. One of his most attractive traits is his genuine care for the poor and for children. His self-appointment as a judge of last resort means that even before dawn, he is sought by petitioners. He is lucky he doesn't require much sleep!"

"We can hope that this kindness will endear him to the people, but I'm not so sure," observed Worqenesh. "We are a recalcitrant lot."

"What else, John? What about the Church and the army? I know the boys and I must soon be involved." Fenta was earnest in his concern.

"I am not sure about the Church. For now the King has made his peace with Abune Salama and the *Ichege*, and I understand that doctrinal divisions have been mended. What would you say, Giyorgis?"

"You're right. The issue of *Sost Ledet* seems to have vanished, but with the prospect of enormous outlays in salaries to administrators and soldiers, I would be surprised if he didn't begin to covet some of the wealth of the Church."

Worqenesh, John and Fenta all looked at the young priest in astonishment. "For example," he continued, "there are a good fifteen of us at the Church of Iyasus in Debra Tabor – debteras and priests. Two thirds of us are a luxury. And do you realize that the Church controls a good third of the country's taxable land? That means the Church controls the wealth generated by that land, not the King."

Now John looked distinctly uncomfortable. It was true. He had heard Tewodros mention the wealth of the Church, but had paid little attention. It was not something he knew much about. The army was another matter. Here he believed he might be of use to the King. "We must let Giyorgis be our expert on church matters, but as to the army, Tewodros has already begun to effect reforms. As well as trying to convert to a salaried force; he has begun to organize his men into groups of tens, hundreds and thousands, and the soldiers are to be mixed so that men from the same province are separated and regrouped with men of different provinces. Again, their loyalty is to be to their commander and to the King – not to their tribal chief. And the King is trying to make the army leaner; that is, without so many support groups such as cooks and grass cutters, and without camp followers. Part of Tewodros' success has been due to his army's mobility. You cannot move quickly when those who accompany you are twice your number."

"John," interrupted Fenta, "what can I do? Could I be of some help to you? If I return to fighting, I should want to serve with you, and not be sent off with folks in other provinces."

Bell's eyes twinkled. "I think I can fix that." Then turning serious again he continued. "I have promised the King that I will help him with training the troops in some European methods. I would welcome your help. In a few weeks I am going over to an area on the Zege peninsula at Lake Tsana that Tewodros has set aside for this purpose. We'll go together."

At this point Issete appeared ushering the children across the compound. Susan was eleven now and Aligaz eight, and both were apt pupils of their Uncle Giyorgis. Mary, at three, did not like to lose sight of her older sister, and would sit quietly through Susan's lessons to avoid being separated from her. Fortunately, Susan was as patient as Mary persistent. Mary was the most striking of the three to look at with her pale, blue eyes and dark, curling hair; and while she was as inquisitive as her siblings, she exuded an aura of calm and contentment.

Bell looked at Worqenesh and smiled. He had great hopes for his children in this land he expected to be wrapped in peace and progress.

Worqenesh returned his glance. "Off you go then, you three."

And her eyes followed the children with her brother, walking across the village pathway to a grove of mountain firs. While she did not fully trust the new King, her mother's Uncle, she too felt confident.

* * *

By mid July, John Bell and Fenta Tadese were sitting in a hall in Gondar where Tewodros had called together a convocation of the country's clergymen to present to them his need for greater income, and his expectation of their understanding and full support. Fenta had come with Bell because afterwards, they would continue on to the Zege peninsula to conduct the promised training exercises for the army. Together, they sat in bemused attendance as Tewodros presented his case to the Church.

"I am determined to modernize our armed forces," he began, "so that they no longer support themselves by stealing from our farmers and pillaging the land. To do this, I will need your help."

Fenta had cast his eyes on the face of the *Ichege*, and saw the man's pleasant smile fade into stern attention.

The King continued. "Our fellow Christians in foreign lands pay their standing forces so that the fields do not suffer and the poor are free from fear."

The *Ichege* glanced at the Abun. The direction of the King's words assured him that he and the Bishop would be in accord.

While Fenta watched the clergy, Bell kept his face turned toward the King's, and his eyes held the monarch's with confidence. Tewodros was articulate and succinct. He was sure of his position. "In the days of King David of Israel, the House of Levi produced priests and the House of Judah, kings. Levi claimed a tenth of the taxes, and no more. Here you hold a third of the land and pay no taxes. I ask for what is right and needful to feed the army that protects you."

The Abun remained silent, but the *Ichege* had the audacity to suggest that the King might reduce the size of the army.

"The army protects the people," roared the Lion of Judah.

"Then it should live off the people's land," replied the *Ichege*.

The King sighed, and tried a new tact. There were far too many clergymen, who lived well and produced nothing. No local church needed more than two priests and three *debteras*. The excess should be turned out to work the land, earn their own livelihood and pay taxes.

The bickering continued for hours. In the end, there was a sort of draw. The King would not reduce the size of his army. The Church insisted that what had become its property could not be taken away. It acknowledged the King's right to tax, but the two sides agreed that, for the moment, nothing would change. The non-solution held for about four years. Bell remembered his brother-in-law's acknowledgment of the vastly corpulent religious institution of his country, and now recognized its equally enormous political clout. Few of Abyssinia's clerical hierarchy shared Giyorgis Yilma's high ideals. Heading for the door, John Bell and Fenta Tadese left the great meeting place and turned their steps to Lake Tsana and the Zege peninsula.

## Chapter 26

"It is based on a simple fact and it is, indeed, irrefutable. There is not a horse in this world that will charge a solid wall." John Bell and Fenta Tadese had arrived in Korata on the eastern shore of Lake Tsana where Haylu had arranged to meet them. They were staying with Bell's old friend, Ayto Cassai, and would cross the Lake as soon as Haylu appeared.

"As long as you are not trying to fight in the mountains, a cavalry force can prevail anywhere in this country because they can simply run down and hack men on foot to pieces. The foot soldiers have no defense. But if these same men were armed with guns and presented themselves as a solid wall, a cavalry could do nothing against them."

"But, Yohannes," his old merchant friend interrupted, "if the infantry tried to appear as a wall, it would be stuck standing in one place."

"No, no – there are maneuvers. What I call a square can move, but it must do so in a disciplined way. My countrymen have used such methods since very early days when Norsemen raided our shores and there were only spears and shields for defense. Now, with guns, it can be even more successful. Many of you have heard of Europe's Napoleonic wars which took place some forty years ago. It was the discipline of Wellington's foot soldiers that stymied Napoleon's cavalry again and again."

"What is your plan then? How will you proceed?" Cassai was full of questions and so interested in Bell's progress in his adopted land. Already, King Tewodros had named his friend a *liqemekwas*, a distinct honor which made Ayto Cassai enormously proud. As such,

Bell was recognized as a high court official, acting as the King's chamberlain; and he was one of only four men in the entire army allowed to dress as the King in battle so as to act as a decoy to protect His Majesty's person. Cassai recalled Bell's early days in the country when they had first met while traveling; and later, when he had taken Bell into his own home to nurse him back to health after the shifta had attacked him. He loved this tall, pale Englishman who was so loyal to all he held dear.

"I intend to work with small groups – perhaps one hundred men or so at a time. It will be a completely new concept for the men, but I hope to demonstrate its merit. It will take rigorous training. Maneuvering a square in battle requires strict obedience and discipline, but such a background is critical to success."

"Yohannes, you will not forget our traditions of reckless courage," Fenta remarked quietly.

"Indeed, my friend, it takes courage to stand still in the face of a cavalry's charge. There is no question of the need for courage."

"I am simply suggesting that ours is a less static and a more precipitate characteristic," murmured his cohort, while Cassai raised his eyebrows and nodded wisely.

Haylu Yilma arrived the following afternoon with the latest news from Diddim and messages from the family. Everyone was well, Aligaz was beginning to ride with Welde and all sent their love.

Early the next morning Ayto Cassai walked the three men down to the Lake's shore where there were a number of *tanquas* pulled up on the sand. The small, canoe-like boats where made of local papyrus reeds lashed together, and were reasonably buoyant until the material became waterlogged. They had plied the waters of Lake Tsana for centuries and were a secure, if sometimes moist, means of transportation. The Lake was as still as glass in the early light. The Zege peninsula was clearly visible looking directly west from Korata, and their paddlers would have them across the waterway in less than an hour. They would alight near the ancient monastery of Azuwa Maryam where there would be mules ready to carry them the short distance to the new army training grounds. The little boats seemed to glide on top of the water in a world that was still gray and dull green until the sun lifted above the mountains to the east. Then, with its light suddenly beaming across the lake, the world turned golden and bright. Bell noticed a large gray hump appear nearby. A hippopotamus was rising to the surface to enjoy the warmth of the morning sun.

* * *

"Left, left, - no stop!" Bell was almost beside himself, and had to remember once again that the brave men of Abyssinia were just that – brave, but untrained.

"Once again, go back to the square." This was the third group to come in for indoctrination, and no more successful than the first and second had been. The new group formed up one more time. Each side of the square contained four lines. In the first two lines men held the butts of their muskets firmly to the ground with the glistening bayoneted ends pointed skyward. To a horse carrying its rider at full tilt, the rows of infantrymen looked like a solid wall of wood and steel. The men seemed to grasp this concept and to understand its benefit. Once the first two lines had fired a volley they would kneel, and the lines behind could then sweep their shot across the field. An approaching horseman would be forced to turn aside, and be fully exposed to this second line of fire. But then to shift the position of the square without opening it up to attack seemed impossible. The concept of swinging out the sides to march and then swing them back to reform on command was something Bell was unable to convey. It was not just the men who had to respond - it was their company leaders who needed to understand how to direct them. Bell drew elaborate pictures in the lose soil, Fenta shouted orders and Haylu physically intervened to grasp individuals and move them; but it was as Ayto Cassai had foreseen. Once the square was formed, with reasonable facility, it would freeze. The soldiers had no background of complex orders or drill. Men who could race up the side of a steep mountain without panting, mount a horse in motion or slide down a gully leaning backwards over their animal's haunches; were having difficulty discerning their right hand from their left.

"Let's try again," called Bell, and the latest group of fighters reordered themselves into yet another square.

The King was due to visit in a few days. John Bell had hoped to present him with a busy and well-ordered camp, leaders shouting out orders and men wheeling and marching as if governed by an omniscient magnet. He had thought to deliver so much, and was loathe to present his royal friend with failure.

The next evening, after yet another day of frustration and disappointment, he sat down with Fenta and Haylu to discuss his options. Was there another way to explain the European methodology to the army? Was there any other way to appeal to the men to exercise a stern self-discipline? Fenta, who was having almost as much difficulty watching Bell's chagrin as Bell was having admitting his ineffectiveness, tried to reassure his friend.

"As Heaven is my witness, you have tried. It is simply counter to our culture. When a people have behaved in certain ways for a thousand years, you cannot retrain them in a few weeks. The King is your friend. I think he will understand."

Haylu spoke up next. "You will not want King Tewodros to arrive here with high expectations only to witness the impossibility of our task. Why don't you go to him? He is probably still in Gondar. Fenta and I will continue the work here until you return."

And so, with the faithful Gabriote by his side and ordering a few of the militia to accompany them, Bell marched off the following morning. A small flotilla of *tanquas* carried them first to an overnight stop on the eastern shore of the Lake where the Rib River flowed into Tsana, and then on to the northern shore. From there they were able to secure mules to carry them up the incline of the land to Gondar.

In later years Bell was able to smile at his embarrassment. The King scarcely seemed to notice his negative report, but was much more interested in the advent of an unexpected visit from the Coptic Patriarch of Egypt, Cyril IV. The news of his approach had put the royal household in a flurry of activity, and Tewodros had simply waved John Bell aside and told him not to worry. It was no doubt a mistake to try to impose British methods on Abyssinian soldiers. He much more needed Bell's thoughts as to why Bishop Cyril was only a few days away. The King decided to receive the high ranking dignitary in his quasi capital, Debra Tabor. John Bell sent a message back to the Zege peninsula to disband the training effort and break up camp. He would meet Fenta and Haylu back in Diddim for Christmas after the Patriarch's arrival.

Tewodros fretted as to the purpose of Cyril's visit, but his greeting was cordial, if not deferential. This was the highest ranking foreign dignitary yet to visit his government, but as the days passed the King began to sense a critical tone in the Patriarch's conversation. There were an inordinate number of days of fasting in the Abyssinian church calendar. It seemed that the saints and the cross were worshipped more ardently than the Savior. Superstition exceeded biblical understanding. At length the King heard the rumor of an Egyptian cavalry brigade of camels on his western border and was convinced that the Patriarch connived to assist in his overthrow. He placed the Patriarch under house arrest along with Abune Salama, and ordered a high hedge of thorns to be placed around the building.

Both John Bell and Walter Plowden, who had been in Debra Tabor, had suggested to King Tewodros he might appeal to the English Queen to act as a balance to Egyptian aggression. The King had rather stubbornly refused, citing distrust of any foreign power. Did his English friends think he was afraid? Did they think he could not protect his own country? Bell had subsequently asked for leave and invited Plowden to join him in Diddim for the family's celebration of *Ganna* early in January.

*\*\*\**

"What can he have been thinking of? The King cannot imprison the Patriarch! Has he no respect for God's church," protested Worqenesh.

"I believe he truly thinks he is above the hierarchy of the Church. He sees himself as God's elect, and will broach no conspiracy, no matter what the source." Walter Plowden was walking to the village church with Worqenesh, John and their young family. "I do fear, John, that he has not thought out the consequences of this action. He will regret what he has done, and undoubtedly apologize when he comes to his senses. I wish he would not act so hastily."

Bell nodded in agreement. He was thinking of earlier starlit Christmas eves, but tonight was dull and overcast. He was grateful to be home and away from the intrigues of the court. It would be good to be in the little church at Diddim. Abba Barhe would celebrate the

Mass in the ancient language of Ge'ez, but he would also have a few words to say in the people's language of Amharic. The atmosphere would be one of comfort and confidence. He glanced at Worqenesh who was walking on ahead with Susan by one side and holding Mary's hand along with Issete. Aligaz had drifted back to walk with his father and Plowden and to listen to their talk. A sleepy bird called in the woods, and Bell remembered Shakespeare's Horatio describing the bird of dawning that sings all night at Christmas time, "…so hallow'd and so gracious is the time." As if she felt him letting go of the cares of his life away from home, Worqenesh turned around and smiled.

# Chapter 27

---

"It is just as Walter predicted," Bell remarked to Worqenesh. "The King now regrets his hasty seizure of the Patriarch and confinement of him and the Abun. Tewodros has just called together a large congress of officials, and included a thousand churchmen, to apologize for his action against Cyril and Salama."

"It all makes him look foolish and, indeed, it was foolish, John. The church in Abyssinia is the greatest force we have for unity. Now he has offended her highest officials. In doing so he turns the people against him and he has made an enemy of the institution that could do him the most good. Do you understand, John? You must try to curb his suspicions and his intensity."

"I do understand. He is losing the good will of the people at large. All he really has left is the army. I have heard that Ras Wube's grandsons are making trouble in Simien again."

"Will the King now march against Neguse and Tesemma in the Simien mountains?"

"Strangely, no. There is also trouble at Meqdela and the area of the Galla peoples. We shall go there next. When you look around, there are small pockets of rebellion breaking out in a number of places. It is strange to think that it is becoming more and more dangerous to travel through the country again. A couple of years ago, just after the coronation, it was fairly safe. Walter Plowden has been ordered by his Foreign Office to go back to his official post at Massawa on the coast, but he is reluctant to do so because of the rebels on the roads. Anyway, what I need to tell you is that when we secure Meqdela, the King is going to bring Tewabach there. I thought you might like to come too – for a while, anyway. What do you think?"

Worqenesh's face seemed to lift with pleasure. "Oh, John, it would be joy. We could have a little more time together. I should like it so much."

"Then Meqdela it is. I shall come back for you myself," and his eyes shone. "I will love having you with me for a change."

\* \* \*

Late in February of 1857, King Tewodros turned his back on the rebels in Simien and Tigre, and marched toward the Galla countries. Off in the distance John Bell could see a huge amba rising out of the plain like a great ship riding the ocean. It was the natural fortress of Meqdela, and it was here that the King had decided to store his treasure, imprison his captives, build a home and even erect a church dedicated to Medhane Alem (Savior of the world). His hand-picked governor of the outpost had chosen to join a group of rebellious Galla chiefs, but on seeing the King approach across the upper reaches of the Bashilo River they all fled without a fight. Tewodros' image of invincibility still held, but he spent a good part of the rest of the year crisscrossing the Galla countries putting down insurrections. Probably the King's only political success of the year was that his appointed governor in Shoa remained loyal, collected taxes and sent the revenue to Tewodros at Meqdela.

In the meantime, a few weeks after Easter, but before the rains; John Bell found time to return to Diddim, as promised, to escort Worqenesh to Meqdela. They decided to take Susan with them. It was past time for her to see something of her country other than their small mountain village and the town of Debra Tabor. Aligaz and Mary would stay with their grandmother, and Issete would travel as companion to Worqenesh and Susan.

Mounting their mules and horses, and escorted by Bell's militia, the family party started off amid voices calling family farewells, animals snorting and neighing, and the clash of spears and lances. The people of the village lined their path out of deep respect for their much loved *liqemekwas* and his noble wife, and called out their greetings. Susan rode off at Issete's side with her head held high waving to Mary, who buried her head in her great grandmother, Ribca's knees.

They rode down the side of their mountain and then turned east, and somewhat south. Their way gradually climbed past well-cultivated fields interspersed with trim little villages. In a day or so, the country turned wild and the scenery grand. The firs and cedars thinned out, and Bell pointed out white patches of sleet on the shaded sides of the hills bordering their path. Worqenesh's face reflected her delight in the beauty of the country around her, and Susan could barely contain her excitement. Her village home was lovely, but this land was majestic. There were thousand foot precipices to carefully creep down and then clamber up the opposite side to gain the next plateau. Before she knew it, they had left Begemder on its eastern border and, climbing yet higher, gained the plains of Delanta. When Bell would turn in his saddle to monitor his daughter's progress, he would recognize his own delight in her face and nod in happiness to Worqenesh. What an inheritance for their child! What an extraordinary land to grow up in!

Each night they pitched tents to protect themselves from the cold of the heights, and slept under layers of clothing and animal skins. It was on the tenth day that they traversed the plateau of Delanta covered with its golden fields of grain and green meadows where herds of cattle and horses grazed and myriad sheep nibbled down the grasses. Scattered about were picturesque villages with their tidy, circular huts. At length they came to the edge of the plateau where yet another chasm greeted them. Off in the distance the travelers could see the silver line of the Bashilo River skirting the base of Meqdela. It would take at least another day to attain the banks of the river, find a suitable location to ford it and begin the ascent of the giant amba.

Approached from the west, Meqdela resembled a vast crescent with flattened peaks on either horn. Bell pointed out the features to Worqenesh and Susan as they prepared to ford the Bashilo. "See, to the left is a small, raised plateau that is called Fahla; and it is connected to yet a higher peak called Salassie (Trinity). Then let your eyes move to the right across the lower plain known as Islamgee. The Meqdela plateau is all the way to the right."

"How isolated and remote it all seems," observed Worqenesh, "and just look at the gigantic masses of rock all about."

"Papa, where are we going," asked Susan. "How shall we climb up the side of this great rock?"

"There is a narrow track up to the Islamgee plain, and then there is a better path up to Meqdela itself. In all, it is about nine thousand feet above sea level. That is where the King has built his house and where a whole community has been constructed. The country surrounding the amba is barren and bleak, but you will be able to look out across into the distance to see mountain peaks in Galla covered with frozen hail and snow. Let's cross the river and then camp for the night. We shall want a fresh start for our climb in the morning."

The early daylight was dim at their camp in the shadow of the amba, but Worqenesh could see light striking the mountains to the west that they had just crossed.

She rose to organize a substantial breakfast to lend strength to their ascent. Examining the sheer granite slabs in front of them she was hesitant, and wondered if they would have to scramble up on their hands and feet for part of the way.

\* \* \*

Looking out across the mountains after their trek up the side of the rock, Worqenesh caught her breath in wonder. It was late in the afternoon, they were standing on the very edge of Meqdela and she was exhausted; but out under a sky of intense blue spread a land that was rugged and wild with mountain tops tinged with the brightest colors. Her mind went back to her childhood when she had traveled to Gondar with her father. It had been lovely to see hippos frolicking in Lake Tsana and the royal buildings of kings, but the splendor now laid out in front of her was spectacular. Glancing at her husband she mouthed a thank you, and then smiled across at Susan. There were no words to describe what she felt.

The three weary climbers turned back toward the amba's village as the sunlight began to fade. Issete had already begun to cook their evening meal and Bell needed to go and settle his militia. Worqenesh hurried to help Issete and Susan followed. They had been assigned to two newly built huts away from the center of the village, and Issete had already organized a cooking area and lighted a fire. Bell rejoined them and, after a hasty meal, all four succumbed to their physical weariness and slept.

Tewodros was expected any day. His campfires could be seen to the south and Bell knew that as the *Itege* was on the amba and not campaigning with her husband, Tewodros would not be absent for very long. In the meanwhile, he would present his wife and daughter to Tewabach.

"Should we not wait until the King returns," demurred Worqenesh.

"The queen noticed our arrival last night, and has sent word that you must come. You will like Tewabach. She is nothing like her grandmother, Menen; but is a kindly, quiet person."

Bell led Worqenesh and Susan through the village to a hut built of branches and twigs like all the others, only a little larger. Their approach was announced and Worqenesh stooped under the door lintel to bow to a delicately built woman of about her own age with a dark complexion and sparkling eyes. For a moment it was as if Issete had suddenly attained royalty and was reclining on an *alga*. Then Tewabach smiled, and all the quiet warmth of her person flooded the room. "I am so happy to see you at last," she said. "We must be good friends, like our husbands," and she held out her arms to embrace Worqenesh. Then Susan came forward and was greeted in turn.

"You are like your mother, but not so tall – and you are nearly grown. How old are you, child?"

Susan confessed her twelve years and was waved to sit on a pile of skins nearby.

"I have no children, but God will provide in his own time," and the queen drew Worqenesh down to sit beside her. "I remember your other two children from our visits in Begemder," she continued. "I understand your reluctance to visit our household because of the King's position on marriage, but between ourselves there must be no barriers. I need a friend and would value your company."

In the weeks to come Worqenesh spent many happy hours with Tewabach. The two noble women would sit together and talk about the country that they both understood and loved, and about their families. They learned of each others losses, and their newly found affection comforted each of them. Tewabach spoke of her father, Ras Ali, isolated now in poverty in Yejju not far away. She acknowledged that she sometimes smuggled food and money to him, and that her husband looked the other way and never interfered. Worqenesh told the queen about her beloved father, Asfaw Yilma, who had lost his inheritance at the battle of Chenti Ber and seemed to slowly die of a broken heart; and she described her home in the little mountain village of Diddim to which, she declared, she would always return.

One day Worqenesh and Issete were strolling with Susan toward the Church of Medhane Alem when they suddenly came upon the Queen accompanied by an attendant. Tewabach stared at Issete and then burst into laughter. "Oh, my dear, forgive me. Seeing you is like looking into one of those European glasses. I thought I saw myself." After that she would always ask about Issete and sometimes, if she was not feeling quite well, she would beg Worqenesh to let Issete sit with her. Then Tewabach would reminisce, and tell Issete about her childhood in the Yejju country of Galla, and Issete would dredge her mind to recall a few stark images of her own early years somewhere in the Galla country – she thought perhaps in the central country of Were Himano - before she had been captured and carried to Begemder as a slave. "But I have always been grateful to be a part of Asfaw Yilma's family. Worqenesh is dearer than a sister to me. Where else could I ever have learned to read and write? Where else could I have grown up feeling safe every night?"

So the days at Meqdela passed happily for Worqenesh and those around her. Messages passed regularly back and forth to Diddim to assure her that all was well, and it was a delight for her to spend more time than usual with her husband and to share his world.

The King spent the remainder of 1857 quelling eruptions of discord in the Galla countries. Bell was at his side as he moved in first one direction and then another, defeating armies but seldom capturing their leaders. Early in November Tewodros suddenly left Yejju, Were Himano and Wello, marching rapidly to the west to fight in Gojjam. Again, he decisively defeated the malcontents, and even seized some of their leaders, but the elusive Tedla Gwalu slipped through his hands. This time, instead of generously pardoning the captured leaders, he executed them. They had already been pardoned once.

# Chapter 28

---

When the King, campaigning in Wello, suddenly turned west to Gojjam, John Bell sent Gabriote back to Meqdela to escort Worqenesh and Susan to Diddim. Tewabach had already joined Tewodros' retinue, and Worqenesh was ready to return home. There she was greeted with joy and, in turn, welcomed her husband home for *Ganna*.

But it seemed that King Tewodros was never free to settle in any one place for very long. The Gojjam campaign was barely over before he was forced to move to the east again. This time the area in revolt was in the province of Lasta, just north of Meqdela, so he moved his headquarters back to the huge amba. As usual, John Bell was by his side and the *Itege* never far away.

This year, seeing her mother in the midst of packing for a second trip, little Mary was distraught. "Please, Mama," she begged, "do not take Susan away from me again." And so it was decided that Mary, who was now almost five, would join the women and go to Meqdela; and that Aligaz would remain with his grandmother and continue his reading with Giyorgis and his tutelage in the martial arts with his other uncles.

Bell's family arrived at Meqdela shortly before Easter while he and the King were still campaigning in Lasta. Worqenesh went immediately to embrace the *Itege*, and was surprised to find her friend lying on her *alga* in some distress.

"Oh, what delight to see you. Do not take me seriously," said Tewabach. "Come and help me up, and we will walk a little together."

The sun was low in a cloudless sky, backlighting the mountains to the west. "It is a beautiful land," sighed Worqenesh; and the queen, holding her arm for support, smiled in agreement.

"I do not want to leave it yet, but I must accept God's will for me," she breathed.

Worqenesh started, and then held her close. "Issete is here with me. She and I will nurse you back to good health. Do not lose hope so quickly. We shall do everything for you – you will see."

\* \* \*

With their mother and Issete spending hours of each day caring for the *Itege*, Susan and Mary were left to explore the flat surface of Meqdela which dominated the other sectors of the mountain. As the daughters of the King's beloved chamberlain, their safety was assured and they were free to wander as long as they remained on the amba itself. There were children to engage their attention and families to visit, but they soon gravitated to a small group of European missionaries who were skilled craftsmen and teaching their artistry to a cluster of young people. In turn, they were struggling to master the complexities of the country's language.

Susan and Mary presented themselves to the woman of the group, a Mrs. Rosenthal, although their communication was with signs and smiles rather than words. Both girls knew a few words of English because of their father, but Hilde Rosenthal and her husband were German, as was their companion, John Brandeis. They had been sent to Abyssinia as lay missionaries by the Anglican Bishop of Jerusalem, Samuel Gobat, at the King's request. Susan understood that their work had to do with Tewodros' dream of modernizing the country and had heard of the little group from her father. She also remembered having heard the name, Samuel Gobat; an Englishman who her Uncle Giyorgis sometimes mentioned and Father Barhe had praised.

In the days that followed she took delight in helping Hilde Rosenthal through the complexities of Amharic and enjoyed listening to the young woman read portions of scripture translated into her native tongue. Little Mary would sit at their feet, entranced by Mrs. Rosenthal's voice and the quiet beauty of the words. Raised in Abyssinia, neither of the girls was familiar with any of the biblical text other than the Book of Psalms and Luke's gospel.

As Easter approached they all rejoiced at the *Itege's* seeming recovery. Between them, and through their love and skill, Worqenesh and Issete had worked a sort of magic. The King could barely contain his joy as he walked beside a smiling Tewabach and they all followed the priests in procession to the Church of the Medhane Alem to celebrate the holy day. In the afternoon there was a great feast on the amba and all relished the plenty spread out before them and the warmth of the April sun. Susan noted that the Europeans had celebrated Easter the previous Sunday. Hilde Rosenthal had explained the difference in their church calendars.

Almost immediately after Easter the men were back in the field; this time chasing Agew Tesemma, who had left the safety of the Simien Mountains to campaign near Gondar. Tewodros forced him back through the mountains to his home turf in Tigre, but it was finally apparent to the King that his strategies were not working. He would have to leave larger contingents of soldiers in place after quelling a revolt so that its instigators could not infiltrate back to repeat their rebellion. To do this he would be forced to revert to the old Abyssinian custom of allowing soldiers to live off the land. His people were blind to his vision of change. How ironic that because they were so accustomed to fighting, the peasants would again suffer the ravages of a fighting army rather than enjoy payment for their produce. The system was put into place in the provinces west, north and east of Lake Tsana and the King rushed back to Meqdela to face a large cavalry force in Wello. He no longer disciplined his soldiers to protect the local population, but allowed the men to pillage wherever he suspected disloyalty.

To add to his concerns, his beloved Tewabach, whose health had seemed to have been restored, was ill again. This time Worqenesh and Issete could do little to alleviate her pain and distress. The King appealed to the European missionaries for any help they might supply, and left her side only when urgently called to battle. When he had to be away, Issete kept a twenty-four hour watch. She alone seemed able to ease and comfort the *Itege*. In the middle of August Issete and Worqenesh sent an urgent message to the King fighting in the Galla countries to hurry back to Meqdela, but he arrived too late. Tewabach had died. The King's grief was palpable. For hours he sat by the *Itege's* bedside. Then, when her body was embalmed, he placed it in a coffin and had it carried on a stretcher wherever he fought. Through the nights he would sit by the coffin until at last the *Itege* was buried at Amba Gishen, whose flat topped surface resembled a cross. Far off, in the Yejju country of Galla, a grieving Ras Ali mourned in hiding.

\* \* \*

Worqenesh stayed on at Meqdela until well after Meskel. For the last two or three years, most of the King's battles had centered around the Galla countries, although there were certainly occasional sorties in the direction of Gojjam or Tigre, and Tewodros had only just returned from a quick trip to Gondar to oust a rebel from that ancient capital. Now he was back. Meqdela was roughly located between Yejju and Were Himano, so that when there were pauses in the fighting, her husband could quickly join her for a few days, or even weeks. Their two huts on the amba had multiplied to become a comfortable compound, and it delighted both John and Worqenesh to share each other's company whenever there was a respite in the ongoing rebellions. As always, she was his chief advisor about her country and its people, and he trusted her unerring understanding.

"What about the missionaries," he asked one day. "Are they useful, or simply busybodies?"

"Oh, John, I think they are fine. Unlike earlier groups who have sought to influence governance and policy, these are simple folk genuinely concerned for the people. Indeed, I am sure that they would delight in conversions, but their emphasis is on helpfulness. They are generous in teaching their practical skills, and do nothing that would cause harm."

"The King seems to trust them, so you feel that his trust is not misplaced. They were certainly kind to Tewabach during her illness."

"Yes, John, and they seem to like the King. The missionaries must know that we are here on Meqdela because the King is in constant warfare with the Galla peoples, but they appear to overlook his aggressive behavior and instead, cultivate his humanity. He needs that."

"I enjoy speaking with them myself. My German is rusty, but I manage well enough; and they are beginning to master Amharic," her husband continued. "Susan and Mary do enjoy Mrs. Rosenthal. She has told them that a few more of their colleagues from their school in Switzerland are on their way to join them. By-the-way, do you want to stay on at Meqdela, or would you like to go back to Diddim for a while? I think the King will be busy here in Galla for a long time to come."

"John, I think I would like to go home for *Ganna*. It is so long since I have seen the family, and Aligaz will be growing up without me. Send me back to Diddim for two or three months, and then the girls and I will return to Meqdela."

Bell remained with the King as he continued his campaign in the Galla countries. The monarch had lost his wife – his dear and trusted companion. He could not bring himself to part with the one other person in whom he relied implicitly. Bell ordered Gabriote to escort Worqenesh, Susan, Mary and Issete back home. Worqenesh grieved to leave John behind, but as their small party approached the familiar chain of mountains to the south of Debra Tabor her heart lifted, and a smile of delight danced across her lips. As always, it was joy to come home.

# Chapter 29

"Worqenesh, it just appears as desperation to me now. What began four years ago as a reign full of promise, now looks hopeless."

"Oh, do not say so, Mother," pleaded Worqenesh. "John has worked so hard to serve the King and this country. We both wanted to believe that Abyssinia could enter a new age and join the countries that are striving in what John calls 'an industrial revolution.' It is dreadful to think our dream will evaporate into a miasma of rebellion."

Worqenesh and Wishan were in the courtyard of Asfaw Yilma's old compound. It was still the central place for family gatherings – a place to exchange thoughts and hatch new points of view. Fenta Tadesse was sitting with them, faithful to his old friend's memory; and Abba Giyorgis had come up from Debra Tabor with him to spend a little time with his sister.

"Do you think the King's mind is stable," asked Fenta. "We begin to hear rumors of harsh reprisals and cruel executions."

"I do think he is driven almost mad with frustration," answered Worqenesh. "He seems not able to share his vision of unity and modernization with his people. He has lost his beloved queen who was always a calming influence. You would wonder at how they used to sit together for hours just talking and sharing their thoughts. Now there is only John to ease his moods and keep him focused."

"The church used to be a force for unity," observed her brother, "as was the old Solomonic dynasty; but King Tewodros has quarreled with the church over both dogma and property, and now threatens the Abun himself."

Aligaz had come to sit by his mother, and she reached out to clasp his hand. "John still hopes," she said. "He says that within the core of Tewodros there is still the young Kassa Haylu, the man of the people who reaches out to the poor and dispossessed. Underneath all of the stress is a man who never gives himself airs and who lives simply in spite of his position, and I do think that the King still believes in his ultimate success. The girls and I are going back to Meqdela in a few days. They enjoy the company of the European missionaries who have established a station there, and I long to be with my husband," and she drew her young son into a warm embrace – torn by her affection for the different members of her splintered family.

\* \* \*

Theophilus Wladmeier was sitting on the edge of the precipice when he first saw them. A tall young man with reddish gold hair and just the beginnings of a beard, he had arrived at Meqdela very early in this new year of 1859, full of pluck and enthusiasm. The journey had been appalling. He and his newly met friend, Karl Saalmuller, had been joined by four other lay missionaries sent out by Samuel Gobat. The six of them had taken the train from Alexandria to Cairo, and then hired a boat to carry them against the current up the Nile River. It was slow going when the wind slackened so they had opted to save the miles of a great curve in the river by crossing the Nubian Desert by camel. Barely surviving the awful heat, they had regained the Nile and sailed on to Khartoum. By the time they had traversed Sudan and reached the deadly heat of Matemma, all five men of the party were dangerously ill. Miraculously, Pauline Flad did not suffer from the fever contracted by the others. Somehow she managed to nurse her husband, along with Karl and Theo, back to health. The two others died. As the four survivors slowly climbed the foothills of western Abyssinia, they were amazed to see clear streams and wild roses, and to feel the clean, bracing air. The land was enchanting. They were referred to John Bell, who introduced them to the King and sent them to join their brethren at Meqdela.

He had heard that Bell's family was expected back at the lofty amba any day. Looking down he saw a small, armed militia struggling up the steep ascent. In their midst were three, well-dressed women and a little girl, reaching for anything to grasp and pull on and laughing at their awkwardness. As they drew closer he saw that one of the women was quite young.

"Don't just gape," she called out. "Pull me up!"

Waldmeier slid down a little way and grasped Susan Bell's hand.

"I'm Susan," the young lady beamed up at him. "Who are you?"

"Theo," he grinned back, pulling her up and over the last step. "Here, let me help the others."

Mary came next, followed by Issete and then Worqenesh. By the time they were all up and over the edge of the amba and standing on level ground, Waldmeier was laughing uproariously with them. "What an armful I have just caught! This has been a good day's fishing."

Then Worqenesh saw her husband hurrying toward them across the open field, and ran to throw herself into his embrace. "It has been too long, too long," she murmured as he crushed her to his chest.

"Is it always so exciting when you people arrive," asked Waldmeier. "And who is this?"

"My sister, Mary, and this is our dear friend, Issete. Really, this is just a few of us. We have left the rest at home in Diddim."

Waldmeier grabbed hold of Susan's arm to help her along, while Issete and Mary hurried to follow. "I have heard of all of you. Issete is the wonderful lady who nursed the Queen last summer," and he looked behind to motion her forward, "and Mary is the one with her father's amazing eyes."

"What about me, then," asked Susan.

"You are Hilde Rosenthal's great friend and instructor. I know of no better recommendation. I only hope that you may help me with my struggles with Amharic as well."

Susan dropped her eyes for a moment, and then looked back up at him. His was an open and intelligent face, exuding kindness and good will. "I shall like that," she answered softly, looking directly at him. "You seem already to have made a good beginning."

Late that night, holding each other close, Worqenesh and John caught up with their news. "It is not a good campaign this year," Bell confessed. "We are locked in a continuing struggle with the Wello

Gallas. The King no longer tries to protect the local people, but lets his soldiers steal their cattle and trample their grain. There will soon be famine. He cannot understand this continuous rebellion. Now there are mutilations of captives. In the past the King repeatedly forgave rebels: he does so no more. There is not much I can do to stay his hand. I do what I can."

Worqenesh shuddered at his recital of violence. "Now I only pray for your safety, John. I do not know what to pray for my country."

"I have not yet given up hope, because the King has not," replied her husband." He clings to his visions, while calling his people donkeys. If only there was a little more loyalty among the tribal chiefs."

"The new missionaries make a good impression. What does the King think of them?"

"He likes them. They are agreeable and hard working. He is particularly delighted with young Waldmeier and Saalmuller who have begun a class in mechanics and who have pleased Tewodros no end by repairing some of the army's damaged muskets. The King enjoys Waldmeier's company."

"I think Susan does too," whispered his wife.

\* \* \*

The fighting in Wello continued and Bell was most often away from Meqdela, campaigning with the King. The people on the amba heard reports of atrocities and of dreadful mutilations, including the cutting off of both hands of hundreds of rebels. In May the King's trusted governor of Amba Meqdela, who had served since the early days of his reign, deserted. The rains came, but the fighting scarcely abated. Only late July and early August saw a brief easing of the conflict.

For Worqenesh, the days without her husband were long and difficult. She was acutely aware of the ferocity of the battles and the duplicity, now, of some of the King's men; and she constantly feared for Bell's safety. Both she and Issete missed their friend, the *Itege*, and were grateful for each other's company. They sometimes visited the two women at the mission station, but it was Susan and Mary who were most drawn to the company of the Europeans. The girls were happy to share their language skills with the gentle foreigners; and Susan's mirth and energy were always welcome, as was the quiet presence of her exquisite little sister.

When he was not mending muskets or teaching mechanics to a group of young men chosen by the King, Waldmeier gravitated more and more to the sprightly company of Susan Bell. She spent happy hours with him, detailing the thirty-three letters of the Amharic alphabet and the six vowels which, when joined with these letters gave each a variant form. In addition, there were diphthongs, each with changes when taking up with vowels. There were two dots between words and four dots at the end of a sentence. The language was complex, and there were delightful opportunities for close study and merry laughter at awkward mistakes. Mary was usually in attendance and Theo's friend, Karl, frequently joined in the fun. Susan learned that while Karl was German, as were most of the others at the mission station, Theo was Swiss. He had been raised by a harshly strict grandmother and had run away from home to eventually become a student at the St. Chrischona College at Bale. It was there that he had one day heard Bishop Gobat speak, and had determined to come to Abyssinia.

Theo had been delighted with the country to which he felt called. The people were cheerful and intelligent, and after the rains the whole land burst forth as a lovely garden. And he was impressed with the country's leader. Where was there another such powerful monarch who lived almost austerely and who often called upon his Creator, trusting in His help. In turn, the King admired the young man's practical skills. This was not a self aggrandizing theologian, but a person who tried to help. Tewodros hoped that Theo and his friend would remain in Abyssinia and contribute to its industrial development. The best way to assure their continuing residence was to marry them off to Abyssinians.

And so slowly, with the King's encouragement and her father's consent, Theo began to court Susan. It was no surprise to anyone that the two were married in December of that same year. King Tewodros insisted upon organizing the festive occasion. After all, Susan Bell was a relative - if somewhat distant - and the daughter of his greatest friend. He gave Waldmeier a beautiful saddle ornamented with gold, and contributed eighty oxen and five hundred sheep to the wedding feast in which the entire amba participated and which lasted for a week.

Worqenesh had quietly agreed to the union for her own reasons. "John, Theo will give her a means of escape from this disintegrating land. I like the young man. He is a good person – intelligent and kind. He is also a European, and not as integrated into this land as you are. One day he will leave."

John Bell looked at his wife in complete surprise. "And you are glad of that?"

"Yes," she said. "I believe I am."

# Chapter 30

Almost immediately after the wedding in early December, the King decided to confront the rebels, Niguse and Tesemma, in Tigre. Tewodros had long been aware of Wube's grandsons dominating conditions in the northern province, but now he had learned of a French delegation that had been sent there in response to an appeal by Niguse to Napoleon III for recognition and aid. The group of French Catholic missionaries that Tewodros had expelled from the country at the urging of Abune Salama had lingered on the border and encouraged the rebels in their disaffection.

"What a difference there is between Waldmeier and those meddling Catholics," the King exploded to Bell. "Young Theo strives to save souls; the Catholic clergy posture for power."

Bell nodded in agreement. Indeed, the French delegation was in Tigre to see how they could help Niguse and Tesemma wrest power from the King. It was, as always, politics and the jostling for position.

So, in January, the royal army raced north to Tigre. If there was one thing that the King could still do extraordinarily well, it was to move his forces at amazing speed. Niguse's army was no match for the onslaught, and many of his chiefs deserted at the sudden reality of Tewodros' army. Niguse escaped with his brother across the receding Mereb River.

\* \* \*

Tewodros had just returned to his capital at Debra Tabor and was sitting with the well trusted Ras Ingida waiting for Bell to join them to discuss strategy, when the Englishman burst in on them. "They have killed him. They have killed Walter Plowden," he cried out.

For once their roles reversed and the King rose to calm his friend. "What has happened, Yohannes? What is this that you say?"

Bell sat down suddenly and put his head in his hands. "Plowden," he said. "You know that he had been ordered to the coast by his superiors, and was under considerable pressure to return to his official base. He was only waiting until he felt it was safe to cross through Tigre. After your defeat of Niguse and Tesemma at Adwa he decided to set out immediately for Massawa. This must have been about two weeks ago. He planned to cross paths with you in Tigre on his way out, so as to make his farewells, and was headed east from Gondar. His small party was attacked as they were crossing the Keha River."

"Who has done this," questioned Tewodros. "Who has killed my friend? Niguse and Tesemma were out of the way."

"Yes, they were not there, but I was told it was one of Niguse's supporters who led the assailants – a man named Gared."

"My nephew," groaned the King. He is a remaining son of Kinfu – probably a half brother to your mother-in-law."

Bell listened in horror. How inevitably they were all intertwined, but always seemingly in disaster. "Walter was hit in the side by a lance, but was not killed instantly. He was carried back to Gondar where he was carefully nursed, but died some days later." And to himself Bell mused at the irony of it all. Walter Plowden had long thought that if King Tewodros would just confront the rebellious Tigrian duo and subdue them, all of Abyssinia would settle down and order could be established at last. Instead, he had been murdered.

*  *  *

While the King remained in Debra Tabor, John Bell was able to spend a few short weeks in Diddim. It seemed to him to be almost a new experience; it was so long since he had been able to relax at home when it was not the rainy season. He and Worqenesh received visitors, attended to village business and had time to spend with Aligaz who was now twelve years old and usually in the company of his younger uncles – Welde and Haile.

"Poor Mary is at loose ends," remarked her father to Worqenesh, "but it is a treat to be here with Aligaz. I don't know when I have felt so comfortable and rested – certainly not for some years now."

"Mary does so miss Susan," observed her mother. "I wish she were a little closer to us myself."

"She will be soon. I meant to tell you," said Bell. "Theo Waldmeier asked me to speak with the King. He feels that a huge amba sitting like a fortress in the middle of active rebels is hardly the best place for a mission station. He wants permission to move the little group to a more rural and peaceful situation. The King has agreed, and the mission will move to Gaffat in June. I think the King is so grateful to our son-in-law for his proficiency in the mechanical arts that there is little he would deny him."

Worqenesh noticed a shadow briefly cross her husband's face and remembered that Gaffat had been Walter Plowden's home just a short while ago. "Oh, John, it will be grand to have Susan close by. I shall be so happy to see her, and Mary will be able to visit. Gaffat is a lovely place, and convenient to Debra Tabor. It's a perfect site for the mission station."

A few days later most of the family was gathered before supper in Wishan's compound. It was a large and boisterous, but cohesive, group; never lacking in either cheerful camaraderie or well buffeted opinions. Wishan's children were all grown now, and all were married, with the exception of Giyorgis. Even Haile who, at nineteen, had seen service with the King's army in the Galla countries and, like his brother-in-law, was home while the King remained in Debra Tabor, had taken a bride. The next generation, which had begun with Susan, was well underway.

"What an impressive group it is, Giyorgis," Bell remarked to the young priest. "Asfaw Yilma would be proud, and so should Wishan be. It is years now since she has been alone, and she has held this group together, educated them and set Yilma's standards for them to strive for."

"My mother has done a remarkable job. We have always understood what she expects of us, but she has also always made clear her love and support."

"And you, Giyorgis, you are not in Debra Tabor so much these days."

"It's true, John. Abba Barhe is feeling the weight of his years, and I really believe that he needs me here more than I am needed in the capital. This is where I can best serve now, and this is where I belong."

"Do you remember," continued Bell, "the early days when Worqenesh and I were first married? I used to ask you to look out for her when I would go off to campaign with Ras Ali."

"I do remember, Yohannes, and I shall always be here for her. You need never ask."

Bell nodded his head in acknowledgment of his enormous debt to this man. "In recent years she has been able to travel with me and it has been a joy for both of us. This year I think that she may decide to remain in Diddim. Susan and her new husband are moving to Gaffat, and I think Worqenesh will want to be near enough to be able to visit."

Dinner was served outside. The now salaried servants, who had once been slaves, brought out piles of *injera* and numerous bowls of spicy *wats* to scoop up with the flat bread. There was both grilled chicken and roasted lamb. The family ate with hearty enjoyment knowing that the fifty-six days of the Abyssinian Lent would begin in less than a week. Then their stews would be made of lentils and family meals would be much less festive. Bell went to sit by his wife's side, knowing his hiatus from the court was bound to be short lived.

After supper Welde pulled out his *bagana* and began to play. At first he chose lively favorites to match the gaiety of the family's mood, but as the sun set and the evening air blew gently through the compound, he changed his pace to softly pluck a haunting melody. The family began to break up and drift away – first one and then two or three. John Bell beckoned Mary and Aligaz to move on ahead of him, and then reached for his wife's hand. Their little family group walked slowly along the path that circled the village that they had followed so often. There was no moon that night, but the sky was alight with a myriad of twinkling stars.

"John," asked Worqenesh in a soft voice so that the children ahead would not listen, "what is next?"

"I am not sure," he replied. "I shall return to be with the King in a couple of weeks. There is still unrest in Wello, and I am not sure what he plans. After Easter, I expect that Susan and Theo will be moving with the mission station. We can look forward to that."

"Yes, it is helpful to have something to anticipate with happiness. There has not been very much recently." Then she visibly shook herself. "Goodness, I seem to be in the doldrums," and she took a deep breath. "I think while you are gone I shall spend a little more time with Mother. I have been away from Diddim so much recently that I have lost touch with the people's needs. I must become more involved again." She squeezed her husband's hand, and he could feel her physically lift her mood and smile in the dark.

# Chapter 30

---

Bell was back at Meqdela with the King in good time to see the mission group off to Gaffat. In spite of it being the beginning of June, with the rains about to begin, Tewodros planned an expedition to Wello. Bell was able to visit Susan and Theo, and to map out a route for their little group to follow. The King sent a guide to lead them and mules to carry both the people and their supplies, and it was with a spirit of expectation and adventure that the Europeans packed their belongings and descended the steep sides of the giant amba.

Within seven days they had crossed the Delanta plateau, climbed the mountains on the eastern side of Begemder and were skirting Debra Tabor to the north. Then their guide led them into the wide, green valley of Gaffat with its open fields and wandering stream; and their mules were trotting toward a few abandoned buildings on a small hill overlooking it all.

The missionaries were ecstatic. "Susan, it is a little Eden," exclaimed Theo. "How kind of the King! What do you suppose the buildings on the hill are? They seem to be empty."

"They must be where my father's friend, Walter Plowden, once lived."

"I should think they could be used for common purposes, and certainly as shelter until we build our own homes. We'd best begin with individual huts, but in time we shall be able to construct a proper, two-story house such as in Switzerland. I can envision a small colony, a school for Abyssinian children and an industrial area powered by the central stream," and his face was glowing in anticipation.

\*\*\*

Those early days at Gaffat were halcyon. The mission group built twelve small huts just above the base of the hill– two for each couple or individual. They were constructed of staves of wood and of straw on the outside, and carefully plastered with mud and ash within. It was the rainy season, but the mornings were clear and calm and the work was not arduous. The missionaries strove together in a pioneer atmosphere to build a community for themselves and a center of education and artisanship for their neighbors, and slowly their neighbors were attracted by their cheerful activity and the fascination of burgeoning mechanical works. Toward the end of the summer there were even the beginnings of a water wheel which would provide power for wood working and for irrigation. King Tewodros, though campaigning in the Galla country, began to send the brightest and the best of his people for instruction, and Theo was most pleased when he was able to begin his mission work by opening a boarding school for poor children in the area. Worqenesh and Mary arrived early in September to visit with Susan and stay through the birth of her first child.

As the rains diminished and the sun began to prevail in its annual pattern, the golden Meskel flowers reappeared, and Worqenesh felt herself refreshed. She had always loved this season of renewal, and now she was on hand to welcome her first grandchild, and expecting her husband's return from Galla as well. Rosa Waldmeier arrived a few days before Meskel; named by her exuberant father for the flowers he remembered so vividly when he first climbed the western mountains from Matemma to attain the highlands of Abyssinia. It was a happy time for them all.

By now the King had returned to Debra Tabor, and John Bell hastened to join his wife and daughters in Gaffat. A new generation had just begun, and the prospects for the future were brightening. Worqenesh was touched by Mary's delight with the new baby, and remembered her own youthful pleasure when she and Issete had been allowed to care for her brother, Welde, in his infancy. Knowing it would be difficult to tear Mary away from Gaffat, she spoke with

Susan.

"Would Mary be a help, or a hindrance to you now? I want you to be quite straightforward about this with me. I will not permit her to stay if she will add to your work."

"Oh, Mother, you know Mary is never work for anyone. Why don't you let her stay until *Ganna*? By that time you will know if you are to travel with Father again, and I think Mary will be a cheerful addition for all of us here. I shall love to have her stay."

And so it was settled. Worqenesh and John Bell would go back to Diddim to have a little bit of time together. She would take Issete with her, knowing that her husband could not be away from the King much longer. Perhaps Susan and Theo could bring Mary back home in time for Christmas.

\* \* \*

Worqenesh and John set out on their mules for Diddim on a glorious morning filled with sunshine. Issete and Gabriote fell in behind them, and the usual militia followed at a respectful distance. Susan, holding tiny Rosa and standing with Mary, watched the procession disappear in the direction of Debra Tabor and thought what a handsome sight the small group made, seeming to radiate calm and assurance. It was a rare phenomenon in these troubled times, but she felt a lift of confidence as she smiled at her young sister and turned back toward her home.

When they had walked their animals through the capital and were headed south toward the mountains, John turned to Worqenesh with a smile. "I have a surprise for you," he began, and waited to see her tawny eyes lift in anticipation. "The King has decided to send a delegation to England, and has asked me to lead it. The idea is that some of his brightest people should be exposed to Europeans ways, and bring what they learn back to Abyssinia. I want you to come with me. After all of these years, you shall meet my family. You will especially love my sister, Susan."

"Oh, John, what joy – but will Tewodros agree that I should go? In theory he doesn't even recognize our marriage."

"In theory, perhaps not; but in reality he remembers your

friendship with Tewabach and your kindness during her illness. He has already agreed to this."

"It's grand! When will it be?"

"After Easter. He is soon going to Tigre to clear up the difficulty with Niguse and Tesemma and I shall, of course, go with him. That should open up the roads. After that he believes the country will begin to settle down and he will be able to concentrate more on governing and less on campaigning. This trip to England fits in with his vision of the future."

Worqenesh and John continued to chat spasmodically, riding along on the rocky pathway; and she gradually became aware of a low, rumbling voice and a gentle response behind her. Gabriote had engaged Issete in conversation, and the two loyal companions were talking together as if old acquaintances. 'But, of course, they are,' thought Worqenesh, and she smiled to herself. She had just not stopped to think about it.

"John, you will be careful these next few weeks," she called out and hurried to catch up with him.

"Do you remember, Worqenesh, what I was reading to you just recently? Let me try to paraphrase:

This thou perceiv'st which makes my love more strong,
To love that well which I must leave ere long.

We have a few days now. Then, I must leave for a little while. But when the King and I have mopped up in Tigre, you and I can begin to pack for England."

\* \* \*

King Tewodros, who had just arrived in Debra Tabor from the Galla country, remained for barely another week and then set off for Wagera where it was rumored that Tesemma and Gared were collecting forces. Bell, with Gabriote at his side, had summoned his militia and rushed to join him.

There had been the usual noisy departure from Diddim, with the voices of those packing last minute necessities shouting instructions, the neighing of horses, the clash of equipment and the calls of various of the militia. Then, as John Bell embraced Worqenesh and pushed the door of their home aside to stride to his mount, there was a sudden silence as both the villagers and the soldiers bowed deeply to their beloved *Liqemekwas*. Giyorgis came to stand by his sister as Worqenesh waved and the household prostrated itself to the ground. There was a hearty chorus of morning salutations, and the party moved to form a double line on the well worn village path as they rode toward the trail that went down the side of the mountain. They caught up with the King just as he was exiting the capital, and beginning a forced march to the north.

# Chapter 31

It was Gabriote who, a few short weeks later, rode slowly up the mountain path to bring her the news. John Bell was dead. Worqenesh saw Gabriote riding alone, somberly and steadily making his way along the village path to the compound. The villagers had begun to gather quietly on either side of the track as he moved forward, and there was suddenly one single, sharp ululation of grief, and then there was another and then another. She felt as if an enormous abyss had opened under her feet and that she was about to drop for miles. 'I must stay calm,' she thought to herself. 'I must keep my head up.' Issete moved to stand by her side and she saw Giyorgis running toward her from the village church. Gabriote dismounted and knelt at her feet, holding up the well-worn copy of Shakespeare her husband had always carried. There was no need for words. Worqenesh slowly bowed to Gabriote, grasped the book to her chest, leaned against Issete and walked toward the little *gojo*.

In a very few minutes Wishan was by her side holding her hand and speaking softly. In the distance, she began to hear the deep voice of the *kebbero* sounding. The single large drum at the little church had begun its rhythmic pulse. Giyorgis left the *gojo* to go to meet the body that was being carried on a bier toward the church grounds. Aligaz arrived with his uncles, and Welde moved next to Worqenesh to help her to her feet. As in a trance she had grasped his arm and reached for her son's hand. They would walk to join the villagers and follow John's bier to the church.

The slow thrum of the *kebbero* seemed to lend her strength as Welde maneuvered her to the head of the procession and they paced in time to its somber cadence. When she turned to take up her proper place behind her husband's body, Worqenesh saw Susan and Mary with Theo and Karl. They had been told of the sad cortege passing through Debra Tabor, and had ridden to meet the girls' father on his sad journey home. Worqenesh could feel herself, assailed by shock and grief, being wrapped in the strength of her family; and she walked on.

They buried him in the church grounds near Asfaw Yilma. Worqenesh reached out to touch his body as it was lowered into the grave. Then he was gone and she turned away, never making a sound. Wishan came to hold her through the night, and very early the next morning, before it was light, she remembered the poem that he had recited to her when they last rode together to Diddim. "John," she whispered in the dark, "we did love well." And then she wept.

\* \* \*

The details of the tragedy were shared with the family after the funeral. Gabriote sat with Worqenesh's brothers the next day in the family compound. It was a pleasant afternoon in late December, with a piercingly clear, azure sky such as the highlands of Abyssinia can boast at that time of year.

"We had gone through Wagera and passed over the mountains in Simien. I am, of course, only an attendant; but it was evident to me that King Tewodros was determined to avenge the death of the Englishman, Walter Plowden."

Fenta Tadese, who was sitting with the young men, concurred. "He is right. I believe that it hurt the King's pride that the representative of a powerful and friendly, foreign government could have been murdered within his jurisdiction. He has been intent on revenge for months."

Gabriote nodded wisely, and continued. "John Bell's purpose was not the same. He looked on Tesemma, Niguse and their cohort, Gared, as rebels. He was not seeking revenge, but a cessation of the civil unrest that plagues our land."

Abba Giyorgis raised his eyebrows. This man was subtle. How like the egalitarian character of Abyssinians that even a person of humble origins could differentiate between a manic focus on retaliation and the legitimate defense of the state. The young priest looked at Gabriote with new respect, and sensed the depth of the man's long devotion to his brother-in-law.

"We had reached some woodland in the lowlands of Waldibba, just south of the Takeze River. I suppose there were at least a hundred of us in the immediate party, with many more following at a short distance. The King and John Bell, as they so often did, were talking together and had moved a little ahead. I was perhaps twenty feet behind my master when I saw motion in the underbrush. At first I thought there was an animal, but John Bell had already recognized Gared threatening the King, and shot him through the heart. Just as he fired his pistol another figure lept from behind a large tree and cast his lance at the sovereign. My master threw himself at this figure and the lance struck him instead of the King. At the same instant King Tewodros raised his pistol and shot this second man. Then tossing his gun aside he threw himself from his horse onto Bell's body crying out his name. There was nothing to be done. My master had been hit in the middle of the forehead and had died instantly."

Haylu had been listening with close attention to Gabriote's words. "You know, this is a dreadful loss for Worqenesh and for our family, but it may be a tragedy for the country as well. We all know how King Tewodros depended on Tewabach and on Yohannes."

"You are speaking of his mental stability, aren't you" observed Fenta. "With both of his good angels gone we may need to worry. He always leaned toward excitability, even when they were here."

"Indeed, sirs," Gabriote continued. "That very day that John Bell was killed, the King tricked fifteen hundred of the rebels into surrendering, and then murdered them all."

"I heard yesterday," interjected Welde, "from one of the militia, that when Niguse and Tesemma were finally apprehended in Aksum, the King ordered a hand and a foot of each cut off and they were left to die slowly in the middle of the town square, with no one allowed to attend to them. I think you are right, Fenta. The days when our King habitually forgave rebels are gone. You know, I do think he has been sorely pressed, but this cruelty is beyond reason."

Giyorgis cringed to think of such suffering. This regime, which had begun with such promise, was deteriorating into a reign of fear. "Perhaps now that Niguse and Tesemma are gone the country can rest for a while. It does seem that the most insistent rebels have been nullified. Anyway, our responsibility here is to our village, to our family and to Worqenesh. We must do what we can to ease her situation. Certainly, I know that we can keep her safe here in Diddim. Her return to any sort of tranquility is, I know, largely up to her and will take a long time. John Bell is a hard man to lose, and cannot be replaced."

* * *

The forty days prescribed for mourning were difficult. Theo and Karl returned to Gaffat. They had their work to continue and Susan, carrying baby Rosa, went with her husband. Mary remained with her Mother, but there was little she could do for Worqenesh other than simply to be there. Christmas came and went and then Timket, which was almost immediately followed by the fortieth day after John Bell's death. When the *kebbero* sounded to call the village to the anniversary Eucharist, an enormous flood of people moved toward the little church. John Bell had been universally loved and admired, and people came from the village, from the capital at Debra Tabor and from Gaffat; and Ayto Cassai traveled from Korata to honor his well-loved friend. Worqenesh led a great wave of mourners and remembered the day seventeen years earlier when she and her family had observed this ceremony for Asfaw Yilma. It had been on that day that her mother had seen John Bell newly returned from Malta, and had beckoned to him to join their family group. With sudden recognition she saw that her parents' solid union had been a model for her own marriage, and determined to seek direction for the future from Wishan's brave years of solitude. Leading the crowd forward she resolved to make what was for her a living nightmare into something else.

Giyorgis performed the ritual of the sacrament. Only the family's closest friends could squeeze into the little church, but Worqenesh could feel the press of the affectionate crowd outside and was comforted by their loyalty to Bell's memory. Truly, he had become one of them - their fellow countryman.

Following the service she reached for her mother's arm and, with her head held well up, she led the crowd along the village path to the home she had made with John Bell, where a great feast was waiting to thank all who had come. Refusing any more signs of sorrow she asked Welde to play some simple tunes on his *bagana* while she moved to welcome her guests. It was late in the day before she and Issete, along with Haylu's wife, Sossina; could begin to slacken their efforts to wait on people.

As the afternoon sun began to dip behind their mountain's fir trees, Ayto Cassai approached her; bowing low and politely holding his right elbow in his left hand. "I wonder," he began, "would you allow Aligaz to come home with me to Korata? I am not leaving Diddim until tomorrow morning. He could come with me to see where his father and I used to sit and listen to the waves breaking on the shore of Lake Tsana. His father loved the city. Would you permit me to show it to him?"

It was arranged. Gabriote would accompany Aligaz to his godfather's home to visit, and they would return to Diddim before the beginning of *hudaddie*.

The following day it was Susan who came to her, asking if Mary might go back to Gaffat for a while. Worqenesh knew that the child would delight in little Rosa and the happy company of the missionary children. She was nearly eight years old now and growing quickly. Her mother thought of herself at that age, when she had only to reach out her hand to feel Issete's hand in hers. Mary needed young company. She should go. And Worqenesh began to think that in releasing the sorrow of John Bell's memory, perhaps she would have to let her children go as well. She must think about it. It was still too soon to decide about that.

# Chapter 32

As the days went by, Giyorgis' wishful prediction of tranquility in the country seemed to materialize. With the deaths of Niguse and Tesemma, most of the active rebels had been eliminated and an uneasy peace settled over Abyssinia. The next two years or so represented the height of King Tewodros' success in controlling the country, but feelings of disapproval and discontent continued throughout the provinces just beneath the surface. It was during this period that Worqenesh struggled against her loss and to resist its crushing weight.

In Diddim, Aligaz returned with Gabriote from Ayto Cassai's home at the beginning of Lent, as promised, brimming with stories of a lion crossing their pathway, Korata's busy and colorful marketplace and its numerous churches. Ayto Cassai had taken him out on the water of Lake Tsana, each in a *tanqua* maneuvered by two men plying long bamboo rods with which they poled the little reed boats through the shallow water and paddled through the deep. The weather had been fair, but cool; so the hippos usually to be seen along the banks of the Lake were submerged in deeper water for warmth. Worqenesh smiled at her son's delight in his brief trip. She must be sure that he had other opportunities for travel, and remembered that his father's life had been one of exploration and change.

Mary returned home for Easter, and Worqenesh was cheered by her company, but she recognized her youngest daughter's attachment to Susan and to Rosa, and determined to send her back to Gaffat before the rains. It was Theo's friend, Karl Saalmuller, who had brought Mary home, and Worqenesh became aware of the young man's self-appointed guardianship of her daughter and the genuine attachment between the two. Where Theo was jolly and outgoing - a natural leader; Karl was reserved and pragmatic. He was also, Worqenesh realized, noticeably handsome. As he shepherded her daughter along the Diddim pathway toward the compound, the dark-haired girl with pale blue eyes and the tall German were a striking pair.

Worqenesh also wondered about Gabriote. He had joined her husband in Debra Tabor as a very young man during the early days of Bell's travel in Abyssinia, and had remained at his side for the next twenty years. Did he still have family in the capital? Would he want to go back to them? Certainly, he was welcome to remain a part of her household. It did seem that his loyalty had expanded to include the entire family, and she would be glad if he stayed. He seemed content in the hut that her husband had built specifically for him shortly after their wedding, but she wanted him to know that he was free to make his own choice. She must take time to speak with him and, looking up from her seat in the compound where she was embroidering an over shirt for Mary, she let out her breath and looked with pleasure at Gabriote approaching her with Issete by his side.

"Woisero Worqenesh," he smiled, "just think. It has only taken me fifteen years to persuade this woman to be my bride," and the three of them laughed warmly together remembering the history of Issete's long years of refusal.

"Oh, I am so glad," said Worqenesh. "This means that you will stay with us in the village," and then she hesitated and, for a moment, looked frightened. Would he take Issete away? But in the next instant Issete had thrown her arms around her friend.

"*Isshi, isshi.* I shall never leave you. I have consented to this man at last, but only with the understanding that we shall live here," and the two women held each other close.

Both thought of their childhood together and the strength it had given to their adult years. Life was beginning to seem like a continuous letting go to Worqenesh, but Issete would lend her the comfort of her companionship and the stability of her loyalty in the years ahead.

Issete and Gabriote were married at Worqenesh's compound on a warm day in the middle of May, 1861. Mary had stayed with her Mother to help serve the guests, who included most of Worqenesh's family and many in the village. It was a quietly happy occasion, and when the celebration drew to a close it was Worqenesh and Mary who retired with their family to Wishan's compound, leaving Issete and Gabriote to enjoy the quiet of the home they had both known for many years, in privacy. Walking along the village path with Mary and Aligaz, Worqenesh mused that it was only during these moments of giving that she knew a little peace. She would have to learn to direct her thoughts more effectively.

\* \* \*

It was Gabriote who took Mary back to Gaffat in early June, just before the rains. Haylu had now assumed the role of head of the family and directed the village's militia, so he arranged for a few of the men of Diddim to escort the small party in safety. They were careful not to draw attention to themselves, not wanting to be seen as potential fighting troops, and so they all rode mules rather than horses. With his newly discovered delight in travel, Aligaz went with them, but just for the journey and not to stay. They were able to make the trip in just under five hours, carefully skirting Debra Tabor.

Their arrival found the missionary-artisans working on a new project. Ever since his defeat at Dabarki at the hands of the Egyptians firing cannon from a fixed, protected position; King Tewodros had hoped to replicate their success with large guns of his own. Unable to import such weapons, he had earlier experimented in their construction by hollowing out thick logs, binding them with metal rings and attempting to discharge large, metal balls through them. The result had been disintegrating explosions. Now he had charged the Europeans at Gaffat with the task. At first pleading technical ignorance, the missionaries had eventually agreed to attempt the project. They had never dreamed of arms manufacturing, but with their mission work and the children's school thriving thanks to the King's help, they could not refuse to try.

Arriving at Gaffat in the middle of an overcast afternoon, Aligaz and Gabriote spent the rest of the day watching in fascination as Karl

Saalmuller, a Pole named Moritz Hall and a few others busily cobbled together animal skins to create a bellows. In his homeland Hall had, at one time, worked as a bell caster. Under his direction the men were struggling to devise the means of casting a small field piece for the King.

Returning to Diddim the next day Aligaz could barely contain his excitement in carrying the news to the family. "You should see it all," he exclaimed, sitting under the fir tree in his grandmother's compound. The family had just enjoyed a quiet dinner, and two of his uncles were on hand, as well as his mother, Wishan and the elder Ribca.

"They have built what they call 'a line to assemble.' There is a place to separate iron ore from the local rock, then a furnace for an intense fire which is to be fanned by the bellows they were making. Finally, there is a mold for the cannon that Mr. Hall has formed of clay. It is all wonderful to see, isn't it Gabriote?"

"It is. But they are not yet successful. I think it will take time as it is a new effort, and never yet accomplished in our country. The men of Gaffat are determined, but the *Habesh* (the name Abyssinians used for themselves) assigned by the King to help them, laugh behind their backs."

Haylu and Welde were listening with interest, and quietly determined to go and see the manufacturing process for themselves. The King was a force to be reckoned with when he set his mind to a thing, so they had no doubt as to the eventual success of the project.

Worqenesh sighed quietly to herself. The country had enjoyed a few months of comparative peace since the King had avenged John's death against Wube's grandsons. She had nourished vague hopes for peace, but here was evidence that Tewodros was not content with the quiet in the land.

As an echo to her thoughts Wishan spoke up. "We have just learned that his new wife has given the King his first son, and heir; and here he is still playing with toys of war."

"Mother, will it never end? This country is so lovely to look at and blessed with fertile land, but its people are always straining to take what power another has – in spite of their seeming good nature. John used to try so hard to ease the King's bent for retaliation so as to ease the enmities."

"I think the people are simply not ready for peace." It was the elder Ribca who was speaking now. "We have been fighting among ourselves for nearly a hundred years – ever since Ras Michael grabbed power from the Gondarine monarchy almost a century ago. It seems as if the people are so accustomed to conflict that they hardly know how to accept authority and live in peace."

Worqenesh looked at her grandmother in surprise. Ribca spent her days caring for her family's needs and seldom expressed her own thoughts. As Wishan encouraged and supported them, Ribca was always there to cook and to sew, to welcome and to hold close. Worqenesh told herself that she must make an effort to speak with her grandmother more often, and delve her reservoir of accumulated knowledge. There were five generations of women in the family now, including little Rosa; and none of them had known a time of tranquility.

"Worqenesh," continued her mother, "I do think that peace will come one day."

"But not yet, Mother. I really do believe that when Tewabach and John were alive the King made fair progress toward modernizing the state, but his nature is too volatile to accomplish his vision alone."

\* \* \*

The missionaries continued their work on the small cannon through the following months, with no success. Either the furnace would not heat sufficiently or the mold would crack at an inopportune moment. Theo, Karl and Moritz Hall led the effort and were close to despair. Then there came a day when everything managed to come together. The recently refurbished bellows raised the temperature in the furnace higher and higher, Theo opened the channel in the fiery chamber and the heated brass ran in a golden coil into the large, bell-shaped mold. In ten minutes it was filled and there was nothing more to do but wait. Two days later they opened the mold to find a perfect cast. After that they were able to make more, and larger weapons, and there were no more snickers of derision from the local workman.

Some months later still, the King came to Gaffat to see a

demonstration of the mortars. A number of people gathered in front of Karl Saalmuller's hut and the usual rugs were spread for the comfort and convenience of the monarch. The latest model of cannon was rolled out, charged and primed; and one of the missionaries leaned over to light the fuse. At first nothing happened. Then suddenly there was a loud roar and the gun lurched backward as the shot flew across the open field. The noise echoed back and forth through the little hills in the neighborhood and King Tewodros sat in absolute silence. The performance was repeated, and still he sat. Then slowly he looked around, noticed little Rosa Waldmeier who had snuggled up next to him, and smiled. He put his arm around the child and began to speak with animation of military strategy and to congratulate all those around him.

The King was ecstatic. At last there was technical expertise in his country. He could build anything he dreamed of, but what he dreamed of was larger cannon. "I want one that will fire a one thousand pound ball," he ordered Theo. The amiable Swiss missionary was careful not to appear uncivil. After all, the King had been generous. After their successful demonstration he had insisted on rewarding each of the Europeans with a thousand thalers. He was now a regular visitor to Gaffat and loved to spend an afternoon sitting with Theo to discuss both weaponry and theology. Theo would never be another John Bell to him because he was a clergyman, and not a soldier; but he was now the one European that King Tewodros trusted.

Theo grimaced within and bowed. "We shall try," he responded.

"That is all that I ask," replied the King.

Not many days later Theo Waldmeier happened to be leaving his home – now the two storied structure of which he had dreamed - and looked out across the undulating fields of Gaffat. In the near distance was a young messenger accompanied by two soldiers. He appeared to be carrying a small bundle on his hip, as a woman might carry a young child. As the group drew close, the bundle began to squirm and, smiling, the man set it on the ground.

"A gift from the King," he announced. "I have been instructed to bring this to Theophilus Waldmeier," and a very small lion cub stepped out uncertainly on the grass.

The young missionary understood enough about Abyssinian

culture to know that no one was allowed to keep a lion but the King, the Lion of Judah himself. If this was truly a gift, it was an extraordinary demonstration of the King's esteem. And so it proved to be. Theo called out to Susan who quickly came to the door with Rosa trotting at her heels. The little girl reached for the cub, but was outpaced by her mother.

"He will take goat's milk," the messenger informed the family, and turned to retrace his footsteps back to the capital.

Susan looked at Theo in astonishment, and the two burst out laughing. Their lives were brimming with youthful happiness and success. There could be no greater acknowledgement of the King's good will. "Theo, we must name him Hagos," exclaimed Susan. "It means happiness in Tigrian, and it just seems to fit."

Her husband grinned back. "Hagos it is, but he won't be happy with goat's milk for very long."

Susan and Rosa took delight in caring for the baby animal who thrived on the family's attention. It was not long before the King was sending a sheep each day to satisfy the cub's growing appetite. The family kept him on a long chain, but often set him loose in their company. As the cub grew to adulthood, Rosa delighted in riding on his back with her father holding on to her with one hand and Hagos' leash with the other. But idylls do not last, and in February of 1863, King Tewodros left Debra Tabor for Gojjam at the head of a vast collection of men.

# Chapter 33

His army was reputed to be forty thousand strong. As they passed over the ancient Portuguese Bridge into Gojjam, they seemed never to end. Hour after hour they converged onto the bridge, marching across the narrow roadway and then widening their ranks as they clambered up the opposite slope. The King stood to watch them pass and then leapt up the incline of the river's bank after them. There was a terrible battle against Tedla Gwalu, a representative of the old ruling clan. The King's army triumphed, capturing seven thousand of the enemy; but Tedla Gwalu slipped away. In his rage, Tewodros ordered all seven thousand captives killed.

That same year there were reports that Egyptians had entered the lowlands to the west, penetrating Tewodros' home province of Quarra; and the King's proven governor in Shoa declared that territory to be independent and himself to be its king. At the height of his power Tewodros looked about; and everywhere, his kingdom was beginning to crumble. He now saw himself not as his country's great leader into the modern world, but as the man sent to punish it for its stubborn ignorance.

In 1864 there was more rebellion and all of the land between Lake Tsana and the Takeze River, including the ancient capital of Gondar, fell into the hands of rebels. By 1865 the King was surrounded, holding only Begemder, Delanta and his stronghold at Meqdela. Now his army was confined to the area between Meqdela and Debra Tabor, which was in no way large enough to support it.

On the political front the King was quarreling with various Europeans in his country. The Englishman who had been sent as

Consul to replace Walter Plowden, Charles Cameron, incurred his wrath and was imprisoned at Meqdela. Soon to join him were Hilde Rosenthal's husband and another missionary, Henry Stern. The British Foreign Office eventually realized that they had inadvertently insulted the King and sent a diplomatic Mission to attain the release of Consul Cameron and any other European held against their will. Just after Easter of 1866, all was in an uproar.

* * *

At first King Tewodros, when he had finally allowed the English Mission to enter his country, had welcomed the three men with all of the charm and gentility of which he was so admirably capable. He particularly enjoyed exchanging pleasantries and conversing with its leader, a naturalized Iraqi named Hormuzd Rassam; but he also valued Henry Blanc, a medical doctor, and Richard Prideaux, a soldier. He set them up comfortably in Korata where he promised to release the imprisoned Europeans to their care. To assure himself that they did not feel too much like strangers, he ordered the still favored artisans of Gaffat and their wives to join them. Both Susan and Mary, along with Hilde Rosenthal and Pauline Flad, were in attendance. Mary was thirteen now and had become a part of Susan's household.

The King did, after some procrastination, send for the European prisoners at Meqdela and bring them to Rassam at Korata. But his mood began to darken and his cunning to exercise itself. He had been given an inaccurate translation of the letter from Queen Victoria that Rassam had brought and, thinking that she had offered Rassam to serve in whatever capacity he might require, the King decided to use him as a pawn to force the English government to send advisors in industrial technology. He arrested the three-man English Mission as they were about to escort the European captives to freedom and had come to his camp on the Zege peninsula to take their leave. Theo and Karl had accompanied the Englishmen and were horrified by their abrupt incarceration.

The time that followed was very hard. While Rassam and his comrades were treated kindly, there were daily floggings of Abyssinians, and frequent executions. Then the rainy season began and an epidemic of cholera broke out in the King's camp. The only remedy was to try to move to higher ground, which meant a march down the peninsula, around the southeast corner of Lake Tsana and across the Nile to the higher ground of Debra Tabor. The journey was dreadful. With the rains setting in, the ground was wet; and when thousands of feet trod over it, the earth turned to mire. There were people who were sick, dying and even dead who were carried along in the crowd. Others were trampled underfoot. The smell was appalling and the grief heartbreaking. Theo had Susan and Rosa with him, as well as Mary and Karl. By the time their little group was able to break away from the crowd and head toward Gaffat, Susan had fallen ill.

Leaving his wife in the care of Mary and Karl, Theo rushed back toward Debra Tabor to beg the King to allow Dr. Blanc, who was a prisoner, to come and attend Susan. In a now rare act of kindness Tewodros remembered his grief at Tewabach's death, and hastened to send Henry Blanc to Gaffat with Theo. Susan began to recover, only to be hit with an attack of typhus. Blanc warned Theo to prepare for the worst and urged him to keep Rosa away from her mother, although she begged piteously to see the little girl; but slowly, very slowly, Susan rallied. Soon after her recovery Mary and Karl were married. Much to everyone's distress King Tewodros insisted on acting as the bride's father on behalf of his old friend, John Bell. He provided the bride with a royal cloak heavily embroidered in gold, and insisted on donating sheep and cattle for the feasting.

Then, suddenly, the King turned on his favored artisans. Late in the year, well after the rains had ceased, Theo heard voices outside his home one day and looked up to see his house, and those of his neighbors, surrounded by soldiers. He and his fellow missionaries were accused of secretly corresponding with the English government and they were herded together and marched off to Debra Tabor. Susan, who tried to follow, was pushed to the ground.

The men were imprisoned overnight and then sent back to Gaffat the next morning to surrender their property and all of their possessions. As Theo packed up his precious books and tools, Susan grabbed the elaborate, gold trimmed saddle which had been a wedding gift from the King and slung it out of a second floor window, striking one of the King's soldiers below. All of the European families were removed from Gaffat and taken, with only the clothes on their backs, to the capital.

Of all his accomplishments, Theo had been most proud of the mission school. To conduct its daily operations he had put a young, dedicated Abyssinian in charge. Debtera Sahalu had been educated in the Abyssinian Church, was an apt student of the missionaries' message and devoted to the children. When the Europeans were taken, he was dragged off with them and brought before King Tewodros. To their utter horror the tyrant ordered the young man's hands and feet to be cut off.

A very few of the children from the school who were orphans and had nowhere else to go, had followed Sahalu to Debra Tabor. Theo was just able to take them aside before the King's orders against Sahalu were carried out. "You must flee to the mountains," he whispered, sliding a hastily written note into the hand of the eldest. "Take the southern road out of the city. Go quickly and avoid the soldiers. There is a path to the southeast. Follow it and you will be led up into the hills. Keep going, and you will come to a village. It is called Diddim. You will be safe there. Ask for Woisero Worqenesh, and give this to her."

\* \* \*

There were four of them who slipped away from Debra Tabor in the brightness of a highland afternoon. Terrified that they would be stopped and questioned, they broke apart and faded into the crowd of the city's streets, being careful to keep each other in sight. When they had left Gaffat that morning they had been clean and decently dressed, but already they looked worn and bedraggled. There were three boys and a girl, none of them related but all bound together by their experience of Gaffat and the decency of their lives there. They would stay together and protect each other as well as they could.

Emerging on the southern pathway out of the city the eldest boy, who looked to be about ten, took hold of the little girl's hand and walked on at as normal a pace as he could muster. The other two boys hid briefly in the shadow of some tall bushes, and five minutes later they too emerged on the path to the south. In about an hour, just as

Theo had said, the trail began to climb up a wooded hill, and the two younger boys hasten to catch up with the other children. The trees would lend cover against questioning eyes, and joining together would provide protection against animals. The sun was still well up in the sky and they now felt reasonably safe from human pursuit.

"How far away do you think it is now, Dawit?" asked the little girl.

"Hirut, I hope you are not tired. Ayto Waldmeier said that Diddim is two or three hours away from the capital. I think it will take us at least three hours, and maybe a little bit more, because we left secretly and have tried to stay hidden."

"I am all right," replied the little girl, who was determined to keep up and not make things difficult for the others. "I am only a little worried that we might get lost."

"I think this path only goes to Diddim," chimed in one of the others. "We can't get lost."

Dawit looked at Asrat in appreciation. The younger boy seemed to recognize the need for confidence and Dawit was grateful for his sturdy support. "That's right, and there is still lots of light left in the day."

"We should sing," suggested the fourth child. Tekle was nearly as old as Dawit, and did not want to feel left out. "Singing will keep us hopeful and if we are noisy, we shall frighten any wild animals away."

The foursome continued along the path, climbing purposefully and singing hymns they had learned at Gaffat. They were tired from the fears of the day, but like most of their countrymen they were unfazed by the physical exercise.

Late in the afternoon Asrat held up his hand for a stop. "I smell supper. We must be almost there." And having briefly halted, they hurried on.

*  *  *

It was Issete who first saw the unfamiliar children approaching Diddim. She had been to the stream just below the village and was taking a leisurely course back to the compound, balancing a jug of water on her head, when she heard hurrying footsteps behind her.

Turning to see who was coming, she was surprised to see four strange children without any adult visible nearby. Putting the jug to the ground she reached out toward them and called. "Where are you going? Are you lost? Let me help you." Before she knew herself what she was doing she was stepping toward them.

Dawit bravely assumed his role of leader. "We are looking for a village called Diddim. Is it nearby? We have a friend there."

"It is just beyond the next bend. Who is your friend?" asked Issete.

"I don't know," and Dawit looked embarrassed. "We have been sent by Ayto Waldmeier and we have a letter. Here it is, with the name. I am not sure of it. Can you read?"

"Yes, indeed," and Issete reached for the small missive. "It is sent to my friend. Come, I shall show you the way." Issete retrieved her jug of water and took Hirut's hand. With visible relief the three boys followed behind.

# Chapter 34

A few minutes later Worqenesh read the letter in stunned silence. Then, remembering that Issete was waiting and that the four children were staring at her, she looked up and willed herself to smile.

"You are safe here. Come. We shall have supper together. Issete, please ask Gabriote to go for Giyorgis while you and I put the food out." Then, as Gabriote hurried off to the village church, she opened her arms and reached out for the children. "You have been so brave. There are no soldiers here. We are part of Ayto Waldmeier's family and this will be your new home."

Later, when the children had been tucked away for the night, she and Giyorgis sat and talked with Issete and Gabriote. "I am not sure what has happened to me," she said quietly, "but I am suddenly certain that I must keep these children and care for them. Theo says they are orphans. The country is turned upside down, and they have nowhere to go."

"What has happened in Gaffat?" asked Giyorgis. "What did the letter say?"

"They have all been arrested and taken to Debra Tabor – even Theo and Karl who have been so favored. Theo must have been in a dreadful hurry when he wrote. He said he thought they were safe for the moment, but that all of their possessions had been confiscated. The school's Abyssinian head was facing imminent execution, and they were unable to keep the children safe."

"Of course," said Gabriote. "Anyone who reminds the King of his own excesses would be in danger. The children would have to be sent out of his way."

"They are well spoken, and you can see that they have had some education," added Giyorgis.

"And that's just it," pointed out Worqenesh. "We are going to need children like these to grow up in this country. I have come to think that in time, if they survive, my own children will leave. It saddens me to think I shall lose them, but I want them to have opportunities in the future. These children have nothing. We can make a difference in their lives and perhaps, someday, they will make a difference in the future of our country."

Issete had sat quietly while the others spoke, but she now began to smile. "Are you going to open a school, Worqenesh?"

Her friend started, and then leaped to her feet. "That's it, Issete, we'll open a school! We have everything we need - you and I have been well taught and we have Giyorgis. What a wonderful idea. We will care for these four who have come to us and continue their education, but we shall teach the children of Diddim as well."

Gabriote shook his head in bemused surprise, but he too was smiling.

* * *

In the days that followed the news from Debra Tabor was disheartening. In his frustration King Tewodros continued to kill his own people. Executions of every dreadful sort were devised and carried out, regardless of the victims' status or position. If the King was angered, both friend and foe were at risk. Theo sent word that although there was little to eat the missionaries were protected because they were needed to build weapons, and carriages to transport these weapons. Even so, one or two of the men were threatened; but Theo was able to plead for their lives. He still retained the King's affection so long as the tyrant was in a quiet mood.

But in Diddim new life was burgeoning. More than six years had gone by since John Bell's death. Worqenesh had struggled with her sorrow, knowing that she mustn't burden those around her; but she had lost the very center of her life. She had sought her mother's example of strength and selflessness, but the days were long. Her children had grown – the girls were both married and had left Diddim and Aligaz had joined the European community as well. She did believe that, for their father's sake, the King would not harm them; but her life was empty. Now, for the first time in many years, on the seasonally warm mornings preceding the rains of 1867, she had begun to awaken early with a feeling of happy anticipation. Plans and projects raced through her mind. There were lessons to prepare and classes to teach.

When she opened her eyes it was Hirut she would see first, curled up next to her in the relaxed abandon of the very young. The child had wriggled her way into the *gojo* and into her heart.

"I think she is from the Galla countries," Issete had observed. "She is like me with her dark skin and small stature."

"And she is as bright as she is brave," added Worqenesh. "She cannot be more than six years old, and we are already reading simple verses together."

The boys had been given Gabriote's old hut, and had settled in happily together. "These children have known both dearth and plenty," he observed, "and have been hurt by neither. It is good to see how full of gratitude they are, and how loyal to each other."

In the early mornings the oddly disparate household would gather for a hot breakfast to begin their busy day. Worqenesh and Issete had decided that classes would only meet in the morning so that the village children were free to work in the barley fields during the rest of the day. Young children had herding responsibilities and could not be spared for more than one or two hours. Every village child was welcome, but none were forced to come. Worqenesh and Issete taught reading and writing, using the book of Psalms as their principle text. Giyorgis would come for an hour each day to work with the boys of Dawit's and Tekle's age. He was developing lessons in history so that the children would learn to value their unique cultural heritage. There were stories of the ancient land of Punt and early trade with the Pharaohs of Egypt. He told of the Aksumite Kingdom and its Queen who visited Solomon of Israel and returned home to bear the first King, Menelick. Then Giyorgis described the beginnings of Christianity in their land, and the story of young Frumentius who went to Egypt to asked Athanasius of Alexandria to send a Bishop to his country, and who was ordained and sent back himself. A century later there was the coming of the nine saints, a group of Greek-speaking missionaries who had an enormous cultural impact on the country by establishing monasteries throughout the north and introducing a Christian educational system. He described the marvelous churches hewn out of stone in Roha in an area that came to be known for the king who inspired them, Lalibela; conflict with the great Muslim warrior nicknamed Gragn, or the left-handed; and the rise of the Gondarine Empire. The children sat enthralled as they listened to the tales of ancient grandeur.

Then he would begin to explain the current situation by first telling of the Solomonic kings' loss of power nearly a hundred years ago, and King Tewodros' struggle to re-establish a central government. It was a little less frightening for the children to hear rumors of the King's excesses if they could understand the situation in the context of their history.

As the days went by and the village children heard about the classes, they were drawn in by curiosity and held by fascination. Their parents were happy to free them, for a little while, to absorb the wisdom of the Woisero Worqenesh, Abba Giyorgis and their friend Issete. Even when the rains came there was usually enough sunshine in the morning for the classes to gather across the village pathway from Worqenesh's compound, under the tall fir trees. Gabriote was always on hand to tidy up the school area and make things comfortable for everyone; and when lessons were over for the day, he enjoyed teaching the boys from Gaffat to ride. It was something that none of the three had had much experience with.

Meskel followed the rains. Worqenesh had always loved the festival with its gay dancing and feasting. The people would dress in their best clothes and the priests in their colorful finery. This year the family knew they would not travel to Debra Tabor; no one now voluntarily approached the environs of the King. Giyorgis had promised a worthy local celebration of the day and their beloved Abba Barhe, who now seldom officiated, would join him to make it special. The school children would fashion a cross and tie bunches of the gay, yellow Meskel daisies to it. Then, just at dark, it would be burned on a bonfire. It was important to continue the old traditions for the children, and they were a safe distance from the capital.

Early on the morning of the holy day Worqenesh, Issete and Gabriote, with their four children and joined by a number of the children from the village, took the trail down the side of their mountain. The youngsters skipped along happily until they reached an open area filled with the blooms of Meskel daisies. Then everyone set to work to pick the golden blossoms and tie them together into brilliant nosegays. Returning to the track Worqenesh looked down the mountainside to see the familiar figure of Fenta Tadese climbing toward them, and ran to meet him.

"What has happened? Are you all right?" she called, and Fenta nodded his head as he hastened toward her.

"The King has burned Debra Tabor and headed east. There is news that a large force of British soldiers has been sent from India to rescue their Consul and the other European prisoners. I will tell you everything when we get back to the village."

"The children! What news is there of my children," begged Worqenesh.

"In truth, their situation is dangerous. The King is using Theo and his colleagues to build a road as they go along, but he needs them so I do not think he will harm them. Your family was safe when last I saw them."

So the day's Meskel celebration was tempered by Fenta's news, but there was still happiness in watching the children's pleasure. The bouquets of yellow daisies were tied to the roughly constructed cross, a representation of the true cross that the Empress Helena of Constantinople was said to have discovered in Jerusalem in the fourth century. There was dancing through the village. Dawit and Tekle twirled and stomped their feet while Hirut caught hold of Asrat's hand and tried to copy their gyrations. Then the family gathered in Wishan's compound, and was joined by many of their neighbors to enjoy a generous meal supervised by Ribca.

As evening fell the two priests led the villagers to an open area where a large fire had been laid and the flower-decked cross had been placed. Giyorgis set the brush alight while the people sang psalms and the women uttered ululations of joy.

# Chapter 35

"It has been very bad in the capital," said Fenta as he began to explain what was going on in the rest of the country. "You do know how fortunate you are to be out of the way here and easily overlooked." The adults who had gathered to listen nodded wisely, but with concern. They knew they were fortunate to be up in the mountains in Diddim, but they also cared about Worqenesh's children, who were in harm's way.

"I confess I have wanted to escape my own home and come here," he continued; "but it was not possible until the King set fire to the city, allowing me to slip away in the confusion. All of the Europeans have either been sent to Meqdela to be imprisoned in chains, or they have been forced to manufacture weapons. When we heard that the English were mounting an enormous rescue operation some of King Tewodros' advisors, in their anger, urged him to kill the artisans; but now that the King has large cannon he needs carriages to transport them and roads for the carriages. He cannot manage without men like Theo and Karl, and he has put them in charge of road construction. When I left they had already laid a few miles to the east, blowing up rock and building supports as they went along. King Tewodros himself moves rock and urges his workers on."

Worqenesh sat is silence. It was unbearable to think that her daughters were frightened and her son in danger, and yet she held out hope for them. If the British were sending a large force into the country to rescue the Europeans, perhaps their fates would be resolved as she had predicted to John years ago. Theo would be Susan's means of escape from this warring land, and now Karl would be Mary's. How very hard it was, but she had really let them go a long time ago. If only they remained safe and kept Aligaz with them it would be all right. She, of course, would remain. That too was appropriate.

It was Haylu who broke the silence. "Will there be an invasion, Fenta? Are we to be conquered?"

"It is hard to know," their friend answered. "I have never had the feeling that the British wanted to become involved with the internal problems of Abyssinia."

"A powerful European country cannot let its people be put in chains in a foreign land and not do anything about it," stated Welde. "Why does the King not understand that?"

"Worqenesh," asked her mother, "how long does it take to get to Meqdela?"

"No more than ten days, usually less. But if you have to build a road for cannon, I have no idea."

"It will be months," said Fenta. "The English have not yet arrived in the country, but they could reach Meqdela before the King does!"

Wishan spoke up again, thinking about the days ahead. "Fenta, will the King survive this challenge? I do not know how he can continue. It seems that the country is falling apart and he has surely lost his aura of invincibility. He came with such promise, but now he causes such suffering."

"I think it is doubtful that he will survive a British intervention, but that is simply my opinion. Do you all remember the young heir to Shoa that the King captured and then kindly educated at his court? His name is Menelick. He escaped from Meqdela two years ago, and I am sure men will be rallying around him. There are also others who aspire to power. It is impossible to predict who will prevail. For now, I hope to spend a few days here with Giyorgis. In about a week it should be safe for me to return to Debra Tabor and I shall see what damage there is to my home and begin to rebuild. King Tewodros will be long gone by then, and he has taken all that is his with him. I really don't think he will be coming back – certainly not any time soon."

"Mother Worqenesh," asked Dawit as she and the children were walking home late that afternoon, "what will happed? Will the country fall apart?"

"No, Dawit, you must not think it. Our country has existed for thousands of years and will continue on. Remember your lessons with Abba Giyorgis. You know, my husband really loved King Tewodros and he believed in Abyssinia. Perhaps the King has tried to do too much at once. I am convinced that even if he fails, he has laid the groundwork for a strong monarchy and that someday, someone will come along who will succeed."

Continuing along the village path she thought to herself, 'these four children who Theo sent to me are the future. I shall be diligent in their care and prepare them for the time that is coming;' and she smiled to herself, acknowledging how quickly she had come to love them.

\* \* \*

As he had said he would, Fenta Tadese returned to what had been the capital in a little over a week. He soon fell into his former habit of routinely visiting his old friend's family in Diddim It gave him a break from the labor of restoring his compound and helping his neighbors to rebuild, and he was able to bring news of the King's progress to the mountain village. As news filtered back to Debra Tabor, he relayed it to Wishan's family. First they learned that Theo had been gravely ill, but that Susan had found a woman to concoct a restorative medicine and he had recovered. Then he told of the immense gorge at Beit Hor three thousand feet deep and seven miles wide. Theo and Karl had engineered a road to the bottom and back up the opposite side. Fenta had also heard that in a moment of rage the King had fired a pistol at Theo, but that the gun had misfired. He decided to keep this information to himself. Obviously, the trip was harrowing and anyone close to the King was in constant danger, but the road progressed. It was an enormous undertaking, and it continued on. He learned that the British Expeditionary forces had arrived at the port of Zulla on the Red Sea and were marching southward to Meqdela. Various groups of rebels were assisting them with supplies along the way.

In Diddim Worqenesh, Issete and Gabriote spent their first Christmas together as a makeshift family with their four adopted children. The day before was a time of fasting and then, very early on the morning of *Ganna*, they donned their best clothes and their white shammas and walked together to the village church. Gabriote carried Hirut, who was having trouble waking up. Worqenesh held Asrat's hand and Issete was flanked by Dawit and Tekle. As they drew near they joined others in circling the church three times and then splitting by gender to enter for the Eucharist.

Later in the day they enjoyed the traditional family feast at Wishan's compound which meant that Wishan, her six children, their spouses and numerous children, and many special friends were all gathered together. Issete along with the younger Ribca, Worqenesh and her three sisters-in-law were kept busy seeing that all the family was served and that there was plenty for all to eat. They insisted that the elder Ribca sit and enjoy the fruits of her labor while they waited on her. It was supposed that Asfaw Yilma's mother was now well into her seventies, but no one was her match in organizing the preparation of large quantities of delicious food for festive occasions. Afterwards, while the women talked and the younger children raced about in the compound, the men and older boys withdrew onto a field across the village path to play a game called *ganna* with a rounded wooden ball and curved sticks. In a little while Wishan came to sit next to Worqenesh and took her hand. Here in Diddim they were all well and safe, but her gesture was an acknowledgement of the danger she knew three of her grandchildren walked in.

After Christmas their lives settled back into the comfortable routine of school days. There were between twenty-five and thirty village children who usually attended now. Along with his regular history lessons, Giyorgis began to include a smattering of the history of the Abyssinian Orthodox church. Worqenesh continued her classes in reading and Issete honed the children's penmanship skills. She also began a class, for a few of the older girls who showed interest, in the identification of various trees and plants and the use of specific species for medicines. These were busy days for both the children and their teachers.

Fenta Tadese continued to deliver his news updates as the weeks rushed by. The King had persuaded the people of Delanta to provide him with supplies and labor. He had reached the Bashilo River where another deep drop and rise in the road must be engineered. He was poised at the base of Amba Meqdela, with a terrifying incline to construct. And all the while the British were drawing closer.

* * *

The King's road reached the huge level plateau of Islamgee nearly three quarters of the way up to Meqdela a few days before Easter. From there he would position the cannon on the ridge called Fahla, where they would overlook the approach of the British from the north.

In Diddim as in the ruined capital, the ravaged ancient city of Gondar, and indeed in all of Abyssinia people knew that a dramatic climax was imminent. King Tewodros' undefeated army was about to meet a major European military power on the field of battle. The King had bragged that he should be called a woman if he did not prevail against an army led by a woman (Queen Victoria). But the King who could well boast of bravery, power and even military genius; lacked imagination. He had never seen an army other than one developed in Africa, and was unable to envision the implications of rigid discipline and technically superior weaponry.

The last news that reached Fenta at Debra Tabor before the two armies met was of King Tewodros' rage and the resultant terrible executions of his own countrymen. In a moment of clairvoyance the King saw that the road which he had built with such care across the Bashilo River had unwittingly provided the approaching British army easy access to Meqdela. Realizing the irony, it did not take much to drive him into a state of manic fury. To everyone's horror he spent an entire afternoon throwing Abyssinian prisoners over the precipice from the heights of Amba Meqdela.

On Good Friday, April 10, 1868, it was King Tewodros' army that attacked the British forces. In a typical display of bravado, the Abyssinian cavalry swept down the mountain's steep side to attack the British who were slowly advancing upward. The King, who had remained on Fahla with his beloved artillery to cover their charge, had little effect. As soon as the riders came within range of the well placed British soldiers armed with breech loading rifles, they were mown down. Between seven and eight hundred Abyssinians died that day.

Two British soldiers succumbed later to their wounds.

Toward the end of the next day, in spite of the advice of most of his chiefs, the King released the European prisoners. He asked Theo and Karl, along with another of the artisans, to escort them down the side of the amba to the British camp. Karl and Theo were given lodging there for the night, but could not sleep knowing their families and the Europeans who had not been imprisoned were still in the King's hands. Early the next morning they climbed back up the side of the amba, and King Tewodros gave the order that the rest of the Europeans might leave. It was Easter Day. The remaining families hasten to gather their possessions together and began their descent at about noon. Theo and Karl had the courage and grace to step aside and take leave of the King.

It was nearly over. The next day the British gathered for a final assault on Meqdela. King Tewodros barricaded the gate giving access to the amba and stood with his remaining faithful chiefs to face the enemy. As the British broke through the barricade and Ras Ingida fell at his side, King Tewodros put his pistol in his mouth and fired. The Lion of Judah was dead.

# Chapter 36

Worqenesh knew nothing of the outcome at Meqdela until late in April. Rumors began to filter into Debra Tabor as survivors of the dreadful denouement straggled back to the former capital. In Diddim word came first of the arrival of the British, then of the terrible battle and finally of the King's suicide. Then a day came when Fenta Tadese came trotting up the mountain path on his mule, waving a piece of paper. He rode straight past Wishan's home before she realized who it was, and continued on to Worqenesh's compound at the back of the village just as the school children were leaving for the day. Worqenesh looked up with surprise, and immediately realized that Fenta's expression was relaxed and that his news must be good. Then she saw that he held something in his hand and rushed to his side.

"It is from Theo," he said. "One of the soldiers returning from Meqdela brought it."

She clasped the letter to her chest, remembered to wave Fenta on into the compound, and dropped onto a nearby stump calling to Issete. Quickly her eyes scanned the hastily written message and then her body visibly relaxed and she looked up in relief. "They are safe," she said. "They are all safe."

"Tell us what he says," insisted Issete as Gabriote came running to her side. "Where are they and where are they going?"

"When Theo wrote, they were at a British camp on the Bashilo River. Aligaz was with them. Theo says that they were about to leave for the coast with one of the British Divisions. There they hope to find a ship going to Suez and from there they plan to travel either to Alexandria or to Palestine, whichever seems best. He will write again when they are settled."

Issete hugged her friend. "It is wonderful to know they are safe. Knowing that they have managed to keep together is very reassuring."

"Issete, I shall never see them again," and quiet descended on the three friends. For a while they all sat in silence, not knowing what to say. Then Worqenesh spoke again. "You know, long ago I told John that this is what I hoped for. They will be free to live productive lives without fear. Look, here comes Mother with Giyorgis."

"Is there news of the children," called Giyorgis as he and Wishan hurried to join Worqenesh.

"It is good news; they are safe," replied Worqenesh as her mother and brother came up. "They must now be on their way out of the country with the British, according to Theo. He will write again when they decide where to settle. Come, we will get something together for the children to eat. Are you both hungry? We can eat with them and talk at the same time."

As she and Issete walked toward the kitchen area Wishan hurried to follow. "Worqenesh, you sound almost indifferent. I know that is not so."

"No, Mother, I care terribly; but there is nothing any of us can do to change things. I think it is a miracle that they all have survived the last six months. Now they have a chance to make a new beginning and I must be glad for them. They have each other and they will do well."

Wishan looked at her daughter with new admiration. Both she and Worqenesh had lost well-loved husbands, but she had always been surrounded and sustained by her children. This golden child whom she and Asfaw Yilma had so loved had met both the joys and sorrows of her life with courage and grace that few could match.

"Hirut," called Worqenesh, "come and help us carry." The mood in the compound lifted as the women brought out *injera* with whey and horns of *tej*, and the family sat on the ground to enjoy the food and their accustomed conviviality.

"Fenta," began Giyorgis, "what are they saying in Debra Tabor? Who will take up the job of governance?"

"It is much too soon to know. What we can be sure of is that the country is split again – almost as fractured as when Kassa Haylu had himself crowned Tewodros II."

"I have heard that Wagshum Gobaze of Amhara and Lasta is asserting himself," said Gabriote.

"Yes, so have I heard; but he is already being challenged," answered Fenta. "When the British Expeditionary Force marched back to the coast they left behind a great quantity of weapons with Dejazmach Mercha of Tigre. He had helped to supply them with food and fodder during their assault on Meqdela, and he will not tolerate an upstart from Amhara."

"And don't forget the little boy from Shoa who the former King took under his wing and educated, along with his own children," added Worqenesh. "He grew up, escaped from Meqdela, and is bound to be interested in the job."

"Who are you speaking of?" asked her mother.

"Menelick. He is of an ancient royal family, well educated and proclaimed himself King of Shoa back in 1865 after he slipped away from Tewodros."

"What do you think, Fenta?" Wishan looked toward her old friend. "My guess is that he who rules in Tigre controls the flow of arms into our country."

"I think you are right, Wishan. Dejazmach Mercha already has the arms given to him by the British, and he controls the gateway to acquiring more. There will be talk and there will be maneuvering for advantage, but the man with the guns will carry the day."

"If he has some of the rifles that the British used at Meqdela," added Gabriote, "there is no question. I have heard that they were able to fire six shots in a minute." There was a murmur of surprise, and appreciation of such technical prowess.

The diverse company of friends and family sat in quiet companionship for a few minutes. Then Gabriote rose and stretched. "I'll call the boys and walk down to the barley fields. I think the first crop is nearly ready for the scythes."

"Wait, and I'll walk with you," said Giyorgis. "The clouds are beginning to gather this afternoon: the rains cannot be many days away."

\* \* \*

It was not long after this cozy family conversation that the people of Diddim learned of the first successor to King Tewodros. Wagshum Gobaze had moved quickly to have himself crowned at Gondar. The old capital that had been so rudely burned by Tewodros in 1866, supported a new monarch in 1868; and Wagshum Gobaze emerged as the self-proclaimed ruler of Abyssinia. He would not reign unchallenged for long. Just as Fenta had predicted, Dejazmach Mercha of Tigre opposed the new monarch almost immediately. As well as weapons, Mercha had acquired the services of a member of the British forces who had promised to train his army in European techniques and strategies. Having observed for themselves the amazing efficacy of the British methods against Tewodros, Mercha's army was more receptive to this training than Tewodros' forces had been years ago when John Bell had tried to educate them.

There came a day in 1869, well after the rains had ended and Meskel had been celebrated, that Gabriote had taken the children to weed in the barley fields and Worqenesh sat quietly with Issete, each spinning the cotton thread that would be taken to Debra Tabor to be woven into cotton cloth for the family. The village was quiet in the early afternoon when the two women became aware of the steady, soft hoof beats of a lone rider coming along the village path. Worqenesh saw Issete rise suddenly, her spindle dropping to her feet, and then a familiar voice uttered the single word, "Mother."

In an instant she was on her feet and then crushed in the embrace of the young man she had not seen in nearly three years.

"Aligaz," was all she could manage to blurt out, and she was laughing and tears were streaming down her cheeks.

Then there were voices coming along the village path and the sound of running feet. Gabriote had seen the young man from the fields and Giyorgis had heard the children racing along. Soon it seemed as if most of the family and half of the village were crowded into the family's compound with shouts of recognition and joy.

It was well into the evening before Worqenesh could sit quietly with her son and hear his story. Gabriote and Issete were with them and Gabriote hushed the four children as Aligaz began to speak. He told of the dreadful road construction led by King Tewodros from Debra Tabor to Amba Meqdela, of the English attack on the supposedly impregnable fortress and of their rescue. Their family group had been able to join an English Division of soldiers on their march back to the coast. From there they had taken a ship to Suez and then a train to the city of Alexandria. But while Susan and Mary had eagerly looked forward to immigrating with their missionary husbands to the land of Palestine, Aligaz had held back. "I knew that Tewodros was dead and that all of you were up here in the mountains. I longed for home. Theo and Karl gave me what money they could spare, and I set out."

Worqenesh felt a shudder pass through her body. Any route that Aligaz might have chosen would have been treacherous. "How did you come?" she asked. "Was it across the desert or over the mountains?"

"I did not want to travel alone from Massawa over the mountains of Ethiopia. The times are too uncertain and there is too much unrest. I took the train back to Suez with the money that Theo had given me, and then was able to earn my passage on a ship down the Red Sea to Sawakin on the coast of Nubia. From there I planned to cross the desert to Berber, on the Nile, and go down the river to Khartoum."

As he spoke Worqenesh remembered the young boy who had delighted to travel to Korata with Ayto Cassai after his father's funeral, and who had gone back and forth to Gaffat with Gabriote.

"Oh, please go on," whispered Asrat, his eyes shining with wonder. "Did you cross the desert on a camel?"

"I did," continued Aligaz, sensing the rapt attention of the four children. "I had just enough money left to purchase a few tins of sardines, some water skins and a camel. He did not look like much, but he seemed to have a certain aura of spirit and fortitude. It took two weeks to reach Berber, and I traveled in the company of a caravan of merchants. The desert is an amazing place, teeming with life even where the sun burns in the middle of the day. I found live insects in the sand where there could have been no moisture. In some places there were rocks and in some the camels sank with each step in the lose sand. Sunrise and sunset amaze the eye with their color, and the nights are beautiful beyond belief with thousands of stars overhead and a pure silver moon. Our path was strewn with the carcasses of dead camels shriveled in the heat as there are no scavengers to clean their bones. We were fortunate, and arrived safely in Berber."

"What then? Did you take a boat down the Nile?" Asrat was hanging on every word, as indeed were the other members of the family. Hirut had crept over to sit by Aligaz's knees and hold Worqenesh's hand.

And so Aligaz continued describing his saga – how he had caught a ride on a dahabeah from Berber to Khartoum with money from the sale of his camel, and how he had actually worked for Ismail Pasha in Khartoum to pay for the rest of his trip. There had been another camel and another crossing of a desert from Khartoum to Matemma, which the Egyptians were calling Qallabat, and the exchange of the second camel for a mule to climb the hills to Wehni and on to Chilga and across the plain to Gondar.

Worqenesh looked at her son in amazement. How very like his father he had grown – not so much in appearance, although he was tall and well made as his father had been, but in his love of adventure and freedom. And like John Bell, Aligaz had given his heart to Abyssinia.

"I am so glad that you are home," was all that she could manage to say.

# Chapter 37

In 1871 Gobaze's army, now 60,000 strong, advanced toward Adwa in Tigre to confront Dejazmach Mercha's men. It was soundly defeated at Assam on the 11$^{th}$ of July by the overwhelming strength of Mercha's men and equipment. By January of 1872, Mercha had himself crowned Yohannes IV. During the remaining years of the nineteenth century his reign was intertwined with that of the Shoan monarch, Menelick. In succession, these two men were able to defend against both neighboring and European advances, and to accomplish the unity of the country of which King Tewodros had so earnestly dreamed.

\* \* \*

With the beginning of the reign of Yohannes IV, one could almost feel an easing of the country's tensions. Perhaps the people were finally tired of continuous warfare; or perhaps their new monarch was not quite so demanding, either of himself or of his people.

Almost four years to the day after Worqenesh had received the letter from Theo and had sat in her compound, chatting of the future with her family; they were again assembled under the fir trees on a warm, cloudy afternoon portending the advent of another rainy season.

"So it is the Egyptians who threaten us now," noted Wishan, "but somehow I do not feel worried."

"I agree – the country has a feeling of solidity now. Perhaps it is because the threat is external rather than a squabble among ourselves." Fenta had ridden his mule up from Debra Tabor and was sitting in the shade with a cool drink in his hand. "I can see it in the town. It is no longer a bustling capital, but it has come back to life and trade is brisk. There is a feeling of energy; but it is a peaceful capacity - not aggressive."

"How different Yohannes is from Tewodros," Worqenesh chimed in. He is content to think of himself as the first of many, and is able to coexist with independent rulers in the provinces so long as they pay their taxes."

"And he supports the church," added Giyorgis. "This is such an obvious thing to do, as it assures him of the people's affection."

Gabriote had been quiet, but now spoke up. "You know, he is every bit as much of a patriot as Tewodros was – he is just more comfortable," and they all nodded and smiled their approval.

Issete got up and motioned to Hirut to help her in the kitchen. Fenta watched the child skip after Issete and turned to Worqenesh. "How about the school: are the children making progress?" As Giyorgis and Gabriote nodded their affirmation, Worqenesh told of her delight, and of their plans going forward.

"Fenta, we really believe that here, in our little corner, our school is the story of things to come. The children have learned so much, and we know it will help them. You mentioned that the markets in Debra Tabor are thriving. Well, I see a few of our village people beginning to move to the town. Their children will help their families to succeed. They have a good knowledge of numbers, and they have a healthy understanding of their culture and of what is important in their lives. They will make positive contributions to their community."

"Worqenesh, don't forget to tell Fenta that we are adding to our subjects again," urged Giyorgis.

"Oh, yes – this is something that Gabriote has come up with," and she nodded to Issete's husband. "You explain, Gabriote."

"It is the Royal Chronicles. We do not have official copies, but we have been able to write down pieces that people remember or new excerpts that we hear."

By now Issete was back and listening. "Oh, it is wonderful," she broke in. "It combines memory, penmanship, history and literature. It is something that Gabriote and I do together with the children. He helps them to listen and remember, while I help them to write bits down. They love the rhythm of the words, and sometimes make up music to go with them."

"I should like to hear such," said Fenta.

Worqenesh beckoned to Hirut and whispered in her ear. The youngster dashed off and was soon back with Dawit, and pulling Asrat along with her. The children were smiling, and Worqenesh turned to Fenta as Tekle slipped in to join them. "I have asked them to sing a part of one of the new Chronicles for you. Dawit, please tell Ayto Tadese what it is."

"This is a piece of a Chronicle that our father, Gabriote, heard a few weeks ago in Debra Tabor. It was written by Alaga Walde Maryam, and it is about King Tewodros." The four children looked at each other and then clapped their hands as they began to sing.

> The King who had ruled from one frontier to another
> Is so wretched that he swallowed [pistol balls].
> Over there, at Meqdela, a cry echoed:
> 'A male is dead who had nothing of woman about him!'
> Have you seen the lion die there?

When they had finished everyone was silent. Their minds had gone back to the time of the late King – to his early promise and to his inexorable march to destruction, and they remembered their own lives as his reign had played out. It was Worqenesh who at last broke the spell to thank the children and praise their performance.

That evening, when the family had scattered and the children had gone with Gabriote to check on the animals for the night, Worqenesh and Issete sat in quiet companionship under the darkening sky. There were some clouds overhead, as the rains were not far off; but still a few stars peeped out to lend magic to the sky. Both women let their minds drift back over the years. They had been privileged to participate in some of the great events of their country's recent history. Worqenesh knew that the women in her family were long lived and she noted, with a little surprise, that she looked forward to the years ahead. Her son had survived a terrible ordeal and had come home, her new family was very dear to her and developing the village school was a continuing challenge.

In a little while she turned to see if she could hear Hirut and the boys coming back with Gabriote. Without thinking, she let her hand fall behind her back; and there was Issete's to grasp it, as it had always been.

© Black Rose Writing

CPSIA information can be obtained at www.ICGtesting.com
Printed in the USA
BVOW081711311012

304328BV00003B/86/P